BOOKS BY

KEN BYERLY

GHOST DANCE

RUNNING FREE, AND OTHER STORIES

MOUNTAIN GIRL

INSIDE THE CITADEL

GOOD LOOKING BLOKE, AND OTHER STORIES

All available, in print and E-book versions, through
amazon.com, barnesandnoble.com and other outlets.

GHOST DANCE

KEN BYERLY

ISBN 10:   1481065955

EAN 13:   9781481065955

Library of Congress Control Number: 2012922379
CreateSpace Independent Publishing Platform
North Charleston, South Carolina

"When I look back now from this high hill of my old age, I can still see the butchered women and children lying heaped and scattered all along the crooked gulch as I saw them with eyes still young. And I can see that something else died there in the bloody mud, and was buried in the blizzard. A people's dream died there. It was a beautiful dream...The nation's hoop is broken and scattered. The center is gone..." Black Elk of the Sioux, on the massacre by Custer's old command, the 7th Cavalry, 1890, at Wounded Knee, South Dakota.

CHAPTER 1

Montana is a big state, 700 miles across at the top. Drop it down on Europe and it begins in Holland, crosses Germany and edges into Poland. Montana is flat and dry in the east and heavy with mountains in the west. Today's tourists like the mountains, but the Indians and the buffalo preferred the plains.

Kyle Hansen drove a rented car across the plains on a cold day in early autumn. The wind blew from the north and smelled of snow. Two Indian boys, oblivious of the weather, played one-on-one with an old basketball in a ravaged roadside playground in Hardin and Kyle slowed to watch. The two kids reminded him of himself, eleven years old, playing pum-pum-pull-away in the snow behind the junior high school in Thermopolis, Wyoming.

They began those pum-pum-pull-away games with one boy alone in the middle of a field. The rest sprinted across and the kid in the middle tackled someone. Now two boys waited in the snow, and when the others ran again they tried to drag two more down. This process continued until a crowd of the fallen stomped about in the middle of the field and only a few stronger runners remained.

As a sixth grader, running against bigger seventh graders, Kyle Hansen began to find himself among these few. He still remembered the day he turned, breath steaming in the cold, and saw that he faced 40 or 50 boys alone.

He hesitated, savoring the moment, before he dashed into the mob. He dragged one tackler, felt others hit him, and relaxed finally as they pulled him down. The next day in school several seventh grade boys actually nodded to him in the halls.

Two years later the Hansen family moved four hundred miles north to Montana, a different state, the same culture. What war? What recession? It all began with sports in these little prairie towns.

On this late September day Kyle drove south along the Little Bighorn River. The wind blew. The river looped among willows and hayfields and on each side stark, treeless ridges extended. He spotted the white monument and drove up an approach road. Yellow leaves blew from cottonwoods along the river and fluttered in dry grass along the road. Halfway up the hill it began to snow.

Kyle Hansen had lived in Montana so snowstorms this early did not surprise him, but the suddenness of this one did. Flakes blotted the far mountains and hissed in snaky streams across the road. Kyle squinted through the windshield of his car. It seemed that he had never left, that he became young and vulnerable again.

He parked at the Little Bighorn Battlefield visitors' center, zipped his coat and drifted with the wind among the white headstones scattered along the ridge. It was Kyle's temperament to root for the underdog, and he returned to this place because here the Indians had won.

It rained often that spring of 1876 and by June, they say, the grass grew so high it touched a horse's belly. Families of Sioux and Cheyenne fled the "reservations," where the U. S. government sought to confine them, and rode away into the hills to hunt buffalo.

U. S. Army Chief of Staff Gen. William Tecumseh Sherman ordered army units to pursue. "Attack," Sherman proclaimed:

"attack," no matter if "...it results in the utter annihilation of these Indians... these Indians, the enemies of our race and our civilization."

On June 25, 1876, Gen. George Custer and 650 cavalrymen topped the ridge where Kyle now stood and stared down at a forest of teepees extending three miles along the Little Bighorn River. Custer acted excited, witnesses said. His Crow Indian scouts noted the size of the encampment below, conferred among themselves and quietly rode away.

Custer shouted orders. He dispatched about 200 men to block an Indian retreat south, and a similar group to attack from that direction. He led his remaining 210 troopers north, swung left, and galloped down toward the river, intending to slaughter the Sioux and Cheyenne when they fled, as he anticipated they must, in this direction.

The Sioux and the Cheyenne did not flee. They chased the soldiers back up the hill. White headstones now speckle the long, bare ridge on which Custer and his 210 men died.

Blowing snow stung Kyle's cheeks and the warmth of the visitors' center beckoned. He lingered at maps and bought a book, *Cheyenne Memories*, from an Indian woman in braids and an embroidered blouse. He guessed, from the look she flashed him, that she herself might be Cheyenne.

They talked; she told him she lived in Garyowen, a hamlet a few miles south on the interstate, and yes, her parents were Cheyenne. Kyle said he grew up Montana but worked now as a newspaper reporter in Washington D. C. "My editor sent me out here to write stories about the Lewis and Clark Bicentennial."

"Ah, the bicentennial. You ought to talk to that woman over there."

Kyle glanced and saw a red-sweatered elbow disappear behind a dividing partition. A high elbow, it seemed, vigorous in intent. He advanced around a bookcase and a striking, tall-shouldered woman stood, hands on hips, as if waiting for him.

"I'm Ginny Foster and I'm with the Montana Lewis and Clark Bicentennial Committee." Her straight blonde hair framed a wide, handsome face and, flaunting her height, she wore boots with platform heels. Kyle straightened. Though he stood six-foot-three, she in her clunky footwear looked him almost directly in the eye.

"Kyle Hansen of the Washington Herald," he introduced himself. "I went to high school and college in Montana and I'm back to write about the Lewis and Clark Bicentennial." The Herald carried a certain cachet back East and he wondered if she might react.

"I'm sorry about the weather," she said, "but if you're originally from out here, you know about that. You ought to visit us in June; every year we do a reenactment of the battle."

"The Indians still win, I hope."

She flashed him a look and seemed to rise on her toes. "That hasn't changed," she said.

Possibilities? It was Kyle's routine reaction, as transitory as a glint of sun on a passing car, when he met a woman so physically attractive. "What is your role with the bicentennial commission?" he asked.

"We expect many tourists, as you know, and my quest is to scout the various Indian battlefields and see to explanatory signs and clean restrooms. Where did you live in Montana?"

"Hightown," Kyle said. "I won an athletic scholarship to the University of Montana." He bragged a little. For her, he thought.

"My husband coached in Hightown. Do you remember Harley Hawkins?"

"I do. Very well. One day in football practice he broke my brother's arm."

Ginny Foster stepped back and seemed to consider this. "He was not my husband then. Hightown was his first coaching job. He coaches football at Montana State in Bozeman now; successfully, I might add. You think he deliberately broke your brother's arm?"

"He didn't do it with his bare hands; he did it with malice aforethought. He positioned the two biggest kids on the team opposite Terry and had them assault my brother."

"How long are you here and where do you stay? You may not agree with this, but I think Harley might enjoy seeing you."

Was she serious? Or just diplomatic? "I've got two weeks; I'll probably work mostly out of Helena." Kyle named the state capital. "I may drive up to Havre to see my old college friend Salmon Thirdkill."

"Well, you see, there we go again. Everybody knows everybody in Montana. I roomed with Salmon's wife, Judy, in college. She and I volunteer together in Save the Land – that's an environmental group – and if you're near Helena next weekend you ought to check us out. We gather at the Vigilante Hotel and I think both Judy and Salmon intend to come."

"Next weekend – I'll point for that. You live in Bozeman? I worked my first newspaper job there, as a reporter for the Chronicle."

"The Chronicle endures. You should stop and say hello."

"It's been ten years. Most of the people I knew have probably moved to California."

"These days people from California move here. Hopefully some of them Democrats." Ginny looked around for her coat. "I must go. I'll mention our conversation to my husband."

"Next weekend? The Vigilante Hotel, you say?"

"Right. Talk to Salmon and Judy for details." She started for the door.

"Ginny," Kyle called. She stopped. "Will Harley be there?"

"Maybe on his way home. His team plays in Idaho." She strode away.

The mysteries of life, Kyle thought: this woman married to manic, whistle-blowing Harley Hawkins? It seemed an offense against nature.

It stopped snowing, blue rents raced in a gray sky. Kyle drove west on Interstate 90. Tomorrow, Sunday, his "leisure day," he intended to visit his old college town, Missoula, and Monday the Governor's office in Helena. Near those cities, everywhere he roamed on this trip, he hoped to immerse himself in the legend of the explorers Lewis and Clark.

He admired, from a distance, the Crazy Mountains. He drove over Gallatin Pass. The mountains ringing Bozeman shone white with new snow and Kyle picked out Baldy and Saddle in the Bridgers and the jagged Spanish Peaks. He had climbed many of these during the three years he lived in Bozeman. He drove on past the city, though, and stayed the night fifteen miles further west in a motel in Belgrade.

He set down his suitcase and looked in the local telephone book to see where Harley and Ginny Foster lived. Prairie Smoke Drive. Yes. He remembered that area; high, great views.

Did Ginny Foster maintain a separate listing? She did. Same address as Harley's, different telephone number. Kyle liked that. It seemed important somehow, as if she left a zestful opening. She listed a business under her name too, something called the MOD SHOP. The bold type called, "Look at me," proclaimed independence.

Kyle sprawled on his bed, turned on the TV and saw that Montana State won its third straight football game today. A film clip showed Harley Hawkins on the sideline. Same face, same wavy hair, same bulky stance. Kyle snapped off the TV and listened to the wind rattle the windows. A vision rose, Harley Hawkins in his sweatsuit, prancing on a football field, a whistle on a string around his neck.

"Come on, Moore, run at me. I won't hurt you, come on." Harley taunted one of the Hightown players, Lane Moore. Lane took a tentative step forward and Harley knocked him down.

"Get up, Lane, and hit him again," Kyle's brother Terry, who deserved his reputation as a smartass, said loud enough for all to hear.

"What's that, Hansen?" Harley's voice sounded different. "Come over here." He positioned P. J. Rolfness and Larry Hauser, two big ranch kids, side by side opposite Terry. "All right, Hansen," he said to Kyle's tall, skinny brother, "let's see you run through them."

Terry ran forward. Rolfness and Hauser, friends of his, cuffed him aside as they might a calf.

Veins rose on Harley's forehead. "Hauser, you candyass, Rolfness, you cunt, I want some hitting here!"

Shoulder pads popped. They knocked Terry sprawling.

"Again," Harley said. The other players stood quietly watching. It reminded Kyle of the eighth grade when Ed Putra sat on Bob Tilley hitting him in the face and neither he, Kyle, or any of the other boys had the guts to try and stop it. Kyle looked at assistant coach Ed Cass. Cass avoided his gaze.

"Hit him!" Harley yelled. "Hit him!" It seemed to Kyle that even the horses over in the field near Casino Creek lifted their heads to watch.

Terry ran at the two big kids and Kyle heard a crack like a branch breaking. His brother sat on the ground holding his arm. His wrist sagged at a funny angle.

"Get up, Hansen," Harley shouted. "Get up, I say!"

"Harley, can't you see? His arm is broke," assistant coach Cass said.

"What's that?" Harley leaned to look. "You okay?"

Terry scowled, didn't answer. "Okay, Ed," Harley said, "you drive him to the hospital."

Kyle walked his brother off the field. "The prick," Terry said. "He doesn't want me to play basketball." Basketball season would start in three months and Terry had grown four inches since the previous winter. He lived for basketball then.

He healed fast, and when winter came Harley wanted to win so he started Terry at one of the forwards and Kyle at center. They had the smallest school enrollment in the Big 16 that year, but the Hansen brothers and their teammates scored many points, little Hightown took second at the state basketball tournament, and Harley Hawkins got voted coach of the year.

That was 18 years ago.

Seated in a restaurant in downtown Belgrade, tilting a second stein of local Octoberfest beer, Kyle gazed out at dark mountains and considered his goals for his journalistic career. He must make the most of this trip. He had to. At age 35, another birthday soon, he experienced this first night back in Montana a scary sense of urgency.

#

CHAPTER 2

Kyle Hansen faced less than a four hour drive next morning, a ho hum travel day in the great sweep of Montana, like scooting down to the market for milk. It was Sunday, and he did not need to call his office. The sun shone after yesterday's snow, blue sky spread forever, and he shot west on the interstate toward Missoula.

He wondered as a boy if you could see state lines, painted in yellow maybe, like basketball courts or highway lanes. Instead, yesterday morning, he stared out a plane window at a creased, seared landscape cut every 200 miles or so by another green squiggle. These rivers, the Knife, the Yellowstone and the Musselshell, flowed north and into the Missouri, and Lewis and Clark had pushed and pulled their wooden boats past every one of them in 1804 and 1805 on their way to the Pacific Ocean.

The explorers and their party wintered once in today's North Dakota and once on today's Oregon coast near the mouth of the Columbia River. They crossed the Rocky Mountains twice, and floated down the Missouri in 1806 back to their starting point, St. Louis.

It was now September, 2003, and in a few months three years of bicentennial observances began.

Yesterday's snow melted in the morning sun. A smell of cured grass and sagebrush blew into Kyle Hansen's car, an elixir of spice and dryness that after the humid East always amazed him. He had missed the summer's wild flower explosion, but arrived in time for autumn, his favorite season.

The highway left the prairie, climbed up and over the Continental Divide and descended toward Butte, once Montana's largest city. They dug for silver here, found copper instead, and whole city blocks caved in. Remnant buildings spread like old ore buckets across mangled hills, greenish water filled the Berkeley Pit, and contaminated mine tailings streaked the flats along the Clark's Fork River.

Kyle played high school football on gravel here, no grass, because in those days the fumes from the Anaconda Smelter killed anything green. Basketball season he and Terry dropped paper bags filled with water on peoples' heads from their rooms in the old Finlen Hotel.

Brothels flourished in those days, along with prizefights and miners' union parades. Today, in contrast, Kyle saw signs touting warm, fuzzy things like a farmers' market and, for the tourists, a Gold Rush Cafe.

Beyond Butte, Interstate 90 tracked the Clark's Fork River west along a wide, brown valley hemmed with mountain ranges. Ugly logging roads, worse than Kyle remembered, zigzagged denuded slopes. He crossed the Blackfoot River at Bonner, where it tumbled into the larger Clark's Fork, and approached a dramatic final notch in the mountains, the Hell Gate.

Early settlers to the area borrowed this earthy name and applied it to a trading post and a surrounding settlement. The more commercially acceptable "Missoula," based on a Salish Indian word meaning "near the cold, chilling waters," later took hold. Today's Missoula sprawled across an ancient lake-bed, now a wide valley, just west of the mountains, and Kyle steeled himself for high rises and shopping malls.

He looked around in pleasant surprise. New homes did clutter surrounding hills, and new motels with trendy patios did line the Clark's Fork River, but Kyle saw little evidence of the fast-food wasteland he expected. Modern Missoula, this side at least, looked actually inviting.

He checked into one of the new motels along the river and drove across the Madison Street Bridge to the University of Montana campus. He strolled across The Oval, a grassy sward dating to the University's founding in 1893, and walked around, but not inside, the journalism school where he attended many classes. A new football stadium and fresh brick buildings beckoned, interspersed among grass and trees.

Kyle drove next to the Sigma Nu fraternity house on leafy Gerald Avenue. Ah. Through a window he glimpsed a piano. "We hail from the State of Montana, boys, we're wild and wooly and rough. We drink lager beer and smoke cigarettes, and do everything else that's tough..." They sang that song Monday nights after Chapter meetings. Kyle had arrived, age 18, a know-nothing kid, and the brothers took him in.

He returned to his motel and swam laps in an indoor pool. A twilight sky glowed outside, and Kyle remembered that his former wife had loved sunsets. He glanced down from his room at the outdoor terrace of the motel restaurant and noted a hostess striding vigorously. She wore her hair piled high and her nipples surfaced as perky little buttons on her dress. Kyle changed to a friskier shirt, hurried down, and let her lead him to to a table overlooking the rushing Clark's Fork.

"Enjoy," she said.

Several times he tried to catch her eye. She rang up the tabs when customers left, and he chose a moment to leave when no one else waited in line. "Business major?" he asked, and presented a credit card.

"Does it show?" She raised one leg and fondled the calf of the other with a sleekly stockinged foot.

"Just a guess. I graduated from here in journalism." Suddenly Kyle felt harried; now two departing couples jostled into line behind him. He left, picked up a house phone in the lobby, and asked for the restaurant.

"I'm the journalism major," he said. "What time do you get off?"

"I finish at ten."

"Want to do something?"

"I'll meet you outside at the fountain."

Nicely done. Kyle credited his no-nonsense approach. When the time came he lathered on aftershave and parked his car near the designated fountain. Mount Sentinel bulked against a sky heavy with stars. He did not see his date approach until she tapped on his car window and slid in beside him. Mona was her name and she looked as fresh in her little dress as an unopened package. She smiled, loosened her hair, and became suddenly youthful beneath its tremulous, brown wave.

Kyle guessed her age as early twenties, but he felt no gap at all. It had been his experience in the South and the Mountain States, land of the good ol' boys, that women shaded their expectations lower. If they liked you, they gave you a shot.

He drove to a bar on the flats south of Missoula, mountains black-edged against the sky, and they talked over the click of pool balls and the whir of video poker machines. Mona came from a small town where she played team sports and someday she wanted to work in Atlanta or San Francisco. Resolutely she tipped her bloody Marys.

They returned to his room and lay together, windows open to the rustling river, and after a while she began to cry.

"I can't climax," she said.

"I went too fast?"

"It's not that," she said. "It's this way with everyone."

Now Kyle understood why she agreed so quickly to come with him. "What happens when you're alone, when you try by yourself?"

"I can do it then."

"Show me what you do." Mona placed his hand, whispered instructions. She fought, she struggled, she teetered at the edge, but she could not push over.

"Try some more? I'm not tired."

"No, now I'm self conscious. You see? It's no good."

How long, Kyle wondered, had she hopped from bed to bed seeking the magic man? The "insolvable problems of life," Tolstoy wrote in Anna Karenina. "It's probably mental, not physical," he said, thinking, she's probably heard this forty times. The Clark Fork's River whispered by outside.

"Knowing that doesn't make it any easier," she said.

"I've had problems too," Kyle said. "Not so much the climax, but getting it up on schedule. You know. Things don't always work the way we want them to. Now if we relax..."

"No," Mona said, "I think it's time I go."

"Someday you'll meet someone with patience," he said.

The sun sparked on the Clark's Fork River in the morning. Mona was gone, and only a spot of lipstick on a pillow marked her passing. Kyle did not see her at breakfast. He walked outside and squinted up at a seamless blue sky. Such flawless weather might continue for weeks, he knew, but by November that Pacific Coast gray would glop in and you'd wonder for the rest of the winter if you'd ever see brightness again.

It was Monday morning, seven-thirty in Montana, nine-thirty on the East Coast. Kyle telephoned the national editor at the Washington Herald.

Jack Leventhal had opened a drawer deep in applications when Kyle applied for a reporting job on the Herald's prestigious national desk four years before. "See all these? Get in line."

"Doesn't anybody ever leave or die?"

Leventhal handed him a printed sheet of scrambled facts. "A murder," he said. "Give me four graphs." Kyle banged out a four-paragraph story while the older man glanced through his clippings. The editor read what Kyle had written. "It just so happens we do need someone," he said.

But since that day Kyle had covered crime and local politics, rather than working Capitol Hill and the destiny-altering assignments he wanted. Two weeks ago, hoping to jump start his career, he suggested this Lewis and Clark series and, miraculously, Leventhal went for it.

He pictured the editor now, balding, fortyish, restlessly swinging his arms. Kyle played shortstop on the National Desk team in the Washington Herald summer softball league and

Leventhal played first base. Kyle suspected this had advanced their relationship.

"Where are you?" the editor asked. "How's the weather out there?"

"I'm in Missoula, Jack, near where Lewis and Clark made their toughest mountain crossings. The sun is shining."

"Good. Plan on four feature stories. We want to stress the Native American angle. You've got ten days."

Stress the Native American angle? He could do that, Kyle thought. He drove south along the Clark's Fork and turned west. It took the explorers eleven days to cross the tangled Bitterroot Mountains from today's Montana into Idaho, autumn, 1805. On today's paved Route 12, Kyle tracked their route over Lolo Pass in two hours.

"I find myself growing weak for want of food," Meriwether Lewis wrote in his journal. "Most of the men complain of a similar deficiency and have fallen off very much."

The Nez Perce Indians found them, fed them dried fish and roots, and saved their lives. The 33 expedition members, slowed by diarrhea, floated down the Columbia River and built wooden huts on the misty Pacific Coast. They hunted and fished and counted only 12 days that winter when it did not rain. The following spring, 1806, the snow lay so deep they could not start back across the mountains until June.

Kyle snapped pictures of canyons and peaks and lingered at pullouts to study terrain. Returning through Missoula that afternoon, he turned off the interstate into town. One place he still wanted to see.

On Woody Street near the railroad tracks the honky tonks of his college days gaped broken and empty. In one of these bars, several times a night, a country band called the Snake River Outlaws once performed their signature tune, the *Orange Blossom Special*. A fiddle led the way while the mythic train gathered speed. Old winos and college kids danced and threw up on the sawdust floor.

The band leader invited people in the crowd to come up and sing and one evening Kyle's brother mounted the platform.

Terry, that night, possessed a sense of the tragic illumed by several beers, and Kyle remembered how confidently his brother leaned to the microphone: "I know you tried your best to love me, you smiled when your heart told you to weep. You tried to pretend that you were happy, but last night I heard you crying in your sleep..."

Conversations halted. Heads turned. Terry zapped them with that old Hank Williams sadness, and behind him even the Snake River Outlaws exchanged glances as they wove their musical spell.

Terry returned several more times that spring and band members and bar regulars recognized him and pressed him to sing. Always he chose from his Hank Williams repertoire. He did *Your Cheating Heart* especially well, and it became his most requested song.

Terry drowned in the Blackfoot River that May, on a raft trip that Kyle organized. Kyle stood now on Woody Street, remembering.

He saw the river running dark and fast, the black rocks shining. He saw a flash of blue, the color of the raft bottoms, and he knew his brother had overturned in the rapids ahead. He had relived this moment many times and, to the slightest detail, it always happened the same way.

Kyle walked down Woody Street, stopped once and looked back, got in his car, and drove east through the mountains. A rooster comb of peaks straddled the horizon ahead, a glowing Shangri-la. His highway coiled upward over McDonald Pass. He thought of the many times, in sunshine, in rain, in the snowstorms of winter, that he drove this road in college, on his way home, or returning to Missoula.

He crossed the Continental Divide in darkness, stepped out to urinate, and began to descend. Far below, across the miles, the lights of Helena seemed to reach for him, as if they wanted to tug him in.

# # #

CHAPTER 3

Helena. The copper-sheathed dome of the state capitol shone in the morning sun. Kyle Hansen mounted stone steps and clattered down an echoing marble hall ten minutes early for his appointment with Lars Bjornson, Governor Otto Cloninger's press secretary.

Lars glanced up, sprang to his feet. "Still the quickness of a mongoose," Kyle said. He and Lars played basketball against each other in high school and Kyle remembered the other's left-handed jump shot and quirky, blond hair.

They eyed each other, two small town boys in business suits. Each wore his hair longer now, Lars brushed straight back; Kyle, dappled brown, parted on the left at the two-thirds mark. Lars beckoned toward a door. "Want to meet the old man?"

"I'm ready." Kyle sought gubernatorial quotes to add heft to his stories, and he followed Lars into a large office where a short, fat, bald man stared out a window.

"The sun always shines on judicial selection committee days," Montana's elected leader said. He sipped a viscous, dark liquid from a styrofoam cup. "Lars, procure the man some coffee."

"Just had some, no thanks," Kyle said.

"The Governor likes on occasion to fish," Lars said. "But today it was not to be." He faced the older man. "Kyle will write some stories on the Lewis and Clark Bicentennial for the Washington Herald."

"That's good. We like to think of ourselves as their home state, you know. On that both Republicans and Democrats agree." Cloninger, a former wheat farmer, identified himself a Republican.

"I assume you're enthusiastic about the bicentennial," Kyle said.

"Some see a financial windfall in the tourists who will come," the Governor said. "Others fear we will desecrate the state with hot-dog stands. Some want to protect the natural beauty of our Lewis and Clark sites; others prefer signs, parking areas, picnic tables."

An image of Ginny Foster pounding stay-off-the-grass signs next to picnic tables rose in Kyle's mind. "Where do you stand?" he asked. He liked this sad-eyed old man.

"I'm hopeful," the Governor said.

Lars Bjornson cleared his throat. "The Governor cares about the environment. He also welcomes tourists. Our state Lewis and Clark Committee will work closely with the National Bicentennial Council, you can be sure."

The Governor made a teepee of his fingers. "Thank you, Lars."

"You've read The Book?" Lars asked Kyle. "Ambrose?"

"Oh, yes." Lars referred to Stephen Ambrose's *Undaunted Courage*, published in 1996, a history of the Lewis and Clark expedition and its aftermath. "Got a fresh copy in my car," Kyle said.

A woman entered, trailed by a visiting delegation of school children, and the Governor glanced wistfully outside. "Quote me as eager to do the right thing," he said to Kyle.

Lars had scheduled Kyle's next appointment, an interview with the Montana Bicentennial Coordinator, also in the Capitol building. "Our projects include observances at Pompey's Pillar along the Yellowstone, a Fort Benton remembrance, and a host of local festivals," a tanned woman of about 30 told him, legs neatly crossed.

"What about Native Americans?" Reporters love controversy and Kyle instinctively probed for possible division.

"We want to get them involved whenever we can."

"Who's handling that?"

"We all are," the woman said. Kyle made notes and collected brochures. The size of his pile grew, and he pretended to stagger under the weight. The woman smiled.

Kyle walked down the hall to another office and interviewed a man with the national Lewis and Clark Bicentennial organization. He picked through guidebooks and other things for sale. "What about this?" He hoisted a video from the pile.

"This recreates Indian songs and sounds as they may have been heard by members of the Corps of Discovery themselves."

Kyle wanted details. He made notes and collected brochures. He asked directions to the Montana Historical Society, walked down a street to another building and assembled another pile of brochures.

Free at last, he gazed up at an endless blue sky. He had collected enough paper for one day. He hopped in his car and drove in September sunshine to the Gates of the Mountains Wilderness twenty miles north of Helena.

Here, as Lewis and Clark pushed their boats upstream, gigantic limestone cliffs seemed to block their way. Then a narrow gorge appeared in the rock ahead and the Missouri River came rushing through. The mountains, the explorers said, appeared to open like a gate. Dams now lifted the water level and gentled the current in what was once a rugged canyon, and Kyle purchased a ticket for a boat ride.

He trailed a hand in the water, he smelled the pines. He took pictures, he interviewed tourists. "Did Lewis and Clark fight Indians?" ranked as number one question.

"Only once," Kyle answered. He studied a Montana map. Great Falls, near where the expedition had first entered the Rocky Mountains, offered more Lewis and Clark lore than any other Montana city and he had time to reach it before dark. He drove north along the Missouri, looped over minor mountains and topped a final rise. Ahead, on the plains below, surrounded by rolling brown prairie and yellow fields of wheat, he saw a distant crosshatch of streets,

That night in a Great Falls motel he studied the explorers' journals. It took the men of the expedition about a month, from June 16 to July 14, 1805, to carry their boats and supplies twelve miles overland around the rapids and five waterfalls that eventually gave Great Falls its name. Lewis climbed a hill above the largest of the cataracts "to gaze on this sublimely grand specticle...the grandest sight I ever beheld." A grizzly bear chased and almost caught him, not far from the future site of Kyle's motel.

Tuesday dawned cloudless, mountains bluish with smoke from distant forest fires. Kyle drove a road along the Missouri River and took pictures of concrete dams, built to produce electricity. These dams now obliterated the largest of the five "specticles." Only two lesser waterfalls still remained.

Kyle hiked a section of rocky soil over which two centuries earlier Lewis and Clark portaged their boats. He telephoned his editor in Washington. "Jack, I'm driving north to follow the Missouri around the Big Bend. I may visit an Indian friend in Havre and I could do a story on gambling casinos on Indian land or on reservation living conditions in general."

"If you see something out of the ordinary, sure," Leventhal said. "Otherwise, let's stick to script."

It didn't hurt to try, Kyle thought. He drove a lonely highway north to Fort Benton, where on Front Street along the Missouri River a historical marker noted that William Clark camped here June 4, 1805 while Lewis explored the nearby hills. The marker depicted Clark and Lewis, one kneeling, the other pointing, eyes searching the horizon.

These brown and white signs awaited tourists across Montana. And justly so, thought Kyle. The explorers covered many more miles here than in the Dakotas, Idaho or Oregon, and it seemed to him that today's Montanans, more than other Westerners, clung to their memory.

He took pictures of the brick, three-story Grand Union Hotel, built before the coming of the railroads, when Fort Benton served as the upriver terminus for steamboats from St. Louis. Kyle liked it that the hotel's Better Days Are Coming Saloon still offered liquor "by the glass, by the quart and by the gallon."

Back on the highway, he sped north again. A gravel backroad veered away toward the elusive Big Bend, where the Missouri River turned unequivocally east. This road vanished into forlorn hills and Kyle decided to stay on paved Route 87.

Further north, another gravel lane angled off into space. "Rudyard, 596 people, 1 old sorehead," a sign proclaimed, suggesting a settlement beyond the horizon. Kyle gazed across flinty, endless prairie. He had read that a homesteader fleeing this part of the country painted on his wagon, "Twenty miles from water, forty miles from wood; we're leaving old Montana, leaving her for good."

He drove toward black clouds and watched the sky clear slowly from the west. Humped mountains emerged into view, the Bearpaws. Kyle imagined he felt the curve of the earth.

In Box Elder on the Rocky Boy Indian Reservation the pumps in front of a gas station blazed in a passing burst of sun. The Milk River near Havre, described by Lewis and Clark as the color of "a cup of tea with a spoonful of milk," flowed the same whitish-brownish today.

Green Burlington and Northern Railroad engines shuttled loaded wheat cars on twin tracks along Havre's Main Street. Why, Kyle wondered, in a state so large, did people build their houses so close together? Salmon and Judy Thirdkill's home gasped for breathing room at the western edge of town.

Kyle parked in front. Hemmed on both sides, the house had instead grown forward and backward, here a deck, there a sunroom, adding tree rings as its owners' resources grew. Kyle stepped on the grass and a man in a University of Montana sweatshirt exploded from the front door.

"Eighty-seven," Salmon Thirdkill said.

"Twenty-six," Kyle responded. Each recalled the other's college football number.

Salmon bounded about, heavier, his bristly, black hair so electrically alive it seemed to throw sparks. He excelled in college at running back and his senior year the other players elected him team captain. Kyle played at end, but now, reversing their college roles, he crouched as a quarterback might and nodded toward the Bearpaw Mountains. "Post pattern, Captain Courage," he called a play.

Salmon sprinted down his suburban street, faked right, faked left, angled right again. Kyle back-pedaled, gripping his imaginary football. He waited. He set his feet, he heaved a mighty throw.

Salmon never broke stride. Glancing over his shoulder, he followed the trajectory of the mythic ball. He leaped, grasped – a spectacular catch – slowed, did a full turn and in triumph spiked the illusory ball upon the startled ground.

Kyle, awed, flung his arms upward. "Touchdown," he shouted, "touchdown!"

# # #

CHAPTER 4

A woman with blond ringlets appeared at the door. Kyle saw a fleecy sweater, a snub nose. "I'm Judy," she said.

"I'm Lieutenant Loyalty," Kyle introduced himself, "college teammate of your husband, Captain Courage."

"At last we meet, Lieutenant Loyalty." Judy dusted flour from her arms. "I'm making bread. Don't forget, Captain Courage," she called to her husband, "Dad's coming to dinner."

Kyle surrendered his suitcase to Salmon. "Too bad about the view," he said. The picture window in their living room opened onto about a hundred miles of prairie.

"Feels pinched, I know." Salmon plopped Kyle's bag in a guest bedroom. "Bathroom's across the hall. Get yourself settled and we'll wash the trail dust from our throats."

Kyle splashed water on his face, changed shirts and studied pictures on the bedroom wall of high school football and basketball teams that Salmon had coached. They represented small towns in Montana, Wyoming and Idaho, and according to the captions one of his basketball teams won the Wyoming State Class B championship.

23

He returned to the living room and Salmon handed him a clinking glass of Scotch and water. "Must have been hard for you to leave coaching," Kyle said. Salmon now served as principal at Hays-Lodgepole High School on the Fort Belknap Indian Reservation.

"Well, your goals change. What's so great about coaching anyway, other than the money, the prestige, the power, the fun?"

Kyle chuckled. "Can't someone principal and coach too?"

"It's frowned upon, but I wander down to the gym or the football field from time to time. Got your phone message kind of garbled. What does the Washington Herald want you to do out here?"

"I'm our designated Lewis and Clark Bicentennial expert, and I'm in search of insight. If there's any special site you'd care to show me..."

"Captain Courage, ask Lieutenant Loyalty if he wants some carrot sticks," Judy called from the kitchen.

"Yes, please," Kyle called back. She emerged with vegetables and dip and for herself a glass of white wine.

"Judy teaches at Havre High School," Salmon said.

"You mentioned that in your Christmas card. What courses? How long?" Reporter Kyle flung his questions.

Judy cited a course or two. "Teammates, huh? Every September Salmon wants to run laps and do calisthenics." She swung the conversation around.

"We reported every fall about three weeks before the other students arrived," Kyle said. "We practiced twice a day."

"Sweaty. Hot. Little time for women. Not if you are dedicated, as we were." Salmon smiled.

"And where did he find you?" Kyle asked Judy.

"Country dance at Wild Horse, twelve years ago; he coached in Shelby. I came home for the weekend from Seattle, where I taught school. Salmon possessed wit. And I liked it that he didn't plaster American flags all over his car when we invaded Iraq that first time, like some of the guys around here did."

"Don't care for this second invasion either," Salmon said. He touched Judy's hand. "Her father, however, holds different views, so we don't talk about it. He farms up near the border off Route Two-Thirty-Two."

"I skidded a car off that road in high school," Kyle said. "Two Havre girls picked up Terry and me after a basketball game; I said I'd never seen Canada, they let me drive, we started north, I slide off in the snow. A farmer pulled us out of a ditch at three in the morning."

"Probably your dad, Judy," Salmon said.

"Seriously, it might have been. Dad expected people to bang on our door when it snowed and the wind blew. Terry was your brother?"

"That's right. He was a year younger."

"I hear something bubbling." Judy jumped up and darted to the kitchen. Salmon followed in his stockinged feet, Kyle heard them speak softly, and Salmon returned with fresh drinks.

Kyle lofted his glass. "The joys of the game," he said.

Salmon gazed out his big picture window. "My team won the basketball championship at Lovell," he said, "but my best football guys graduated. We improved in football next year, but my best basketball guys graduated. You can't play everybody; some of the dads complain. It took me a while to realize that nobody gave a damn how many touchdowns I scored in college."

Judy returned, a sprig of parsley stuck on a bare, chubby arm. "Salmon says you played for Harley Hawkins."

"That's right, at Hightown."

"You know he married my roommate at Northern Montana College."

"Ginny Foster, yes. I met her Saturday at the Little Bighorn Battlefield. She said to ask you about the Save the Land meeting in Helena."

"She called. She told me. We'll talk about Helena later."

"What's the Mod Shop? Does she own a store in Bozeman?"

"Yes, yes. It's THE place for woman's clothing."

"Harley Hawkins has coached five years at Montana State and as far as I know he's never recruited an Indian player," Salmon said.

"Harley put a bounty on Salmon when we played at Browning," Kyle said. "He made us each put a dollar in a hat and whoever hurt Salmon bad enough to knock him out of the game could collect the money. Salmon scored four touchdowns. Nobody collected."

"I believe I only scored twice, but I like your version better," Salmon said. "I did wonder why you guys kept pounding on me." He rose to refill their glasses.

"I've heard that story," Judy said. "What a wonderful way to teach high school kids about life. I'm glad you met Ginny. You think you might join us in Helena?"

"I might. If you and Salmon come."

"We probably will." The doorbell rang and Judy jumped up. "Dad's here. Want to wash up or anything?"

Kyle splashed water on his face in the bathroom. A glow of sunset lingered in the west and he leaned on the windowsill and gazed out at miles of open prairie, not a house, not a light. Winter's coming, he thought. He hurried toward the sound of people.

"Little Father," Salmon said to a short, wrinkled man, "I want you to meet Kyle Hansen. He's from Hightown and in college he knocked down bad people so I could run for touchdowns."

Kyle pumped Sam Teigen's raspy hand. "Tell him about skidding off the road," Judy said.

Kyle repeated his snowdrift story. "Might have been me," the old man said. "I pulled fifty out one time or another. Emily used to say if I turned out the barn light they'd go on to the next farm, but I never could bring myself to do that."

Her father had lived alone for the past eleven years, Judy said. A snowplow struck and killed her mother as she drove home from visiting a friend on Christmas day.

"Little Father," Salmon rested his arm on the old man's shoulder, "there's a pot of beans over on that stove."

Teigen eyed his son-in-law cautiously. Kyle, who wondered, saw no sign that the old sodbuster resented a Sioux Indian stealing away his flaxen daughter.

"That's good," the old man said. "I like beans."

"Tiny Oberg's wife grew those beans," Salmon said. "Those are Democratic beans."

Teigen, apparently a Republican, considered. "I will eat those beans. Beans have no politics," he declared.

Teigen had purchased sweet rolls for desert and Salmon accompanied him into the kitchen to warm them in the microwave. Judy looked at Kyle. "You were married, Salmon said."

"Yes, to a girl from Hightown."

"Where is she now?"

"California," Kyle said. "Her new husband's a doctor."

The phone rang and Salmon took the call in another room. Kyle heard his voice rise and Salmon popped one fist against the other as he returned. "Five white guys beat up two Indian kids in a bar in Dupuyer."

"Big white guys?" Judy asked.

"Grown men. Edgar Ware says the five of them killed two deer hunting illegally on the Blackfoot Reservation. While they were dragging back the meat somebody with a shotgun blew out the tires on their pickup. The five of them hitchhiked to Dupuyer. Edgar says they walked in primed for trouble."

"Who's Edgar Ware?" Kyle asked.

"He's the chairman of the Blackfoot Tribal Council."

"Maybe the illegal hunters thought the kids shot up their tires," Kyle said.

"Doubt it," Salmon said. "The young guys maybe mouthed off, maybe teased a little. You know how it goes."

"You shoot out a man's tires," Sam Teigen said, "you expect him to get angry."

"Yes, Little Father, but these boys had nothing to do with it. At least that's what Edgar says." Salmon busied himself piling wood in a fireplace, igniting a blaze.

They finished dinner. "Got to fix a fence tomorrow." The old man rose, touched his daughter on the shoulder, nodded to the men, walked out to his car. Judy found a schedule for the upcoming Save the Land meeting in Helena and gave it to Kyle. "Hope to see you there," she said. She departed for bed.

The two former teammates lounged in easy chairs facing a crackling fire. "If you've got time tomorrow, there is a site I'd like to show you," Salmon said. "You want to see the Chief Joseph

Battlefield now, before the chamber of commerce pretties it up for the bicentennial."

"Chief Joseph of the Nez Perce?"

"Yep, the same tribe that saved the Lewis and Clark expedition."

"Let's do it," Kyle said.

He took two aspirins before bed, but still lay awake. Salmon and Judy married twelve years, no kids: was it intentional? Did rockets explode tonight for Mona in Missoula? What did Ginny Foster wear this instant, if anything? Three days back; already he felt involved.

The sound of the wind outside reminded him of the Blackfoot River and the old pictures rose in his mind. Lane Moore popped up downstream and swam for shore. Kyle stood in the raft he shared with Jerry Anders and tried to spot his brother. A hand rose from the water, reaching. Terry's head appeared and he opened his eyes. He saw Kyle, their eyes met. Kyle wanted to dive in, to try and save him. But he feared those rocks, that dark water. He hesitated, the current spun him and his raft downstream. He looked back, his brother was gone.

# # #

CHAPTER 5

Judy drove away to her teaching job. Kyle Hansen gazed out at a sky of relentless blue. Over breakfast, he and Salmon made plans.

"Interesting," Kyle said, "that Edgar Ware telephoned you yesterday after he heard about the five palefaces beating up the Indian kids. So you're in the loop?"

"Well, I like to stay involved," Salmon said.

"How long has he been chairman of the Blackfoot Tribal Council?"

"I don't know. Ten years. Edgar has come to define the office."

"He's active politically?"

"Very, when he thinks it might be helpful."

Kyle considered that. "Chief Joseph and the Nez Perce," he said. "We know their ancestors befriended Lewis and Clark. It seems Lewis and Clark got along with all the other tribes except the Blackfeet. What is it with these guys?"

"They're high spirited," Salmon said.

Kyle laughed. "If I had time and you had the time, and if you thought we could find the exact spot, we could drive over to Highway Eighty-Nine to see where Lewis and three of his guys engaged in the expedition's only 'hostile encounter' with Indians in three years of exploring to the Pacific and back."

"That would be the Blackfeet, of course," Salmon said. "There's a sign for tourists along that road, but no one knows the exact site. Lewis and his lads shot first, you know."

"He and three of his men went exploring and ran into a Blackfeet hunting party. They accused the Indians of trying to steal their horses and killed two of them."

"That stuff about the horses; that's Lewis' version," Salmon said.

"That's true; the Blackfoot account hasn't come down to us. Salmon, I appreciate you acting as tour guide today, but don't they expect you at your school?"

"I called, told 'em I'm propagandizing an Eastern journalist."

Salmon leading, each in his own car, they sped east on Route 2 through green fields along the Milk River. Dull-eyed descendants of 1880s Texas cattle drives chewed mouthfuls of grass moist with dew. The scene reminded Kyle of pictures he had seen of the Valley of the Nile in Egypt; a ribbon of irrigated lushness, hemmed on both sides by barren, yellow hills.

The town of Chinook preened in early morning sun. Flowers cradled houses. Old trees shed weary leaves. Two water towers rose, one shaped as a tea kettle painted red on top. The other, silver, proclaimed "Chinook" in large, solid letters.

Kyle followed Salmon south out into hayfields and grassland. Gophers risked mad dashes across the road. Conical mountains floated ahead, the northern slopes of those same Bearpaws Kyle saw yesterday from the south. They passed a red corral stranded in barbed-wire vastness. Salmon slowed and turned into a grassy parking area along a shallow stream.

Snake Creek drifted through a depression in an open, treeless plain. Birds played in high reeds and on the prairie meadowlarks darted and sang. "They fought here for five days," Salmon said.

Kyle knew the story. In 1877, a year after Custer's final mistake, white settlers forced Chief Joseph and his band of Nez Perce from their ancestral home in the Wallowa Mountains of Oregon. The by then familiar pattern ensued; a few Indians resisted, settlers and politicians yelled for the army.

The Nez Perce departed in a long column of families and horses. They hoped to join Sitting Bull in Canada and for 1500 miles they fought off repeated attacks by soldiers and vigilantes while following old hunting trails east then north through the mountains. They paused here, along Snake Creek, to rest and let their horses graze, 30 miles from the safety of the Canadian border.

"It was a cold October day," Salmon said. "The Army rode up and galloped in shouting and shooting. The Nez Perce defended themselves." He indicated a stone memorial, erected by the Daughters of the American Revolution, inscribed with the names of 23 soldiers who died in the several days of fighting that followed. Kyle recorded some of their names in his notebook: Whitlow, Mielke, Alberts, Durselow...

He followed Salmon across a plank over Snake Creek, up a bank and along a prairie path muddy from recent rain. He saw no other cars in the parking area; he and Salmon had the place to themselves. Birds wheeled and darted. Views pulled the eye toward far horizons.

A wooden stake printed with crude lettering poked from the ground: "Looking Glass killed here." "He was a chief, a good fighter," Salmon said, "but on this trip he goofed more than once. Sometimes he forgot to post sentinels."

Pink and white fragments scattered the ground and Kyle leaned to look. "Roses," he said, surprised. "Still fresh; somebody must have brought them in just the last day or two."

"Because of this." Salmon indicated a depression in the ground. "Mass grave. As usual in these 'battles,' the soldiers killed mostly the weakest, the old people, women and children."

"Why the fence?" Kyle asked. High, iron spikes ringed the burial grave, a lonely rectangle on a treeless plain.

"Sometimes souvenir hunters dig up Indian bones." Salmon pointed. "See the knoll? That's where Joseph surrendered."

Alvin M. Josephy Jr., in his history of the Nez Perce, and other writers have described what happened that day. According to the military record transcribed by Lt. C. E. S. Wood, Chief Joseph said to Gen. Oliver Howard and Col. Nelson Miles, "Our chiefs are killed, the old men are all dead. It is cold and we have no blankets. The little children are freezing...I am tired. My heart is sick and sad. From where the sun now stands I will fight no more forever."

"...My heart is sick and sad. From where the sun now stands I will fight no more forever..." Kyle grew up in the West and had read that quote many times. He had wondered at it. He had tried to imagine the events and the setting. Today, over 100 years later, on a barren hill surrounded by space, he caught a glimmer, only a glimmer.

"The Army shipped the Nez Perce to prisons in Kansas and Oklahoma," Salmon said. "They moved them again to the Colville Indian Reservation in eastern Washington. Chief Joseph asked the government many times to let him visit his native Wallowa Mountains again. They never did. They buried him on the Colville Reservation. It's a dry, sad place."

"You've been there?"

"Stop by, if you get a chance."

They walked through waving grass. Kyle saw a placard near the path and stooped to read, "'They took it from us. Now we will take it from them. Follow the Holy Road.'"

"What's 'the Holy Road?'" He squinted at Salmon.

"Sorry, I'm not into that medicine man stuff; I'm a college graduate."

They crossed the creek and approached the parking area. An occasional car or truck whooshed by but no one stopped. Salmon sat on the hood of his car and unfolded a Montana highway map.

"Observe," he said, "the government laid out the Fort Belknap Indian Reservation in the shape of a rectangle. But what's this? It appears someone reached in and sliced out a chunk."

Kyle traced with his finger; yes, someone had indeed carved a neat square from the south side of the reservation, and in the middle of the purloined piece he noticed a dot. "Zortman," he said.

"Zortman's got a gold mine."

"Ah ha," Kyle said, "that sign, 'Now we will take it from them' – Montana Indians mean to reclaim Zortman?"

Salmon snorted. "Next week," he said. "At the latest."

They drove north, Salmon again leading, and stopped in Chinook for coffee. "What happens to the five men who beat up the two Indian kids?" Kyle asked. "Police know who they are, right? My newspaper might want a story."

"Police know their names," Salmon said, "but nobody's been arrested. Edgar and some of the others are concerned about that."

"You think he might do something?"

"It's conceivable." Salmon smiled enigmatically.

"Might he tell you about it first?"

"If he does, I'm sure you'd like to know. Where are you headed from here, anyway?"

"East across the High Line. Maybe to North or South Dakota. Scouting the route of Lewis and Clark."

"I was born in South Dakota," Salmon said.

"Oh yeah?"

"...yep, Sioux on both sides, entered the world right there on the Pine Ridge Reservation. I don't remember my mother, but after she left my dad drank himself to death. One of my uncles leased a gas station in Browning. Sure thing, selling gas outside a national park, right? Well, he found out Glacier Park closes from October to June. He made a living, though, and gave me a home. He tried to teach me things. I got my football scholarship to the university before he died."

"My editor wants me to stress the Native American angle in my Lewis and Clark stories," Kyle said. "Perhaps you can help me there."

"Perhaps I can."

A waitress offered more coffee. Kyle declined. "I've got to get going. You and Judy will come to Helena this weekend?"

"That's our plan."

"You guys come, I come," Kyle said.

"Do. The Save the Landers put on a good show. I don't know if Ginny told you; she's leading one of the programs."

"She's a piece," Kyle said. "It pains me to imagine her with Harley. Is she faithful, do you think?"

"I think so. I think she fights them off."

"How do you mean?"

"Guys are always trying," Salmon said.

They stepped outside. The wind blew in their faces and bent the grass along the road. "I'll drive ahead of you to the Agency," Salmon said. "That's my Holy Road, where I turn south to my school."

# # #

CHAPTER 6

William Clark floated down the Yellowstone, Meriwether Lewis down the Missouri, separating their party for over 500 miles during their return in 1806 from the Pacific Ocean. They reunited at the junction of those two rivers near today's North Dakota border, and Kyle Hansen drove east across Montana to see and photograph this spot.

The Missouri paralleled his route somewhere south, but he did not see it until he reached Fort Peck and stopped to ponder today's lake and dam. Feathery, hurrying clouds flecked the sky, and after days of glorious weather tomorrow's forecast predicted rain.

Kyle stayed the night in Wolf Point and rose early Thursday. He felt excited, a detective in quest of the past. He drove past a windmill and crumbling homesteader cabins on a gravel back-road. An abandoned bank and a white, castle-like church high-lighted lonely Bainville. A dog loitered on a corner. An old man leaned into the wind.

Kyle intended to begin at Fort Union, near the junction of the two rivers, depicted in a painting by George Catlin in 1835.

He had read that the National Park Service reconstructed the old traders' post on its original site, even though the Missouri River shifted, in 160-some years, from the edge of the fort to a quarter mile away. He drove lonely backroads and found a fortress of golden logs, surrounded by an equally fresh log stockade. He studied a copy of Catlin's painting of the original fort, prominently hung for tourists to see, and walked outside to compare. The same bald hills rose from the same wooded bottoms.

But where did the Yellowstone flow into the Missouri? He asked a park ranger.

"Drive east, turn right on the dirt road past the Buford Bar."

Kyle passed, on a bumpy, dirt road, a sign that informed him he entered North Dakota. A bar – a beer-drinking bar, not a sand-bar as he had mistakenly expected – appeared ahead. He passed a gaggle of parked pickup trucks, turned on a muddy lane and glimpsed through trees a glint of running water.

A lone picnic table stood in high grass among scattered cottonwoods. Wind riffed the Fat River, the Indian name for the Missouri. Birds wheeled. Blackish clouds scudded. "Ah," Kyle said. Under a bluff across the way, running fast and clear between its gravel banks, rushed the longest free-flowing river left in America.

The Elk River – today's Yellowstone – kicked a noisy chop as it hit the Missouri. Kyle sat on the smooth curve of a drift-wood log and wondered at a thumping, clunking sound, until gradually he realized that the noise came from stones tumbled by the current along the bottoms of the rivers. He took pictures and marveled at the isolation, the loneliness of the place. It looked as wild as the beginning of time.

It began to rain and, looking back occasionally, Kyle drove slowly away. He stopped in Sidney to telephone his newspaper and drove across the prairies of eastern Montana toward Helena on a route chosen to take him through his old hometown.

He stopped in Circle, marooned in dust and sagebrush, and photographed the white Gladstone Hotel and streets that ended precisely at prairie's edge. He drove east on Route 200 through red-clay badlands and long, dune-like hills and stopped to urinate near a bridge marked Timber Creek. East, west, he saw not a tree.

Wild Horse and War Horse Lakes lay out there somewhere. Treeless, endless, the earth extended. For miles Kyle met not a single car and then a dot appeared, a lone bicyclist loaded with saddle bags. He and Kyle waved at each other in passing.

"Do you remember a girl named Betty Admundson?" Kyle asked the waitress at QD's Restaurant in desolate Jordan. It was from here, he remembered, that she moved to Hightown.

"Little white-haired girl? Buck teeth?"

"She didn't have buck teeth when I knew her." Kyle drove by the Jordan school and thought of all the times he and Terry played basketball in little towns like this. He remembered headlights converging in the night and high-ceiling gymnasiums where bands played and cheerleaders strutted. People drove for miles through cold and blowing snow to watch kids play basketball. They gathered for two or three hours, shed some loneliness, and then the headlights of their cars radiated out into blackness again.

A skim of water flashed in Big Dry Creek. Circular protuberances poked from empty prairie, earth hiccups on the land. Kyle approached a ribbon of green across a moonscape of sagebrush and dry grass. He crossed the Musselshell River and entered Petroleum County – larger than the State of Rhode Island, total population about 600 people.

Gaps opened along Winnett's main thoroughfare where houses and stores once stood. Birds drank from puddles in front of a stone building adorned with a faded yellow "Hotel $9" sign. Kyle got to talking with a pair of wizened oldsters in Gershmel's General Store.

"...a homestead every hundred and sixty acres, mostly bachelor boys from Germany, Norway, Finland. Nineteen-Twelve drylanders started to plow high ground. Rained so much in Nineteen-Fifteen, they say, anywhere you dropped a seed it grew. Nineteen-Nineteen the bad years began..."

"...all the big ranches had baseball teams. Grass Range boys said the N Bar field had too many gopher holes. My father played for the N Bar and he complained about the sagebrush on the Flatwillow Field. Moore had the powerhouse baseball teams back then. Read somewhere that when they played in Hightown, the whole town came along on a special train. Nobody left in Moore but the dogs..."

Kyle drove west toward a growing smudge on the horizon, the long line of the Spirit Mountains. No elevations but the Black Hills for a thousand miles behind him, but here in Central Montana it began, mountain range after mountain range, all the way to the Pacific Ocean.

He drove the bypass around Grass Range, another dying little prairie town that peaked 80 years ago. He crossed a ridge of the Judiths and the stubble of wheat fields contoured a sweep of land ahead, a vast basin ringed by clumps of mountains that hunched like islands.

Kyle parked on Main Street in Hightown. A leathery woman tended the cash register in the Jason Forks Cafe and a placard behind the counter advised, "When trouble strikes, take it like a man. Blame it on your wife."

He ordered a Forty-Niner sandwich, liverwurst and onions on rye with extra pickles. He did not see anybody he knew and when he walked back outside a red parking ticket brightened the windshield of his car. "Howdy, Stranger," it read. "You have violated parking regulations, but we're doggoned glad you came..."

Old cowboys wandered back and forth from the Mint to the Stockman Bars. Kyle drove up the hill and his rental car turned as of its own accord toward the house where his family once lived. The metal rim of the basket jutted still from the wooden backboard over the garage. His father put it up and added a light so his sons could practice at night.

They wore gloves to play in January and laid cardboard on top of the ice. In March they scooped up snow-melt water and carried it off in buckets, 46 one day, 35 another; Kyle remembered, he had counted. In May they played until late at night beneath the outside light, the ground perfect now, hard-packed, bouncy. In summer the dust began.

Kyle remembered other nights, eating cereal with Terry, he'd hear his father's footsteps on the stairs and know they would listen again to the same old stories. "Did I ever tell you...?" But Terry never seemed to mind. It was Terry who grieved the most when their father, an insurance salesman and town councilman, died suddenly of heart collapse.

Sprinklers flung water across the grass at the high school football field and Kyle jogged down a sideline, turned, and trotted back. It was expected in small Montana towns that if you were male and healthy you went out for football, but the gridiron glory Kyle anticipated playing pum-pum-pullaway in Wyoming had been slow in coming. He and Terry served primarily as cannon fodder during their first two years in high school. Stoically they took their knocks and waited.

Not all boys were suited, of course, and many stuck it out for dad and pride. It was these, not the quick and the strong, who deserved the medals, Kyle understood now. It was the slow, the undersized, the uncoordinated, who showed the greatest courage.

Kyle shot up in size after his sophomore year and one day he looked around at football practice and realized he had become one of the big kids. He played fullback on offense and linebacker on defense and he loved carrying the ball. During games he liked to get up slowly after a hit, shake himself, and limp slightly as he trotted back to the huddle.

Girls noticed him in the hallways at school. Businessmen recognized him on Main Street. He won an athletic scholarship to the university and played football and basketball there too.

That was over, and Kyle paused at the spot where Harley Hawkins broke his brother's arm. He heard girls' voices and, grateful for a diversion, followed the sound up the hill into the high school gymnasium.

Sixteen-year olds in ponytails sprinted up and down the floor. They did not play their first basketball game until November, but here they were practicing in September. Good pass. How did she see that? These young ladies could play.

The woman coach blew her whistle, her team gathered round. They walked springy, feet apart, that walk that Glenda Lodermeier invented. Loose, hands on hips, they shifted weight.

The coach spoke softly and the girls bounded in a warm tide of bodies down the stairs.

A basketball trembled on the varnished floor. "I played here in high school," Kyle said. "Can I shoot a few?"

"If you take your shoes off," the coach said, and she too disappeared down the stairs to the locker room.

Alone on the shiny court, Kyle picked up the basketball and caressed its pebbled surface. With his right hand he lobbed the ball behind his back, with his left he plucked it from the air. "I'm Kyle Hansen, folks," he thought, "I know what to do with this thing." He dribbled beneath his leg and behind his back, he lobbed up a shot. The net sighed. He shot again.

So familiar, it felt like breathing. He felt the ball and the basket as extensions of his body; an understanding ran from him to them. Memories. He lofted a jumper from the key, another from the corner, and gradually he felt the presence of his brother.

He and Terry played many games on this court, practiced here countless times. I'll toss him the ball, Kyle thought. But something gray darkened the sky and the sun faded from the floor. He realized his brother was gone.

# # #

CHAPTER 7

Kyle Hansen crossed the Judith Basin past grain-elevator towns lost in vastness and stayed the night in Great Falls. Salmon Thirdkill had told him of a mountain canyon to the north where one of the best of Montana writers situated his novel of the mountain men who came after Lewis and Clark. Why not view the place, Kyle thought, and weave it nostalgically and historically into his upcoming series?

He had briefly considered lingering longer in Hightown. Though he departed the streets of home eighteen years ago to attend college, he still knew many people there. But they would ask about Terry. They would ask about Glenda, his former wife. They would ask about his mother, who like Glenda had moved to the West Coast and remarried. He might come back in two years for his twentieth high school reunion, Kyle thought. Maybe by then he'd have something to brag about.

He had suggested this Lewis and Clark series to National Editor Jack Leventhal after a softball game in hopes of advancing his career. To prepare, he read the explorers' journals and Stephen Ambrose's book. He brought with him tomes on Crazy

Horse, the Oregon Trail and other icons of the American West, and this week in Montana he had added more to his collection. But nothing topped this, he thought. Nothing topped the joy of going to see for yourself.

He drove north from Great Falls. The peaks of the Continental Divide, as brilliant as diamonds in the clear air, angled ever closer on his left. Beyond Choteau, where Highway 89 crossed the Teton River, he turned onto the gravel road that Salmon told him about.

The road climbed through scattered trees and swung in beside a clear, rocky stream. Gaps appeared in the Rocky Mountain Front and a canyon gradually took shape ahead. Beside the road, on a knoll above the river, stood a weathered sign:

OLD NORTH TRAIL

Through this immediate region, hard by the mountains, ran the old north trail, its starting point far to the north, its termination to the south, its origins lost in the mists. It is a surmise that long-ago Mongols, crossing the Bering Sea Land Bridge, found and marked their way south and became, or merged with, our Indians of mountains and plains. History runs into mystery here.

"History runs into mystery here." Kyle liked that. He copied the words in his notebook, and photographed the sign.

"There is only one direction – north," Montana poet Richard Hugo wrote. Kyle gazed in that direction now, seeking to follow the line where prairie and mountains met, trying to picture the early ones coming.

Did he look upon the Holy Road? He had to smile. For the rest of his stay in Montana he expected to see Holy Roads around every bend.

Salmon Thirdkill told him that the Montana novelist A. B. Guthrie Jr., in his novel *The Big Sky*, situated an Indian camp in the canyon ahead, so Kyle followed a gravel road into a crease in the mountains and scanned terrain in anticipation. There! A fork of the Teton River meandered, the water slowed by a seemingly endless series of beaver dams. Here's the spot, Kyle thought, here where the ground widens and flattens.

He got out, looked around. Yes. Here beside this mountain stream, after they keel boated up the Missouri River battling Indians and outlaws, the fur trappers Boone and Dick Summers courted Teal Eye, the Blackfoot princess. Here their drama unfolded. Kyle had read *The Big Sky* in high school and twice seen the movie.

A. B. Guthrie, Jr. died in 1991 at the age of 90. He lived in Hollywood but always he had returned to the mountains. Might not he too someday, Kyle wondered, return to Montana to live? Of course he would have to find the magic woman. He worried that since his divorce he lazed into a pattern: romance, find fault, move on.

"East of the Divide...west of the Divide...," he listened on the car radio to the weather forecast. Clear and cool across the state, the announcer said. Kyle nodded approval. He had left Washington D. C. in humid, relentless heat.

The grassy trails of a winter ski area descended ahead, brown slashes on a mountain green with pines. Kyle's road wound up past these trails and deteriorated into little more than a jeep track. He backed around, drove back to the beaver dams, got out of his car and sat on a rock in the sun.

The sky spread so blue it hurt his eyes. Kyle's inner hiker examined and gauged mountain slopes, calculating best routes to climb. Only gradually did his thoughts return to the task at hand.

Sunday, after Save the Land, he would visit the headwaters of the Missouri River between Helena and Bozeman, a mother's lode for students of Lewis and Clark. Monday drive east along the Yellowstone and photograph Pompey's Pillar near Billings, another explorer landmark. Tuesday fly back to Washington D. C. He saw himself writing his articles, his editor happy, he, Kyle, accepted as a newly-minted member of the national desk reporting staff.

But leave Harley Hawkins smug and unscathed? Tonight in Helena, Kyle decided, for pleasure, for revenge, to make a play for Harley's wife, Ginny Foster.

A tang of adventure hung in the air. He sped toward Helena and stopped only once, on Tenth Avenue South in Great Falls, at the first red light he had seen in 300 miles. He saw himself inviting Ginny to his room; that is, unless she invited him to hers first.

He reached Last Chance Gulch in Helena before sunset and registered for a room at the Vigilante Hotel. "Has Ginny Foster Hawkins checked in?" he asked a man behind the desk. He knew Salmon and Judy Thirdkill did not arrive until tomorrow morning.

"You're with Save the Land?"

Kyle nodded. "Ginny Foster's in room two-twelve," the clerk said.

He phoned her room; no answer. He ran up the stairs for sheer enthusiasm and lurched out onto the balcony of his sixth floor room. The Vigilante Hotel fronted a big, scarred mountain and beyond that, higher, ever higher, patches of snow gleamed on the Continental Divide. Down below, along the old whooping El Dorado of Last Chance Gulch, clothing boutiques and art galleries replaced the gold diggings of yesteryear.

Kyle dined alone in a Chinese restaurant, sipping plum wine from a bottle with a dragon on the label. Where was she? He returned to the hotel and looked for Ginny Foster in the bar. He'd suggest a walk, a balloon ride, anything to peel her away from the Save the Land crowd. He took a seat and ordered a local micro brewery beer.

Attractive women sauntered here and there, but none of Ginny Foster's striking stature. As usual when alone, every conversation looked interesting. Impatient, Kyle wandered out into the hotel lobby and noticed an unattended Save the Land registration table. He darted toward it and snatched a program.

"Whoa. I saw that."

Ginny Foster faced him, brash, high-shouldered. "Hello, Wandering Journalist. Judy Thirdkill said you might come."

"She told me you planned to lead a workshop and, by god, that decided it," Kyle said.

"It's a slide show, not a workshop." Ginny flung back her splendid hair.

"A subversive slide show, Salmon says, and if you'd care to tell me about it, they've got the darkest bar in the West back there." Kyle swung his head in invitation.

"Try me on that tomorrow after Salmon and Judy arrive."

"How about dinner then?" He could eat twice, Kyle thought. He could eat three times if need be.

"I've partaken, thank you."

"Can this be? I've run through my repertoire." Kyle sought to charm. At that moment an elevator door slid open, a yellow-haired man stepped out behind Ginny, and before she could turn to see who it was he grasped her around the waist and flashed Kyle a crinkly, wind-burned smile.

"Hello, Jeb," Ginny said, without even turning to look. "Come to Save the Land tomorrow. Maybe you'll learn something."

"Are you kidding?" the man said. "I'd be politically destroyed." Ginny introduced him to Kyle as Jeb Small, Montana's Attorney General.

"Don't go too hard on us cowboys in your stories, Kyle. See you, Ginny." Jeb Small spun out the door.

"Jeb's from the 'if-it-grows-cut-it-down, if-it-moves-kill it' school," Ginny said. "He's probably our next governor."

Kyle remembered Montana's attorney-general-becomes-governor apostolic succession from his reporting days in Bozeman. But it was Ginny's reaction to Jeb Small that interested him. "You recognized his grasp," he observed as they shared an ascending elevator.

"I saw him earlier in the lobby. I knew he was here. Harley called, by the way. He said he'd like to see you. He says he'll try to fly in after the game tomorrow."

"Pocatello has an airport?" Kyle had hoped Harley would not come. His Montana State team played at Idaho State, and Ginny's easy assurance provoked him.

She flung her hair and waited for it to settle, a mannerism so practiced that already Kyle anticipated and hoped for it to happen. He knew the process now; tendrils crept forward, tickled her cheeks, blocked an eye, until, agitated, she tilted her head and primed another throw. Backward flew tumbled tresses, an almost sexual heave of release, and the whole countdown began anew.

"Would you believe it? We're civilized out here too." Ginny touched Kyle's sweater. "I like this color. I sell clothing, you know. Let's have dinner together tomorrow night, okay? We'll sit with Salmon and Judy. If Harley comes, it won't be until later."

The elevator door jerked open at her floor and with a smile she strode away. Provoked, Kyle rode on to the top and back down again. Approximately 20 hours remained for him to work his wiles before Harley's likely arrival. He'd look for Ginny at breakfast. He'd look for her at lunch. That still left the afternoon.

Now he had stories to think about, and the Native American angle.

# # #

CHAPTER 8

"If Judy and I have kids, who do you suppose they will look like?"

"They'll probably come out kind of in the middle," Kyle Hansen said. It was mid-morning Saturday, and he and Salmon Thirdkill sat halfway up a mountain overlooking Helena.

"Should we raise them as Sioux? as Presbyterians? You want them comfortable in the dominant culture and yet you don't want them to lose whatever it is that makes them special."

"Trust your judgement," Kyle said. "You're a school principal."

"Well I've got to get her pregnant first," Salmon said.

"Do Ginny Foster and Harley Hawkins have kids?"

"Judy says Ginny doesn't want kids," Salmon said. "He does, she doesn't, that's not your usual situation. Knowing Harley, I'm sure he's tried to sneak some seed through. What's this? You've got that wistful look, my friend."

"Why doesn't Ginny want kids?"

"She likes going, doing," Salmon said. "You've seen her. I guess she likes her freedom."

"Last night at the hotel Jeb Small snuck up behind her and they kidded around as if they'd run the Colorado River rapids together. Is she like that with everybody?"

"With the throng, yes," Salmon said. "It's my theory that if she really likes a guy she acts more standoffish."

"Hmmm." Kyle lay on his back and studied a cloud.

Salmon plucked a blade of grass and spun it in his mouth. "You know what counting coup is?"

"When you ride in close and touch an armed enemy."

"Right," Salmon said, "that's how young bucks showed bravery in battle. It was a good system a hundred and fifty years ago. Young men counted coup and won glory. Then they courted any girl they wanted."

"I guess the equivalent today is scoring three touchdowns," Kyle said.

"That's my point," Salmon said. "I think it's the kids who do well in the classroom who should get rewarded."

"You could argue that they do, that college grads make more money."

"Yes, but most Indian kids don't go to college. It's not in the culture. I see former students of mine waiting for the bars to open in the morning. I know men on the reservation who mix lysol with water and drink it."

"That's a disinfectant."

"Sometimes it kills them," Salmon said. "How do you instill pride?"

"You made it through," Kyle said.

"Football wrote my ticket; in high school I hung out at the Teepee Village Shopping Center just like the rest of them."

"Remember how after football practice in college you used to lead us in mad dashes up Mount Sentinel? I'd nip at your heels, try to follow close behind, but I could never catch you."

"I remember you out in front of me one time," Salmon said. "Against Idaho State. I had the ball, you blocked for me, you knocked down two men on the same play. A miracle. It was symmetrically perfect."

"I remember that. I hit the first guy and rolled forward and damned if the other one didn't go down too."

"It looked good on the game film," Salmon said.

"I said, 'Coach, could we see that again?'"

They chuckled. Salmon jumped up. "Come on, let's ascend."

Here we go again, Kyle thought. I follow my old teammate up another mountain. Christ. Will he ever stop? Ah. They flopped in the shade of a lonesome pine.

"Montana, as far as I see..." Kyle enjoyed the view. Mountains ringed the horizon, brown at their bottoms, darkening to pine forest in the middle, thinning to gray spurs and spars and streaks of September snow white in the sun.

"I had mixed feelings about coming back," Kyle said. "I expected everybody to ask about Terry and my former wife. It hasn't turned out that way."

"How has it turned out?"

"I'm seeing places I never saw before. It's cool at night. I met Ginny Foster."

"That's good. How much time do you have left?"

"Four days," Kyle said. "It's going fast."

He and Salmon descended the mountain, showered, changed, and joined a flow of Save the Landers into the Vigilante Hotel's Silver Bow room. Judy saved them seats in the second row and they sidled inward along a row of chairs. Kyle looked for Ginny Foster – he had missed her at breakfast – and spotted her up front formidable in skirt, military blouse and clunky hiker boots, where she conferred with a tanned, bearded man. Not likely to be mistaken for the girl next door, Ginny appeared the taller of the two.

The man introduced himself as Larry Cameron of Missoula, President of Save the Land. He tapped for silence, thanked donors, listed program events. "From Bozeman, I give you Virginia Foster."

Ginny rose and swept the audience with her eyes. "Bobby," she said to a young man in sandals, and nodded almost imperceptibly at Kyle while the youth leaped to his feet and closed curtains to darken the room.

She snapped on a projector and a photo of a dead, emaciated deer appeared on a big, white screen. "Note the steel trap holding its leg." Ginny clicked to a pinioned coyote, teeth bared. "Observe; before this animal died of thirst and starvation, it gnawed its leg almost in two." She spoke softly, almost in a monotone.

She showed raccoons and bears dead of starvation, their legs gripped in metal traps. She showed coyotes poisoned and shot from airplanes, their bodies stacked like piles of wood. She showed a pyramid of dead birds atop a pile of sticks. "They pour gasoline on them and burn them. Why? I don't know, but that's what they do."

She stepped forward, directly into the projector's chalky light. "Who's 'they?' Who does these things? I illustrate for you the work of the Animal Control Unit of the U. S. Department of Agriculture. Our government provides this service to ranchers free of charge. Who pays for this? You do. You pay with your tax dollars."

Click. A rangeland cow, the kind that abounds throughout the West, stared at the audience from the screen.

Ginny waited before she spoke. "For this we destroyed the buffalo," she said. "For this we shot, poisoned, trapped and tried to exterminate the wolf. For this we continue, year after year, to slaughter coyotes and countless other wild animals."

A man raised his hand and identified himself as a journalist from a Montana newspaper. "What about wolves and coyotes killing and tormenting cows and sheep, gnawing off their noses, leaving them to bleed to death?" he asked.

"If wolves or coyotes do kill livestock, government and private groups compensate the ranchers for their losses," Ginny said.

The journalist remained standing. "Listen, we're talking about vicious predators here."

Ginny studied him. "Wolves did not invent napalm and torture chambers," she said. "Wolves do not invade countries and start wars. Man is the vicious predator."

Kyle Hansen in his second-row seat turned to Salmon and Judy. "Wow!" He mouthed the word quietly.

He telephoned his newspaper during the intermission that followed and spoke to an assistant editor sitting in for Jack Leventhal on Saturday. "The wife of the football coach at the state agricultural college in Montana just attacked the cattle industry at a public forum. That's like attacking god out here. The local newspapers will pick it up and it could make a good story for us too."

"She attacked cows?" the editor asked. "How?"

"She said a unit of the U. S. Department of Agriculture in Washington slaughters animals – birds, coyotes, you name it – at the request of ranchers, and she showed shots of the dead animals and a picture of a cow as the creature responsible. I could copy her slides."

"Sounds perfect for Sunday," the editor said, half facetiously. "Stir the pot. Send us what you've got."

Kyle returned to the Silver Bow Room, where Save the Landers still roiled about. Ginny talked in a corner with journalists, and Kyle sought out Salmon and Judy. "I called my newspaper about Ginny's program," he said. "They're interested. They want me to seek reaction."

"Reaction?" Judy squinted at him.

"Outrage the locals, tell them what Ginny said." Since Salmon and Judy had invited him here, Kyle now sought to involve them too.

"Shouldn't you ask her first, before you do something like that?"

"You saw the Montana reporters here; story's already out," Kyle said.

"Still I think you ought to ask her," Judy said. "Salmon, what do you think?"

"Ask her."

"Alright," Kyle said. "I will." He worked his way through the crowd to Ginny. "I talked to one of my editors about your program and he's interested. But I need to seek reaction from ranchers or politicians or both."

Ginny understood immediately. "Call Congressman Eldon Lauder," she said. "He usually flies home from Washington to his ranch on weekends; that's in Powder River County, near Sonnette. Try Clinton Mosby. He's Mr. Angry Stockgrower around Bozeman."

Judy, listening nearby, shook her head. "Oh god," she said.

"See those local reporters on their telephones," Kyle said. "What do you think they're doing?"

Congressman Lauder answered at his ranch. "She said what? Hmmm," and then crisply, as if he prepared every morning for this sort of thing, he responded in a gentle voice: "I feel sorry for this woman, who so little understands the backbreaking toil of ranching. I suggest she tell us how much in taxes are paid, how many jobs created, by these wolves and coyotes she loves so much."

Clinton Mosby, summoned from outside his ranch house while Kyle waited, asked him to repeat Ginny's more provocative comments. "A sorrowful thing," Mosby said, "a sorrowful thing. She wants to throw decent working farm families off the range and give it back to the buffalo. What does it matter to her? She and her husband, whose salary is paid in part by taxes on the ranchers of Montana, do not have to make a living from the land."

Kyle looked around for Ginny and Judy, but did not see them. He wrote a story in his room, faxed it and pictures East, and found Salmon watching television in the hotel bar. Harley Hawkins' Montana State football Bobcats had defeated Idaho State in Pocatello 34-7.

"Harley called. He's flying in tonight," Salmon said.

"That's too bad."

"Don't you want to see him?"

"No."

"Come on, it's character building," Salmon said.

Kyle ran up the stairs to his room and looked in his closet to see what clothes he had left. Go for it, he told himself. You'll not like yourself tomorrow if you don't. He stepped out on his terrace. A cold wind raged from the north. Rag-tag clouds raced, dark mountains prodded a blue-black sky. Not good flying weather, Kyle thought hopefully.

He showered. He chose a sports jacket, no tie. He skipped down a series of stairs and joined Salmon and Judy in the hotel dining room.

Ginny Foster in a high-necked, black dress strode toward them. People rose to compliment her on her afternoon program. Kyle jumped up and swept back the chair beside him in invitation.

"Well thank you." Ginny smiled and sat down.

A woman at an adjoining table leaned to speak and Kyle heard her mention the Mod Shop, Ginny's clothing store in Bozeman. Ginny responded, "So right; softy woolies in great colors; what a marvelous season it will be."

Other people stopped to speak with Ginny. Kyle nominated himself wine-pourer and in his enthusiasm overturned his own glass. Waiters brought food and gradually people ceased table-hopping and settled in.

The four of them, Salmon, Judy, Kyle, Ginny, pulled their chairs closer. Salmon told of a Cheyenne Indian named Austin Texas and the seven Sioux brothers who became the stars in the Big Dipper. Kyle quoted Ralph Ellison, "Go curse your God, boy, and die," and "His name was Clifton and they shot him down."

Judy recalled from John Updike's *Rabbit at Rest*, "The U. S., held together by credit cards and Indian names." Kyle glanced outside. A bleeding splash of red splayed across a black sky.

The room lights dimmed, and amid the detritus of dessert they scraped back their chairs to watch the evening Save the Land program, a filmed version of the Jack London story, *To Build a Fire*.

Snow, woods, Alaska; the story absorbed Kyle. The dog respected the terrible cold that the man until too late ignored. "This is well done, don't you think?" Ginny touched him on the knee.

"Yes!" Kyle agreed, startled. Her touch scorched his nerve endings.

Salmon eyed him curiously and nodded toward a door in the rear of the room. A man stood silhouetted there, his face indistinct against a glow of light behind.

"Harley," Ginny said. "Come on. Let's go greet him."

# # #

CHAPTER 9

"Let's not mill helplessly; the bar's this way;" the coach took control. "Judy, Salmon, good to see you. Kyle Hansen, this is a real surprise." Harley Hawkins' eyebrows still touched in the middle and his hair shone as black and shiny as Kyle remembered.

Harley took Ginny's arm and Kyle noticed that again, as with Larry Cameron, she stood the taller of the two. Why did he like this? Kyle felt something stirring down there.

He and the others ordered drinks at a table in the bar and Ginny asked about today's game.

"They scored first," Harley said. "They never scored again. Kyle, what brings you west? You didn't come all this way to write about Save the Land."

"I came to write about the Lewis and Clark Bicentennial, but I did do a story on your wife's slide show today." Kyle sought to avoid slipping back into the old youngster-coach role, and also to provoke a little.

"The dead coyotes?" Harley asked. Ginny nodded, casual.

Harley laughed. "I've suggested to this lady here that if she wants to save humanity she might catalog books for the library, she might collect food for the poor, she might teach crippled kids to ski. I've suggested that in these kill-the-cow extravaganzas she alienates the very people whose support we need to run a championship college football program. But she enjoys it. So..." He spread his hands.

"Democracy thrives on different opinions, husband Harley," Ginny said. "I urged no one to rush out and slit cows' throats. Rejoice, your team won today, and here sits a player from your hallowed past."

Was this normal conversation between these two? Apparently, because Judy and Salmon appeared not at all surprised. "Harley," Kyle sought to change the subject because he was the one who brought up Ginny's slide show, "how is it coaching college football?" He made it a point to address his old coach by his first name.

"It's not just drawing X's and O's. It's motivation and execution at whatever level. I'm proud to say that we recruit most of our players within our own state."

"Somehow avoiding recruiting any Native Americans," Salmon said.

"As you know, Salmon, with the reservation kids we find that discipline's a problem." Harley responded in the same easy tone.

"Bull shit," Salmon said. "It's not a problem at other colleges."

"I'm a coach," Harley said, "not a human relations specialist."

"No one will ever accuse you of that," Ginny said.

"It might be nice if they did, Harley," Judy said. "It might be exciting new territory."

Harley grinned. He seemed to enjoy all this, and ordered another beer. He described Ginny's tennis instructor in Bozeman as, "short, fat, with a speech impediment." He clapped Kyle on the back, suddenly jovial. "The Hansen Brothers. You guys had a dog that used to come and watch football practice."

"The great dog Lance. He especially liked passing plays."

The others dutifully chuckled. Kyle shifted position and inadvertently touched Ginny's shoulder. Harley looked at her, and then back at Kyle. His expression flattened. "I'm sorry about what happened to your brother on the river," he said.

Caught by surprise, Kyle found himself without an answer.

"Well, you still look like you're in shape. It's good to see you again." Harley glanced at his watch. "Sorry to drink and run, but I've two hours of game films to study. Ginny, I'm riding back to Bozeman with Mack and Arlo. Want to come along?"

"More's the pity," she said, "I'm committed to the morning program."

"That's right, I guess you did tell me." Harley drained his glass and extended his hand. "Come back and see us again, Kyle. Judy, Salmon, always a pleasure."

Harley left. Ginny uncoiled her long legs. "Mac and Arlo are assistant coaches. Would you have recognized him on the street, Kyle?"

"I think so. Maybe he's gained two pounds. He looks more relaxed."

"Ginny's soothing influence," Salmon said.

"You think?" Ginny tossed her hair.

"Maybe he's relaxed because he doesn't have to ride those high school buses anymore," Judy said. "Hark! Is that a rock band I hear?" Music boomed from a podium at the far end of the room.

"By god, I believe it is!" Salmon said. He jumped up. "Come on, Judy."

"Shall we?" Kyle extended his hand to Ginny.

They wended toward the noise just as Larry Cameron and other Save the Landers walked into the room. "There you are!" They surrounded Ginny. A lady wanted to discuss tomorrow's program. Larry Cameron hovered. Kyle, shunted aside, caught Ginny's eye and nodded again toward the dance floor.

She pushed toward him and he guessed from her apologetic look that his moment had passed. "I'm sorry," she said. "I know all these people. Don't rush off tomorrow, though. We'll do something after the morning program."

Judy and Salmon returned from dancing and sized up the situation. Judy made small talk, excused herself and retired upstairs. Kyle and Salmon planted themselves at the bar. "Remember, against Wyoming...?" They relived the old stories.

The phone jangled in Kyle's room next morning. "We're in the coffee shop," Salmon said. "The coach's wife is with us."

Kyle dressed quickly and descended and found Salmon, Judy and Ginny in a booth, the front page of a Montana newspaper spread before them.

COACH'S SPOUSE ZINGS RANCHERS

Kyle read the story beneath the headline. "They like you," he said. "This reporter's on your side."

"I must become more outrageous," Ginny said.

"Kyle, what did you write in your story for your newspaper?" Judy asked.

"I won't see it for a few days. I don't know how much of it, if any, my editors used."

"Don't they Email you copies or something?"

"Eventually. Not right away."

Salmon excused himself and Kyle saw him talking on a telephone. "I don't want to break up anything here," he said when he returned, "but Judy and I are wanted in Havre." Kyle saw –he hadn't noticed before – that his friend wore a "Property of University of Montana" sweatshirt.

"What," Ginny said, "and miss the morning program?"

"The natives are restless," Salmon said. "Call me before you fly away in a great silver bird, okay, Kyle?"

The four of them strolled outside. Kyle edged Salmon aside. "Something doing?" he asked.

"Don't know yet," Salmon said. "I got your cell phone number. Something happens, I'll call."

"Please do. By the way, Captain Courage, I heard you use the term 'Native American' with Harley. Do you prefer that phrase?"

Salmon reached with one hand and stroked his crinkly, black hair. "I don't care really," he said. "Perhaps for academic types and newspaper stories. But 'cowboys and Indians' gets the point across better, I think, than 'cowboys and Native Americans.'"

They returned to the others. Kyle cuffed Salmon on the shoulder. "Greatness lies in the unfathomable," he said.

Salmon grinned. "Don't wait so long next time," he said.

"I won't. Drive with caution." Kyle thought of his friend returning to his sagebrush school to graduate kids to crash cars and die of cirrhosis of the liver. He kissed Judy, catching a fragment of lip. He watched their car disappear down Last Chance Gulch.

Ginny led Kyle through the lobby of the Vigilante Hotel to the Silver Bow room. She sat at the head table, he toward the rear. A mining engineer in suit and tie took to the lectern to defend current methods of extracting gold in Montana. They dripped cyanide over freshly dug ore to leach the gold and collect it in settling ponds, he said. "I can tell you," he looked his audience in the eye, "the safety factor in these ponds is one-hundred per cent."

Ginny rose, the audience tilted forward. She named gold mining sites in Montana where she said settling ponds leaked cyanide and poisoned ground water. "I can tell you," she looked the audience in the eye, "the failure rate of these ponds is almost a hundred per cent."

Kyle loved it. He called his newspaper after she finished and pitched a miners-versus-environmentalists story to another new editor sitting in on Sunday.

"Do us a memo for the futures file, okay?"

"I'll work on it." He would forget it; so would the editor, Kyle knew. "Say, did they use anything on the coach's-wife-ravages-ranchers piece I winged in yesterday?"

"I don't know, want me to look?"

"No, that's alright." Kyle found Ginny in the conference room, as usual surrounded. "It seems Save the Land needs you in the lineup to win," he said.

"Come on, I'll show you the capitol."

"The Lewis and Clark mural?" Kyle had photographed it last week, but he wanted to see it again.

Their footsteps echoed down a hall and into the cathedral-like chamber of the House of Representative, where Charlie Russell's huge depiction of Lewis and Clark meeting the Flathead Indians in 1805 dominated the wall behind the Speaker's desk.

Charles Marion Russell rode a steamboat up the Missouri from St. Louis to Montana in the 1880's. He lived with Indians and worked as a cowboy, all the while honing a talent as an artist. In this painting, done a century after Lewis and Clark, he emphasized the power of the landscape, the yellowing aspens, the snow-streaked peaks of Montana's Bitterroot Range. He portrayed the Indians with dignity and Lewis and Clark as but a minor part of the scene.

"You like?" Ginny asked, lips pursed, hand on chin.

"Very much."

"Me too."

They walked along a high-ceilinged hallway to the rotunda beneath the capitol dome where the busts of Montana "heroes" peered from niches in the circular wall. Kyle noted that the inscription beneath the only Indian in the group, Chief Plenty Coups of the Crows, praised him for fighting with the U. S. Army against the Sioux. "Crazy Horse, Sitting Bull," he said, "the ones who fought for their land; they're the 'heroes' who ought to be here."

"Not to excuse Chief Plenty Coups, but don't forget that the Sioux and Crow considered themselves rivals from way back. But...let's see..." Ginny called to a guard who had just entered, "Kevin, these busts, how often do you change them?"

"We rotate in a new bunch next year."

"Any Indians in the new group?"

"Don't think so," Kevin said.

Kyle jotted details in his traveling notebook for possible use in stories. He spotted sunshine through a door and moved toward it. "Do you know everybody in the state?" he asked Ginny.

"Just the men." She laughed.

Outside, they watched a squirrel dance along the limb of a nearby tree. "See how it uses its tail for balance" – Ginny wiggled herself to demonstrate– "nature does everything right."

"Okay, who's the man on horseback?" Kyle eyed an equestrian statue on a pedestal.

"That's Territorial Governor Thomas Meagher. They say he drowned drunk in the Missouri River."

"Editor of my college newspaper used to yell, 'Get me Hansen, I don't care if he's a drunk, he's the best goddamed reporter we have.'"

"Started young, did you? If I were a journalist I would shout, 'Stop the presses!'" Ginny said. "Did you ever?"

"I wanted to. I still hope for an opportunity." Kyle studied the sky, as if to estimate the time remaining in his day. "How do I get to Missouri Headwaters State Park? I ought to remember, but I don't."

"It's just off the interstate near Three Forks. You can make it in an hour; it's right on the way to Bozeman. Remain alert. Look for the state park sign."

"Is it marked, the hill that Lewis climbed?"

"No, but an intelligent person could find it," Ginny said.

Kyle pretended disappointment. "Okay," she said, "I'll show you. Follow along."

"Since you're going that way anyway..." She led in her car and they bulleted south between the mountains.

They crossed a long ridge and bisected what seemed to Kyle the world's largest wheat field. They rolled onto Interstate 90 in the Gallatin Valley and exited at a green "Headwaters Park" sign.

They parked their cars in the dappled shade of cottonwood trees next to a fast, clear river. "The Gallatin," Ginny said. "The Jefferson flows into the Madison just over there. Jefferson was President in 1805, Madison Secretary of State and Gallatin Secretary of the Treasury. Observe yonder bridge" – she pointed – "beneath it the three rivers join together to become what we call the Missouri."

She crouched behind a tree to change to hiker shorts, and rolled on long, clinging white socks that reached almost to her knees. The sun shone, a gentle breeze stirred. Yellow cottonwood leaves clumped on rocks in the river.

Kyle opened his copy of *The Journals of Lewis and Clark* and read aloud an entry by Meriwether Lewis, July 27, 1805: "'We set out an early hour and proceeded but slowly the current still so rapid that the men are in a continual state of their utmost exertion to get on, and they begin to weaken fast from this continual state of violent exertion. At nine a.m. at the junction of the S. E. fork of the Missouri the country opens suddenly to extensive and beautiful plains and meadows which appears to be surrounded in every direction with distant and lofty mountains; supposing this to be the three forks of the Missouri I ascended the point of a high limestone cliff from whence I commanded a most perfect view of the neighboring country...'"

Opposite, across the Gallatin River, a nondescript hill jutted. "There?" Kyle asked.

"That's the spot."

"Let's go there."

"Follow me," Ginny said.

# # #

CHAPTER 10

Kyle Hansen and Ginny Foster walked downstream to a wooden bridge, thumped across and stepped over two railroad tracks. The Missouri River rushed away beneath them into a gap it had slashed over millenniums through a dry chain of hills. It would flow first north, then east, and finally south to Omaha, St. Louis and the Mississippi River.

"'Violent exertion,' I should say," Ginny said. "Look how fast the current flows; remember, they had to push and pull their boats upstream. That would build an appetite, huh? See the flat spot along the bank? That's where they camped. Right there."

Maybe not exactly there, Kyle thought, but probably close. He imagined a campfire, weary men sprawled. Was it just another night for them? How could they have suspected, even in wildest imagination, the changes that would follow?

He and Ginny scrambled up a bank and hopped a fallen barbed-wire fence. They crossed brick-hard prairie and climbed again. "How old were you when you got divorced?" Ginny asked.

"Twenty-five."

"Ten years? You haven't found anybody you liked?"

"You," Kyle said.

"Now you tell me. Do you think we would have liked each other had we met ten years ago?"

"I would have liked you," Kyle said.

Ginny laughed. They topped a rocky ridge, prickled with sagebrush and scrub pine, and worked their way along it to a final emphatic prong of stone. Here, as did Meriwether Lewis almost 200 years before, they stopped and gazed across the Gallatin Valley.

Three rivers glinted in the sun, the Gallatin, the Madison, and the Jefferson. Each entered the broad valley from clefts in mountain ranges to the south and splayed out in different directions. Shadowed by dark lines of trees, the three rivers meandered in great swoops across the prairie and then converged as if they felt each other's attraction all along.

"Let's see what Lewis says." Kyle read from the Journals, "'...from E. to S. between the S.E. and middle forks a distant range of lofty mountains ran their snow clad tops above the irregular and broken mountains which lie adjacent to this beautiful spot...'"

"The 'irregular mountains,' that's the Bridgers." Ginny pointed. "By 'distant, lofty mountains,' he means our Gallatin, Jefferson and Tobacco Root Ranges."

"I'll accept that," Kyle said. "Now let's picture Meriwether Lewis. He doesn't have maps or anything like that, unless it's some rough drawing he got from the Indians. He sits here, he looks down at these three rivers, and he has to decide which one to follow upstream. He and Clark can't just say the hell with it and go home; Jefferson told them to find the best route to the Pacific Ocean."

"Read some more from the Journal," Ginny said.

"'...It is impossible that the S. W. fork can head with the waters of any other river but the Columbia...' Hear that," Kyle said, "the southwest fork, that's the Jefferson. It's summer, it's hot, they follow it upstream. The Jefferson shrivels and dies and they don't find the Columbia. So they wander for weeks and race winter over the Bitterroots."

"They made the best choice," Ginny said. "If they followed the Gallatin or the Madison we might never have heard from them again."

"Nicely phrased. I might say it just that way in my articles."

"Feel free." Ginny sat on a rock and crossed her ankles. With her long, white socks, she looked like a woman soccer player. "Lewis and Clark and their men stagger over the mountains," she said. "The Nez Perce find them and feed them until these guys from the East grow sick of eating salmon. They float down the Columbia to the Pacific Ocean."

"They spend the winter on the Oregon coast and it rains almost every day. In the spring of 1806 they start their long journey home."

"And they all survive," Ginny said.

"Yes. Good." Kyle looked at her, pleased. "How did you and Harley meet, anyway?"

"I sold real estate in Great Falls the year Harley coached his state championship high school football team. We met at the TV station where he hosted a weekly sports program."

"You looked at him? You knew?"

"He had sort of a brooding attraction. He still does, though you may not have noticed."

"I noticed that you are taller than he is."

"So? Because you're tall, you feel superior?"

"I'll bet you're smarter than him."

"I'm smarter than most men." She swept Kyle with her brown gaze.

"A dollar says you seduced him."

"That's none of your business. Who was the first woman you ever slept with?"

It seemed on this day a natural question, and Kyle considered. "Betty Amundson moved to Hightown from dry, lost Jordan in eastern Montana. She wore tight, fuzzy sweaters. I was a senior; she was a junior. We eyed each other in the high school hallways, but we did not speak."

"She was mute?"

"Shy," Kyle said. "I was too, in my bumbling way."

"Who broke the silence?"

"In May, one of the first warm nights that spring, I saw her walking up Main Street and offered her a ride home. She got in my car. I asked if she might sneak out later, not thinking she would. 'Come back at eleven-thirty,' she said."

"She spoke."

"It felt ordained. I parked at her house in the shadows away from the streetlights, still not thinking she would actually do it. I saw her slide out a window. We drove out the highway toward Great Falls and I chose a road – lucky choice – that ended in the world's softest, grassiest field. I had a blanket."

"Ah," Ginny said.

"I said there were six steps that married people followed. I had never speculated on this before; don't ask me where it came from. Step one, the kiss – we did. Step two, admiration, meaning I must fondle her breasts. She did not prevent me. Step three, remove the sweater. I did, she wore a pointy, white brassiere."

Ginny nodded and shifted position.

"She lay on her back, the grass high all around, and her hair looked wispy-silver in the moonlight. I especially remember that."

"'Wispy-silver.' I can see that, too," Ginny said.

"Step four, remove the brassiere. Trembly, perky breasts; dusky, darkish nipples."

Ginny snorted. "Whoa. You're out of control."

"Step five, remove the skirt and panties."

"Now what's she doing?"

"She's quiet. She's looking up at me."

"Knowing full well what step six will be."

"I must be frank," Kyle said. "At step five Betty Amundson stayed my hand. We never reached that golden moment. Her family moved away that summer and I never saw her again."

"So. It wasn't your first time?"

"No. My actual first time occurred with a skinny girl from Juneaux Street under our backyard bushes."

Ginny grimaced. "You're right, best to stick with the Betty Amundson story."

"Tell me about your first time."

Ginny spoke softly: "I loved the feeling of 'Will he or won't he?' I loved it when the boy stroked my breasts and just above

would I? Sometimes – this was later – I liked being on top; you

and just below my panty lines. I liked the suspense: if he did,
would I? Sometimes – this was later – I liked being on top; you
know, the deeper penetration."

"That's zestier than the stuff I offered," Kyle said.

"There's something to be said for frankness." They descended
now toward the river.

"Long winters, little towns," Kyle mused. "A lot of the girls I
knew in high school couldn't wait to leave."

"I grew up in Cut Bank where it's flat and the wind blows.
I wanted to go to Vassar, but I got a scholarship to Northern
Montana College. I got a job and I met Harley."

"I liked Bozeman. I told you I worked as a reporter for the
Chronicle.   Glenda and I liked to explore. We'd drive through
Rogers Pass and stop at Trixie's in Ovando for a beer. We talked
about staying in Bozeman after she graduated."

"What happened?"

"Another woman. Idiocy on my part. It was Glenda I wanted."

"Last week I walked in on Harley and another woman in the
Brick Breeden Fieldhouse. He's got a couch in his office. He forgot to lock the door."

"Harley, at the school?" Kyle said inanely. "Doing...?"

"Yes. A compromising situation. What is it with you guys, anyway?"

Kyle scrambled to assemble some thoughts. "We need to
prove we're irresistible to women. Did Harley offer an excuse?
A reason?"

"He said she started it. He's the hero coach, and she's the new
secretary in the athletic department."

"This is true?"

"It's true," Ginny said.

"Had it happened before?"

"Not that I witnessed, but I suspect so."

"Why don't you leave him?"

"I care for him. Plus, I've achieved a relative freedom. I go
and do pretty much as I please."

"Salmon told me you don't want kids."

"I don't want the anchor, the duties. Mother told me I never
played with dolls when I was young."

"Why did you tell me about walking in on Harley?"

"I know you leave soon; and we were speaking frankly." They approached their cars.

"Pompey's Pillar tomorrow," Kyle said. "Tuesday I fly back to Washington. I could stay in Bozeman tonight..."

"Not a good idea," Ginny said. "I'd enjoy seeing you, though, if you plan a future trip. Just let Salmon and Judy know."

"Good. Yes. I will." Kyle leaned to kiss her, ostensibly playful, ready to pull back, but she met his lips fully and did not close her eyes.

"So you did try. I wondered if you would. Follow me. I'll lead you back to the interstate."

# # #

CHAPTER 11

Kyle Hansen drove east to Billings to spend his last two nights in Montana. He wanted Ginny Foster while he was with her, but now he wanted to return to Washington and write his Lewis and Clark stories.

He tried, in his motel, to compose a lead for the first article, but his mind kept jumping back to Ginny in her long, white socks. Instead of explorers crossing a continent, he saw himself exploring Ginny's thighs. Instead of floating down rivers, he imagined his fingers navigating the terrain just above and below her panty lines.

He tried focusing on St. Louis, where Lewis and Clark started and ended. Bad choice. A vision hovered, himself and Ginny in Missouri, romping in a pillowed room.

Enough. He couldn't afford trysts and pillowed rooms unless he succeeded at his job. Kyle wrote a sentence, another. He forced himself to concentrate.

Monday morning the sun gentled the mountains and the air smelled of sagebrush, as if to remind Kyle what he would miss by leaving. But he was not fooled; he knew that winter waited.

He ate three bowls of cereal and blasted out on the interstate. Pompey's Pillar, an abrupt grayish white pinnacle of rock maybe 200 feet high, climbed next to the Yellowstone River about 50 miles east of Billings. William Clark camped here on his way East in the summer of 1806. "...emence herds of Buffalows, Elk and wolves," he wrote in his journal. "...The natvs have ingraved on the face of this rock the figures of animals & near which I marked my name and the day of the month & year."

A young Indian girl, Sacajawea, served the explorers as a guide and carried with her a young son, Baptiste. Clark named this mound of rock Pompey's Pillar after the boy, known about camp as "Little Pomp," or "Little Chief."

The federal government maintained the area for tourists now, and a contraption of metal and glass protected Clark's signature. Kyle climbed a rocky path and read this inscription in the sandstone:

"W. Clark July 25, 1806"

Words and numerals appeared fresh, so fresh a sceptic might suggest that someone recently enhanced both signature and date. Kyle saw no need to quibble. Better a little creative maintenance, he thought, than surrender to the indifference of the ages.

He stood on top the rocky protuberance and gazed around. Ducks ran along the surface of the Yellowstone River and rose into the air. South, in Wyoming, the pointed tips of the Bighorns gleamed with fresh snow, as naked and bare-boned in the clear air as if viewed with a telescope. Some historians suggest that from this vantage point William Clark cast his last look at the Rocky Mountains.

George Custer and some of his soldiers climbed this same spot in June of 1876. Kyle wondered if they glanced south about the same time Crazy Horse and Sitting Bull looked north from the hills above the Little Bighorn River. Three days later, in any case, all would meet.

Kyle trotted downhill to his car, Clark's journal at hand, and drove further east along the Yellowstone. He dipped his hand in the river. He dined alone beneath a long, purple sky. He packed for his return flight to Washington tomorrow and flicked his television to the Montana news.

"...entrances to the park blocked on both the east and the west. Indians let no one through except tourists who want to leave. They demand the arrest of five men who they say assaulted two Indian boys in a bar in Dupuyer..." The announcer sounded excited.

Kyle's cell phone rang. It was Salmon Thirdkill. "The Blackfeet block all the roads east of Glacier Park," he said. "Guys with guns. Shouldn't you be there?"

"Thanks, Salmon, I just heard. You think your friend, what's his name, is involved?"

"Edgar Ware? I believe he is," Salmon said.

"Do you have phone numbers for him?"

"As it happens..." Kyle jotted Ware's home and cell phone numbers and called both. Nobody answered. He phoned Jack Leventhal in Washington.

"Cable television's doing a live feed from one of the roadblocks," the Herald's national editor said. "How far is this from you?"

"About four hours," Kyle fibbed. A memory flashed of roads disappearing into space, the Rocky Mountain Front sawtoothed against the sky. "I'm trying to contact one of the Indian leaders. Happily we don't face an immediate deadline on the Lewis and Clark series."

"That's right," Leventhal said, "you can work on that later. Okay. Cancel your flight tomorrow. Hustle to the scene. I wouldn't send a reporter all the way to Montana on this, but since you're already there..."

Kyle exulted. Leventhal just gave him his first breaking news assignment for the National Desk.

He called the airline. He called the car rental agency. He tried Edgar Ware again. Now he had a Native American angle he had not expected. He telephoned Governor Cloninger's press secretary.

Lars Bjornson reflected. "What we want to do, Kyle, is to arrest tomorrow the five suspects – white, Anglo, whatever you want to call them – and charge them with assault or something. We'll let local police actually do it, of course. That would seem to meet the key Indian demand. Trouble is, Congressman Eldon Lauder's already up there raising hell, and we don't need that. You media folks can stir this thing up or you can help us cool it down."

"Can I quote you that the five paleface suspects will be arrested?"

"No. Better not. The situation's in flux. Jeb Small's driving up there now."

"The attorney general?"

"Right. Ol' Jeb intends to work his magic."

"I'm in a bar right now," Kyle said. "Television says roads are blocked with hay bales. They're showing people walking around with guns."

"We're not happy about that," Lars said. "Governor Cloninger has ordered police not to shoot except in self defense."

"Who do you talk to on the Indian side?"

"Edgar Ware," Lars said. "He's the chairman of the Blackfoot Tribal Council."

"You reached him? What did he say?"

"We haven't been able to contact him yet," Lars said.

"Thanks, Lars. Talk to you later." Kyle tried Ware's two phone numbers again. Nothing, not even an answering service. A map appeared on the television above the bar and he moved closer to see. The Blackfoot Indian Reservation, a big one, nudged up against Canada and fronted the entire eastern side of Glacier National Park. Indians blocked the popular Going to the Sun Highway and the park's lesser-used eastern approaches. They obstructed roads in and out of the Blackfoot Reservation itself, and had, only minutes ago, shut down a main highway connecting Montana to Canada.

It would be a bigger story, Kyle thought, if the height of Glacier Park's summer season had not already passed. Still, he'd take what he could get. He made one more phone call, to reserve a motel room in Cut Bank, hopped in his car and drove north. An image flashed of Ginny Foster in long, white socks. He'd call her, yes, let her know he was still around.

He listened to news reports on his car radio. It looked promising. Two groups of armed men faced each other across barricades.

Like most journalists over thirty, Kyle Hansen placed little faith in human nature.

# # #

CHAPTER 12

Kyle drove north in darkness. It would take him six or seven hours, not four as he had suggested to Jack Leventhal, but he was on his way. Finally a breaking, national story, a quantum leap from his early days as a police reporter in Washington D. C.

He recalled one fetid summer day in particular. He telephoned his newspaper from the city's police pressroom, hoping for an all clear, but an editor intoned, "Another one before you come in: the George Washington arsonist strikes again."

Kyle hurried to 26th and K where a luggage store still smoldered, flashed his Herald press pass and interviewed merchants in the area. "You wonder if it's your store next." "I won't sleep nights until they catch this fiend." He returned to the office and wrote another Fear Stalks the Streets of Washington story – if he'd done one he'd done thirty – and felt oddly demeaned the next day to see it played first page.

Barricades around Glacier Park seemed more the real thing. Kyle stopped for coffee in Great Falls and continued north on Route 89, worried only that somebody might settle the crisis before he got there.

Tourists continued to flee the park, he heard on the radio. Armed Indians paced atop hay-bale barricades. Montana Congressman Eldon Lauder, not known for subtlety, called a press conference and demanded that state officials rush in bulldozers and forcibly "cleanse" the roads.

Kyle approached Cut Bank near midnight and his cell phone rang. Salmon Thirdkill spoke conspiratorially, as in a football huddle: "What I tell you must remain shrouded in secrecy. Jeb Small met privately with the Blackfoot Tribal Council tonight. He will put on a show for the television cameras tomorrow at one of the roadblocks. He will pretend to negotiate, he will lift his hand, the barricades will tumble down."

Settled already? Kyle's shoulders sagged. "Why the charade?" he asked.

"Jeb likes the cameras and the cameras like him. He expects to become the next Governor of Montana."

"But why do the Blackfeet play along?"

"If Small prosecutes the five dingleberries, the tribal leaders come out looking good too."

"What about Edgar Ware, the tribal chairman? Was he at the secret meeting?"

"The meeting was at Edgar's house."

Kyle recalled that in college Salmon studied football game films for hours, seeking always that tiny edge. Campus politics captivated him, but not as a candidate. Salmon preferred to manage the campaigns of others, to work behind the scenes.

"Which barricade tomorrow, Salmon?

"Route Two where it exits the Blackfoot Reservation just west of Cut Bank. Jeb Small's choice. It's out in the open, convenient to everyone. TV cameras are already in place."

"Shit. I'd like to at least write a story saying what's really going on. Would that create a problem for you?"

"Run it by me before you send it in."

Kyle sprinkled his story with "allegeds" and referred several times to an unnamed, all-knowing "spokesman." He called and read it to Salmon.

Ken Byerly

"How about if you refer to your unnamed spokesman as 'someone close to both sides?'" Salmon said.

"That will work. Does Edgar Ware know you're doing this?"

"He won't mind. You mentioned him four times." Kyle dictated by telephone to a rewrite person in Washington.

Maybe since his story exposed Small's gambit in advance, the deal might fall through. Then the standoff – and his stories – could continue. Kyle wondered why this possibility did not seem to worry Salmon.

He stared at the ceiling above his bed and visualized Montana as viewed from space. In the middle, near his old hometown, stretched the long, dark arc of the Spirit Mountains. The Continental Divide climbed in the west, a frantic tangle of peaks. Where, in this picture, ought he to locate Ginny Foster? Probably, it pained Kyle to admit, in bed with Harley Hawkins.

He had yet to call Ginny. Maybe she spoke with Judy Thirdkill, and Judy told her he was still around. Kyle wished Ginny could see his byline, "By Kyle Hansen," at least once. He envisioned a rather dull headline tomorrow:

ARRANGED SETTLEMENT SEEN IN MONTANA DISPUTE

He finally got to sleep at three in the morning and it seemed only minutes until he dreamed crazed motorcyclists pounded on his motel door. He shook himself awake and saw day light outside. The pounding continued. He opened his door and Salmon Thirdkill and a slant-eyed, bow-legged man about 45 years old with tangled black hair stood looked in at him.

"Kyle Hansen, meet Edgar Ware." They shook hands. Salmon said he and Edgar drove the 160 miles from Havre in a little over two hours.

Ware studied Kyle. "We don't reopen any roads unless the five yahoos the police arrested serve at least token jail time," he said. "I wish you had stressed that in your story."

Salmon looked apologetic. "They quoted your Herald piece on the news," he said. "No, I doubt it will mess up anything. It's a Jeb Small done deal. Come on. We haven't had breakfast either."

Kyle pulled on his clothes.

"Kyle's from Hightown," Salmon said to Edgar Ware "Remember the Hansen brothers?"

"No," Ware said.

Salmon clapped his forehead as if astounded. "Come on, Edgar, flatter him a little. He's from a big newspaper. You want him on your side."

"Oh, THOSE Hansen brothers!" Ware said, and smiled. Unlike Salmon, with his springy walk and war-chief cheekbones, the Blackfoot leader looked as if he had just ridden in from the Mongolian steppes.

He wore a red vest, a fringed shirt, and a scar jagged from one eye to his hairline. Kyle sat opposite him at breakfast. "What's 'token jail time?'" he asked.

"'Token' means bring your toothbrush and extra shirts."

Kyle asked more questions, and learned that Ware and his wife lived on a cattle ranch so remote you had to ford two creeks to get there. They had two kids, who they sent away to schools in the East.

"Schools in the East; do many people do that?"

"No." Ware spoke to the point and made no attempt at good ol' boy backslapping. In that, and in his grain-truck physical stolidity, he reminded Kyle of Montana Governor Otto Cloninger.

They sat next to a window. Cut Bank outside baked in the open like a silk-caravan oasis in the desert, with one long main street and haphazard side streets jutting off into space. A line of waiting trucks and cars jostled each other along Route 2, the town's east-west trade route.

"Looks like everybody expects the Red Sea to part," Edgar Ware said.

Salmon grinned. "Jeb will put on a good show. Edgar, I hope you do your part."

"I could grimace and glower. That what you mean?"

"Give it your best," Salmon said. "Lot of cameras out there. We don't want to disappoint."

Salmon and Ware drove ahead in their car and Kyle followed. The sun beat down, the peaks of Glacier Park ribbed the sky ahead. The blue lights of police cars revolved at the entrance to the Blackfoot Reservation and the wind made waves that ran with cloud shadows along the prairie grass.

A state trooper lifted his hand, spoke briefly to Salmon and Ware, and waved them through. "Jeb Small here?" Kyle asked the trooper, and identified himself as a reporter.

"No sir, not yet."

"You expect him?"

"Yes sir. We do."

Approved, Kyle drove a hundred yards further to an area of brown grass trampled as if the circus had come to town. "Careful." "This way, sir." Situation still novel, police remained polite. A stack of hay bales blocked the highway ahead and ladies and gentlemen of the news media, natty in khaki and safari jackets, occupied center ground.

"Okay if I stroll over and speak with the people on the other side of the barricade?" Kyle asked a state trooper.

"Sorry, sir." The trooper sounded genuinely apologetic.

Young Indians wearing ski masks gazed down from atop their hastily assembled barrier, and though several cradled rifles, Kyle sensed an air of festivity. The bales that blocked the road, stacked three or four deep, exuded a green-brown freshness and smelled of prairie after a rain.

Kyle wandered away from the crowd with his camera. The country opened to brown distances, hardly a tree between here and the abrupt rise of the Continental Divide. Streams descended from gaps in the mountains onto the prairie, escorted by lines of trees. Some of these tree lines thickened and prospered as they advanced, but most dwindled and died, their streams evaporated, lost, gone.

The sun warmed Kyle's face and arms. Meadowlarks darted and sang. A black bus approached on the highway from Cut Bank, nothing showing through its smoky, hearse-like windows. A door opened; dark shapes stirred. Identically dressed forms filed forth, pea-pod bulky in bullet-proof vests, caressing rifles sleek with 14-inch scopes.

"Who are they?" Kyle asked a Montana State Trooper.

"Agents of the Federal Bureau of Investigation and the Bureau of Alcohol, Tobacco and Firearms," the trooper said.

"Why?"

"You'll have to ask them, sir."

A new stimulus, the sound of sirens, diverted attention. Two police cars raced toward the barricade past a line of waiting tourist cars. Brakes squealed, gravel pinged; a red-faced man leaped from the lead car and hit the ground talking: "...Pioneers...wilderness inhabited by savages...churches... schools... return to them the entire State of Montana and do you suppose...?" Middle aged, he wore yellow cowboy boots, leather elbow patches and a Western bolo instead of a tie. An entourage disgorged from the police car behind him.

Reporters crowded close. "Eldon, what must be done?"

"Bulldoze that goddamn barricade." Ball point pens rustled on paper. The Montana reporters knew their man.

Congressman Eldon Lauder offered the most violent opinions earnestly, his shock of gray hair bobbing. Kyle glanced at the barricade, wondering if the young warriors up there overheard. He noticed that quietly, unnoticed, an old car puttered up the road from Cut Bank, no escort, no sirens, a lone man at the wheel.

The car halted. Kyle recognized Jeb Small as he stepped out – white shirt, no tie. A breeze stirred his longish blond hair.

"About time, Jeb." Congressman Lauder flashed a salute.

"Eldon, as usual you keep the folks entertained."

If Lauder resented his upstaging by the state's attorney general, he gave no sign. Arm in arm, the two men strolled away. The scene reminded Kyle of a Western movie as, foreheads almost touching, the two politicians talked on a windswept, empty road. Small glanced at his watch, seemed to sigh, turned, and strode alone toward the Blackfoot barricade.

Edgar Ware appeared and walked to meet him. All around, Kyle heard cameras clicking. The two men huddled close, talking. Behind the silent ramparts of the Rocky Mountains rose.

The hopeful governor-to-be turned and faced the media. He lifted his hand, a signal. A hay bale trembled atop the barricade, dangled a lazy moment, and tumbled down.

"I now declare this highway open," Jeb Small proclaimed. Television beamed it live.

At the request of photographers, several young Blackfeet lifted the hay bale back and pushed it off again. They did this several times, until Edgar Ware motioned, "Enough," and traffic finally began to move.

# # #

CHAPTER 13

Jeb Small leaped into the back of a pickup truck. "The five men who assaulted the two Indian boys in Dupuyer will plead guilty in court tomorrow," he proclaimed to the assembled media.

"Though I do not presume to speak for our independent judiciary, I think it reasonable to assume that each will be sentenced to a certain amount of time in jail. Reason prevailed today, my friends. I salute the Blackfoot Nation who with dignity achieved their objective."

Small looked expectantly around. Photographers called for Edgar Ware or some other Native American to shake hands with him, but suddenly there seemed no Blackfeet to be found.

Where was Ware? Where was Salmon Thirdkill? Kyle wanted comments from someone on the Native American side to balance his story. He walked, ran, to where the hay bales lay scattered along Route 2. No one. The Indians had gone.

Kyle watched as the federal agents disappeared into their dark bus, still cradling their burnished weapons. Were they pleased, disappointed? He tried to read their faces but could not. He looked for Eldon Lauder, confident he could prod the congressman into saying something outrageous, but could not find him.

Strange, everybody leaving. He sat in his car and worked on his story on the candy box-sized lap top he brought with him from Washington. Someone tapped on his shoulder; it was Salmon Thirdkill.

"What the hell, Salmon? Where were you? Where's Edgar Ware? Where's everybody?"

"Gone. They'll wait and see if Small delivers on his promises. Edgar will monitor the situation, you can be sure."

"Salmon, I know you want to go home, but can you loiter a few minutes? I'm fresh out of Native Americans. Let me update my editor, and then I'll interview you."

Kyle got through to Managing Editor Leventhal on his cell phone. "It's over – maybe," he said.

"Why maybe?"

"I don't know. It just went too smooth."

"Wait and see what happens in court tomorrow," Leventhal said. "See if the settlement holds. Is there a town on that reservation? Are they pleased? Sad?"

Kyle turned to his friend. "You heard?"

"Yes. Too smooth, you think?"

"Don't you wonder? Are you pleased? Sad? Speak, man."

"You'll quote me as a 'Native American educator'? Excellent." Salmon furrowed his forehead, looked to the distance. "This incident illustrates the power of working together..." He rambled on.

Kyle scribbled. "Good. Yes. Thanks, Salmon, for taking me to battlefields and flinging a good story right into my lap."

"You're talking about the 'secret settlement?'"

"Yes, that and more. One challenge remains for me, though, Mount Ginny Foster."

"Making progress there, were you?"

"I feel that if I had the time..." Kyle had not mentioned Ginny's walking in on Harley flagrante delicto. If Ginny wanted that story out, she would tell Judy.

"You can visit us again, you know," Salmon said.

"I intend to," Kyle said. "So, you going to the arraignment tomorrow?"

"I've got to get back to my school." Salmon extended his hand. "Until the next time, Lieutenant Loyalty."

They shook hands. Salmon honked three times as he drove away.

Kyle drove west across Montana's Blackfoot Indian Reservation. My god: even at 70 mph, tourist cars zipped past him toward Glacier Park and the mountains. He stopped at a wide spot along the road and called Ginny Foster at her store in Bozeman. "I'll probably fly back East out of Billings, and the interstate to Billings leads past Bozeman. Don't I owe you dinner?"

"Do you?"

"Yes."

"Call if you're passing through. Who can say?"

Kyle lowered the car visor against the sun and whooshed on west through the Blackfoot Reservation. Ahead, across treeless prairie, a dun-colored sprawl of buildings took shape. Hard times, Kyle thought, entering Browning. The town looked worse than he remembered. Rusted cars sagged behind peeling houses. Beer cartons rotted in ditches. Old signs advertised rare rocks, antiques, lost causes. Here, thought Kyle, his friend Salmon Thirdkill came of age.

He stopped for gas and, heeding his editor's suggestion, interviewed several locals. They seemed aware of Jeb Small's performance today in Cut Bank, but suspiciously noncommittal. Kyle took a room for the night in a motel across the highway from the Teepee Shopping Center.

He still had most of his Lewis and Clark series to write. But not today. He bought three beers and drank them in his room, watching the sun sink behind the Rocky Mountains.

A woman emerged from the gas station across the road and walked toward a car with California license plates. Young, she wore her blonde hair in a ponytail. Glenda Lodermeier! Kyle jumped up to stare out a window and the woman paused and glanced toward him.

It was not Glenda. The woman got in her car and drove away. Kyle lay back down, hands behind his head, remembering...

Hightown, the day after he graduated from college, he walked into the Treasure State Laundry carrying a suit to be cleaned and a girl behind the counter took it from him and hung it on a rack. He saw pale blue eyes and a pointy nose and her hair, pulled up in a ponytail, looked bleached pale gold by the sun.

"Wednesday okay?" she asked.

"That's fine." Kyle Hansen and Glenda Lodermeier exchanged their first words. Her parents owned the laundry and she had recently graduated as valedictorian of her high school class.

Kyle took her to movies and Saturday night dances at lonely prairie community houses. He stroked her and kissed her until nervously exhausted while resolutely she clamped closed her thighs. "I want to be liked for my mind," she said.

Kyle knocked at the front door of her house one night, bringing her *Madam Bovary* to read. Glenda stepped out wearing a little girl's nightie complete down to the booties on her feet.

"This is what you wear to bed?"

"Yes."

He hardly slept for nights.

"Glenda Lodermeier?" Kyle's mother said, "she's just a baby."

"She's eighteen, mother. When I'm fifty-four she'll be fifty. When I'm seventy-six she'll be seventy-two."

Her parents planned a California trip in September. "Let's you and I go away too," Kyle suggested. Glenda's aunt and uncle could watch things at the laundry.

"That might be fun," she said.

"I'm talking about overnight."

"I know."

Kyle lived from hour to hour that week, fingers crossed, taking nothing for granted. Saturday they drove the gap between the Spirit and the Little Belt Mountains and stopped at the first motel in Harlowton.

This old railroad junction town sprawled in space along the Musselshell River. A cold wind from Alberta ripped at the motel windows. Big trucks shook the floor. Glenda stepped from the bathroom in her little-girl nightie, toes curled in fleecy booties.

Kyle kissed her hard mouth until she became big-eyed and still. "There's an opening in my nightie," she said. "I don't need to take it off."

She jerked when he entered as if she'd cut her finger.

"Did it hurt?" Clinically they discussed their first time over dinner in the Graves Hotel, an old sandstone building perched on a bluff above a dry channel of the Musselshell River. The peaks of the Crazy Mountains climbed in cold silhouette in the distance.

"A little," she said.

"Did you get a release?"

"I think so." She had not, he felt sure, but they had time.

They coupled that winter in his car and once on her living room floor. Kyle worked as a reporter for the Hightown newspaper and played basketball in the Central Montana adult league. After a game in January – he scored twenty-six points – he asked her to marry him.

"If you find a job in Bozeman." She sat cross-legged beside him in his car, naked except for white socks, her hair up in a ponytail.

Kyle got a job as a reporter for the Chronicle, the Bozeman daily newspaper, and Glenda enrolled at Montana State College as a major in humanities and English lit. She got good grades, she sang in the glee club and she took birth control pills. He advanced to political reporting and played in the local mens' basketball league. As in high school and college, life still moved for him as a succession of sports seasons.

He and Glenda shared flirtatious, outdoorsy lives with other young couples. One day, after too many beers and the proximity of chance, Kyle consummated with one of Glenda's female friends on a blanket in the woods at a lake in the mountains. The friend, aware they had been observed, later confessed to Glenda.

He might have overcome this had he offered genuine apologies and had the girl been anyone else than Glenda's campus poetry-composition rival. Glenda got a divorce and moved to San Francisco. She broke her leg skiing at Lake Tahoe and married the doctor who set the bone.

Kyle wished he had tried harder to save his marriage, but he also recognized that at the time something in him wanted to rebel, to play the game again. Lately, though, when he saw on the street a perky, ponytailed blonde, his heart speeded and he hurried to see her face, hoping it might be Glenda.

He suppered slowly in a fast food restaurant in Browning, Montana. It surprised him that he had so quickly become infatuated with Ginny Foster. Yes, she's sexy and intelligent, but he met women like that all the time in Washington. What made the difference? The Harley connection? Oncoming middle age? He wondered at it.

Kyle returned to his motel room and telephoned Edgar Ware at his ranch in the hills. "What do you think will happen tomorrow at Circuit Court in Great Falls?"

"Five assholes will go to jail."

"Hope so. See you there," Kyle said.

# # #

CHAPTER 14

Mountains paraded, high and distinct, wind whipped dust across the roads. Kyle Hansen felt autumn's tingle. He drove the great open south toward Great Falls and thought of his brother who, the Christmas after their father died, chose as a gift for their mother a red bathrobe.

"She'll like it, but she'll cry," Terry predicted.

"No she won't," Kyle said. She did cry, though; Terry knew those things.

Kyle visited his mother last year in California. He asked her how she and his father had met.

"Let's see, I met your father ice skating in the park at Thermopolis. I think he worked for the railroad then."

"Ice skating: did you do that a lot?"

"Oh, yes; your father was a good skater."

"What about you?"

"I could handle myself," his mother said.

"How long did you and dad go out before you got married?"

"I guess we courted for about a year. Your father liked to travel and after we married, before he decided he wanted to sell insurance, we took free trips on the railroad. Your father liked to drive, too. You remember the summer we drove from Thermopolis to Yellowstone Park? We had to leave Lance at home, and you and Terry didn't like that." Lance was their black and white wonder dog.

"We stayed at the Old Faithful Inn," Kyle said. "Driving home we listened to a comedy program on the radio. You and dad sat in front and Terry and I in back. We watched an amazing red sunset."

"Yes, that's right, we did," his mother said.

They had been a family then, Kyle thought. He felt safe under that red Wyoming sky. "I don't think I've seen a sunset like it since," he said.

"I wanted Terry to be a doctor, did you know that?"

"I remember, Mother."

Kyle and his brother got jobs on a railroad section gang the summer Kyle graduated from high school. Shirtless in the sun, they swung long, thin-handled sledge hammers to drive the spikes that linked the rails to sticky, wooden cross ties. Three strokes and down; god, it felt good – Kyle Hansen, steel-driving man. Trains boomed through. "Hot rail! Hot rail!" Kyle loved that job.

The coming of the railroads in the late 1800s meant the end for the buffalo and the free life of the Indians, though, and last night in his motel room in Browning Kyle started to read *Crazy Horse* by Mari Sandoz. In 1851, Sandoz wrote, the U. S. Government deeded the Plains Indians their hunting grounds "forever" if they allowed white settlers to pass unmolested on a new wagon path called the Oregon Trail.

It wasn't long, Sandoz wrote, until Indians began to refer to the Oregon Trail as "the Holy Road."

Ah ha! Kyle recalled the sign Salmon showed him on the Chief Joseph Battlefield: "They took it from us. Now we will take it from them. Follow the Holy Road." But, follow the Oregon Trail? To what purpose? Kyle saw himself tracing wagon ruts in moonlight, stumbling after mysteries he might never understand.

He drove fast, covering ground. At Black Eagle, near Great Falls, the Sun River flowed from the west through a canopy of naked cottonwoods and merged quietly, almost imperceptibly, with the Missouri. Kyle, taken with the scene, yearned to linger, but he did not have time.

Jeb Small and Edgar Ware fidgeted at opposite ends of a long courtroom bench. Three rows back, Kyle noted with surprise, sat Congressman Eldon Lauder. The five men accused of assaulting the two Indian boys in Dupuyer stood quietly, wearing ties and jackets. The judge asked them to step forward and plead to charges of assault.

"Not guilty," the first man said.

Edgar Ware jumped to his feet. "That's not right!" he said loudly. According to his agreement with Jeb Small, each defendant would answer, "Guilty."

"Please," the judge chided. One by one he asked the other four men to step forward. "Not guilty," each repeated.

Ware glared at Jeb Small. The local prosecutor shook his head, apparently taken by surprise. The judge rapped for order. "Are either of the alleged victims or witnesses to the alleged offenses present in this courtroom today?"

No one answered.

The judge banged his gavel. "Then I have no choice but to dismiss this case for lack of evidence."

"How can you do that?" the local prosecutor asked.

"I just did," the judge said.

Edgar Ware confronted Jeb Small. "I didn't know," Kyle heard Small say. The two men argued. Their agreement, jail terms for the five defendants, had ended the Blackfoot roadblocks.

Ware walked outside. Kyle tried to catch him but the Blackfoot tribal chairman leaped into his pickup and drove away.

"I didn't know," Jeb Small repeated, surrounded by reporters. "I didn't know."

Kyle honed in on Congressman Lauder. "No comment," the man said.

Kyle telephoned Lars Bjornson in Helena to tell him what happened and ask the Governor's reaction.

"We heard," Lars said. "The Governor's pissed."

Kyle reached National Editor Jack Leventhal in Washington. "A congressman intervened, the deal fell apart."

"Roadblocks again, it says on the wires," Leventhal said. "I want you to drive back up there."

Kyle listened to radio news as he rode north. New barricades blocked traffic. Someone shot at a deputy sheriff's car. Young men waved guns. Again, tourists fled. A restaurant in Columbia Falls, near Glacier Park, refused to serve a family of Indians.

Drops of rain spattered Kyle's windshield. He drove through Cut Bank and up against a new barricade on Route 2, apparently constructed from the same hay bales the Indians tumbled two days ago. Already police reestablished checkpoints. Black clouds in the north trailed curtains of rain. As if eager for battle, these dreadnoughts moved, darting shots of lightning. Kyle Hansen donned a blue, plastic poncho and followed Jeb Small, who had returned to the scene.

Last time Small arrived alone. This time he trailed an entourage. Aides made it a point to inform reporters that the Montana Attorney General sped here so quickly he did not have time for lunch. Small entered a hastily erected tent, stood where everyone could see him, and held a cell phone to his ear.

"Another deal behind the scenes?" Kyle asked a member of the attorney general's crew.

"No, no." The aide blanched as if Kyle said an unclean thing.

Small spoke heatedly into his phone, flipped it shut. "Jerry," he called, and the aide with whom Kyle spoke bounded forward. He, Small and and another man conferred and Kyle wondered at the look of unscripted tension on their faces.

Kyle Hansen, like most reporters, had for lack of initiative or for sheer shortage of time too often in the past presented scripted encounters as news. Now he longed for honest conflict, anarchy even. So, apparently, did other reporters. Small stepped forth, his face taut, and Kyle felt an anticipatory stir rustle through the journalists around him.

"I am in contact with officials of the Blackfeet and with officials of the state government and hopefully we will negotiate without interference from those without day-to-day familiarity with the situation." Obliquely the Montana Attorney General rebuked Congressman Lauder.

Did Small confer with Indians? The judge? "Not yet." He batted away questions. Over on the Indian side no one appeared to pay the slightest attention. Young men paced with rifles. Someone passed around coffee.

Kyle attempted without success to reach Edgar Ware on his cell phone. Get away from all these journalists, he thought. There's something more here, he thought, something I don't know yet. Go see. Search it out. He slid under a barbed wire fence and followed the base of a ridge that extended north from barricaded Route 2.

"Hey, you can't do that," he expected someone to shout. No one did. The rain had stopped and he felt cold. Moving shadows of black clouds darkened the prairie around him.

An Indian on horseback appeared on the ridge above. Sitting his mount quietly, a rifle across his saddle, he seemed to look down at Kyle but not directly at him.   Kyle stood motionless, looking up. The man wore moccasins and buckskin leggings.

Kyle had copied an Indian war song from one of his books, hoping to use it in one of his stories: "I have been looking all my life to die. Today I see only the clouds and the ground..." He thought of the song and wondered at the chasm between the culture that produced it, and the culture that produced "We're number one!" flag waving, and canned laughter and fake wrestling on TV.

He looked again. The Indian was gone.

# # #

CHAPTER 15

Kyle dined with other reporters in Cut Bank that night. It was an expectant group and beer bottles littered the table. All possessed expense accounts. They lived free and on their own, away from their offices and editors, and knew they chased a developing story that might erupt at any moment into front-page, career-promoting drama.

Later, driving to his motel, Kyle gazed out at Montana night and thought of Mona in Missoula. He'd like to try with her again. His failure to ignite her still rankled. He'd allow more time, employ more strategic stroking.

But it was Ginny Foster he dreamed of that night. They idled in a pool of some sort. It was dark and the water was warm. He was sexually excited, but someone, a man, approached along the edge of the pool. Harley? A telephone rang in his room, awakening him. The dream lingered, so vivid Kyle expected to hear Ginny's voice.

It was Jack Leventhal at the Washington Herald. Someone had cut the throats of ten cattle belonging to a Montana rancher named Rudy Ottens on a ranch south of the Blackfoot Indian

Reservation. What, Kyle didn't know about it? He should go there at once.

Kyle bolted breakfast and drove the same road Salmon Thirdkill first told him about, the one that led to the sign describing the Old North Trail. An "O" burned into a wooden arch marked the turnoff to Ottens' ranch.

He followed a dusty line of other vehicles and bumped over a cattle guard, a row of steel rails inches apart that cows of all persuasions loathe to cross. He saw a glint. The headwaters of Dupuyer Creek trickled in the sun. A cluster of clouds clung to the peaks of the Bob Marshall Wilderness, but out over the prairie the sky cleared to frosty blue.

The Otten ranch huddled against the south side of a hill that partially protected it from wind. Men in cowboy hats straddled corral rails, spitting for the flatlanders. Rotted, brown remnants of last winter's hay bales sprawled near a barn and this year's harvest, newly stacked, exuded an aromatic odor of green.

Reporters polished sunglasses. "When do we see the dead critters?" All assumed that a direct line ran from the assault on the two Indian boys in Dupuyer through Jeb Small's failed agreement to the ravaged cattle up the hill.

A woman carrying a bucket emerged from the house and disappeared into a barn. A tall, loose-limbed man followed her out and thumped down wooden porch steps. "I'm Rudy Ottens," he announced.

"Why your ranch?"

"I'm active in stockman's associations," Ottens said. "I speak out on issues; I suspect that's got something to do with it."

"Speak out on what issues?"

"I don't believe in free handouts." He nodded north, presumably toward welfare cases on the Blackfoot Reservation. "I believe men should work for what they get."

Questions pinged from right and left. "Any enemies?" Kyle asked.

Ottens removed his cowboy hat and scratched his head. "Not that I know of." The sun hit him from the side and his face looked rutted from wind and weather.

A police car approached and out hopped a man in a big hat. "Hey, Rudy."

"Hey, Mason."

The newcomer, Teton County Sheriff Mason Kimberline, cultivated a mustache and smelled heavily of aftershave. He made a show of conferring with someone on a walkie-talkie. "Can't go see the dead cows until tomorrow, folks. Sorry. F.B.I.'s up there investigating."

"F.B.I.? Why the F.B.I?"

"Proximity to Glacier National Park," the sheriff said. A ranch hand pulled up in a battered truck. Ottens hopped in, and the two of them disappeared over a hill. A deputy, hat pulled low, circled the media as a sheepdog might, ready to chase them back if any tried to follow.

Sheriff Kimberline sat on the hood of his sheriff's car. "Bob here," he indicated one of the fence-sitters, "thinks he saw two Indians in a blue pickup leaving fast this morning, Montana license plate. He didn't get the numbers."

Indians as suspects? Revenge for the assault on the two Blackfoot boys at Dupuyer? Had Ottens in any way been connected with that?

The sheriff shot that one down. "None of the five accused men ever worked at this ranch, or even lived near here."

Questions continued. The woman they saw earlier emerged from the ranch house with a pot of coffee and paper cups. Kyle sidled over to ranch hand Bob, who had volunteered the two-Indians-fleeing-in-a-pickup-truck story. "Know any people over around Hightown?"

"Can't say I do."

"I'm from Hightown," Kyle said. He glanced up the hill in the general direction of the dead cattle. "You been up there?"

"I'm the one who found 'em."

"That ought to be in the story. What's your last name?" Kyle jotted on his notepad. "Were the dead cows close, scattered, what?"

"Like someone had herded them, all inside the circle."

"What circle?"

"Looked like a circle tramped in the grass," Bob said. He was about Kyle's age, and he had an unhurried way about him that reminded him of ranch kids he had known in school.

"What caused that, do you think?"

"I'm thinking someone walked around them to push those cattle together before they killed them. It's juicy up there. There's a lot of blood in a nine-hundred pound steer."

"You live here on the ranch?"

"In that bunkhouse over there."

"Hear anything last night?"

"Toward midnight. I told Rudy it sounded like somebody pounding on something. Wind will do that, blow a gate back and forth; that's why I didn't go up to see."

"Think it could have been the sound of drums?" Kyle asked.

"Drums?" Bob looked startled. "Don't think so."

No matter, Kyle thought, his Lewis and Clark series forgotten for now. He had his lead for tomorrow's story.

# # #

CHAPTER 16

"Unknown assailants apparently walked or danced in a circle – a ritual eerily reminiscent of the ghost dance that swept the American West in the late 1800s – and then slashed the throats of ten prime steers belonging to a Montana rancher last night.

"The cattle bled to death just south of the Blackfoot Indian Reservation, where tribal members, angered by a recent assault on two Indian boys, now blockade roads at gunpoint, denying entrance to the reservation and to vast reaches of Glacier National Park..."

Kyle quoted in his story "an observer familiar with Indian history," (Salmon Thirdkill, last night) who stated that in 1890 a shaman called Wovoka prescribed the ghost dance as a magical ritual to rid the West of invading whites. This dance, the observer noted, eventually led to the slaughter by the U. S. Seventh Cavalry, Custer's old command, of nearly 200 Indians at Wounded Knee in South Dakota.

Kyle started the wave in motion; now he and his editors rode it. They doubted, frankly, that the cattle killers danced the ghost dance before wielding their knives, but by now others in both local and national media, captivated by cowboy Bob's description of a circle tramped in the grass, began to romp and run with the idea.

Reporters clamored again next morning to go up and take pictures. "If you want," Sheriff Mason Kimberline said. "But we took the dead steers away as evidence, and the circle itself is virtually obliterated."

Cowboy Bob, now much besieged by reporters, continued to trickle forth revelations. Kyle bought the man a fifth of bourbon and plopped it down beside him in a paper bag. "Those two Indians you saw driving away, some old grudge, you think?"

"Rudy Ottens hasn't lived around here long enough to make enemies," Bob said. "He only came here from Bozeman two years ago. He ranched over there with his dad in the Gallatin Valley."

Kyle split from the pack and telephoned Ginny Foster at the Mod Shop in Bozeman. "I'm at the scene of the throat-cut cows. The rancher, Rudy Ottens, lived in the Gallatin Valley until two years ago. Ever hear of him? Ever meet him?"

"I've been asking myself that and, no, I don't think so."

"Know anybody at the Chronicle, Ginny? Most of the news staff has turned over since I worked there. Besides, we're competitors now."

"I know just about everybody there. You want me to see what they have on Rudy Ottens? This is fun."

She phoned Kyle back in an hour. "Weed control, school board, volunteer fire department; Rudy Ottens, model citizen. He even gave blood. The Chronicle reporters already had the clippings out."

"Any theory? Maybe Rudy Ottens just happened to ranch too close to the reservation?"

"No, no," she said. "We can do better. I prefer a sinister motive."

Kyle noted and took encouragement from the "we." "Seems to me," he said, "that the situation calls for joint consultation. Let's say you drive to Havre to visit Judy and Salmon Thirdkill and while you're in the area you and I meet and put our heads together." A long shot, he knew. But nothing ventured...

"Interesting you suggest that. Harley and his team depart later this week on a nine-day football trip and in fact I do consider a business journey to Seattle for a clothing show."

Kyle recalled his anticipation when Glenda Lodermeier told him yes, maybe she could spend the night with him in Harlowton. "You could stop here on your way to or from Seattle."

"What if the Blackfeet make peace and your newspaper calls you back to Washington and I'm in the Snake River Valley or somewhere?"

"I'm confused," Kyle said. "You said you planned this trip..."

"But then you said..."

They both laughed. "Tell you what," Kyle said, "You've got my cell phone number? I'll give you my motel number too..."

The sun shone. Kyle basked in a plastic chair in front of his motel and made the rounds on his cell phone.

"The Governor nudges both sides toward a settlement, you can be sure of that," Lars Bjornson said from Helena.

"Rudy Ottens? I don't know the man; maybe somebody stumbled onto his place by mistake." Edgar Ware theorized from his tribal chairman's cubbyhole in Browning. "And besides, why does everyone assume it had to be Indians?"

"Rudy Ottens? Who the hell is he? I think we've reached the point where you ought to arrange a free subscription for me to the Washington Herald." Salmon Thirdkill, summoned from a classroom, spoke testily from his school on the Fort Belknap Reservation.

Kyle drove back and forth from his Cut Bank motel to the road barricade on Route 2 west of town with two goals in mind. One: continue to establish himself as a bona fide national desk reporter. Two: have sex with Ginny Foster.

Harley had his romances; why not her? Sex seemed naturally adapted to the wind and space of northern Montana. Kyle stopped to purchase a sandwich and a bottle of low fat milk. The barricade area ahead, he noticed as he approached, had grown almost overnight to resemble a dusty, little tent city.

Reporters wandered about. Young Indians in sunglasses, rifles slung on their backs, stood guard atop hay bales, while sheriff's deputies and state police sipped coffee in styrofoam cups fifty yards away. Governor Cloninger had decreed "zones of separation" to avoid direct confrontations at all road entrances to the Blackfoot Reservation.

Armed agents of the federal government also returned, but discreetly. Thus far the Governor managed successfully to keep them largely secluded from view. Kyle wanted to interview their leader, whoever that was, but was denied permission again today to approach their bus.

Instead he interviewed participants, on both sides of the barricade, and took occasional pictures. The situation was still novel enough, the chance for serious confrontation likely enough, that ennui had not set in.

He returned to town for supper, hurried back to the barricade, and sat around a campfire with other reporters until after dark. He might, if the standoff continued, purchase a sleeping bag and tent for himself, but now, around midnight, he returned to his motel readily enough.

Kyle lay in bed and listened to the wind outside. He had read of sod-hut homesteaders driven crazy by that sound. Indeed, it seemed to him now that he heard two winds: one just beyond the window, ripping at the roof of the motel; the other higher, deeper, a great roar across the land. That's time passing. That's lost, wild America sighing by. Kyle thought of his brother. He thought of rivers out there in the night.

Clouds shrouded the mountains in the morning. Someone fired rifle shots, but who? As yet, no reports of injuries surfaced. Legal authorities dickered whether to seek new charges against the five men who beat the Indian boys. Roads remained blocked, effectively closing eastern Glacier Park for the winter. The threat of one mistake, a finger too quick on a trigger, hung in the air.

Kyle attended a press conference organized by a ranchers' group at a schoolhouse out on the prairie. A Montana newsman commented that Rudy Ottens' steers died while pastured on national forest land, an angle Kyle realized he had overlooked. The reporter, sympathetic to the ranchers, derisively quoted a national environmental group's slogan for public lands, "'Cattle free in Two-Thousand-Three.'"

"A group called Save the Land campaigns against cattle grazing on national forest land," a second reporter said. "Do you consider them as suspects?"

Sheriff Mason Kimberline, seated up front under an American flag, fielded the question. "We know all about Save the Land," he said. "We will talk to them. You can quote me."

"That's easy. Call the coach's wife at Montana State," Rudy Ottens interjected.

What coach's wife? Reporters stirred to life. "I think the man means Virginia Foster in Bozeman," somebody said. Kyle shook his head. Who would have thought it? Ginny Foster became part of his story.

Kyle called National Editor Leventhal first. "Remember the coach's wife who took on the ranchers? She got obliquely mentioned at a press conference today as a suspect in the cattle killing."

"Please. Does anybody really think she did it?"

"No. But it's an interesting angle."

"Talk to her. Get her to confess," Leventhal jested.

Kyle reached Ginny at the Mod Shop. "My newspaper wants me to check you out."

"You're the fifth reporter who's called in the last hour. Good ol' Rudy Ottens. And I don't even know the man. Harley's not happy. He says he talks to ranchers at alumni fund raisers. 'How can I coach football with this circus going on!'" She mimicked her husband's voice.

"Anything you want to say in defense?"

"I'm flattered that Rudy Ottens thinks I crept through the night and killed his cows. Now listen to this: a doctor I know says Ottens got an Indian girl pregnant. The girl worked for him as a maid when he ranched near here. The doc doesn't think she had the baby. He says she's a Blackfoot, originally from Browning. The doc says none of this is generally known."

"Why did he tell you?"

"Well..." Kyle pictured her smoothing back her hair.

"Where is the girl now?"

"Her name is Sylvia Bright Angel and she works as a nurse at a hospital in Cheyenne, Wyoming." Ginny read Kyle a phone number. "It's for the hospital: she's not listed under residential."

"You checked all that?"

"I was curious."

Kyle phoned his editor again.

"Talk to the girl," Leventhal said. "Maybe she'll come right out and say the rancher knocked her up."

"Could we use that? What about the laws of libel?"

"See what she says and then we'll worry about the laws of libel."

Kyle telephoned the hospital in Cheyenne and someone paged Sylvia Bright Angel. "Hello?"

"I'm a reporter." The line went dead.

Ginny said Sylvia Bright Angel grew up in Browning. Salmon Thirdkill grew up in Browning. Kyle reached his friend at his school.

"Pretty girl, yes, I knew her," Salmon said. "Not Biblically, of course. Rudy Ottens got her pregnant?"

"That's what a doctor told Ginny."

"Ginny? Ginny Foster?"

"She's been helpful," Kyle said.

"You want me to tell this girl she should talk to you?"

"If you would," Kyle said.

"Would you use her name?"

"Not if she doesn't want me to."

"This is important. I'll hold you to this."

"Better she speak with someone friendly," Kyle said. "If the story's true, you know sooner or later word will get out."

Salmon called back in twenty minutes. "Miss Bright Angel will talk to you face to face, but not on the telephone. She wants her boyfriend there. You ready? Here's her address and home phone number."

Kyle jotted numbers. "Thanks, Salmon."

"Cheyenne?" Jack Leventhal said. "Why? The Pope's plane crashed over Wyoming?"

"The nurse says she'll talk to me, but only if I go in person. My friend, the school principal, knew her in Browning. He arranged it. I could drive to Cheyenne tomorrow. I've checked; plane connections are not good."

"Do you want to go?"

"Here's an exclusive that might establish a motive for the cattle killing. Maybe, going and coming, I research more background for my Lewis and Clark series."

"Go," Leventhal said. "We'll put out a bulletin to the people on both sides of the road barricades: 'Don't do anything newsworthy until Kyle Hansen comes back.'"

# # #

CHAPTER 17

Twenty-six years since that winter afternoon in Thermopolis, Wyoming; Kyle and Terry ran home from shooting baskets, no hats, no mittens – as a kid you didn't feel the cold – almost dark, street lights flicking on, the brothers excited because it started to snow, and the preacher who lived down the street climbed their front porch steps pulled along by a black and white sheepdog on a leash. "He's yours," the preacher said. "He likes you best."

Lance, agog at the life of a dog in Wyoming, galloped after the brothers whenever and wherever they rode their bicycles. He loped along when they pedaled to swim in the hot springs across the river, ever eager to harass a big bull elk who periodically jumped the fence from the wildlife preserve.

A ritual developed: the elk lowered its horns and chased Lance, Lance lowered his head and chased Kyle and Terry on their bicycles. Strung out like this, they raced for the railroad underpass, beneath which, happily, the elk apparently feared to go. Kyle Hansen smiled remembering in his rental car on his way to Wyoming.

Last summer in California his mother showed him a drawing Terry did of Lance. She saved his brother's sketches all these years. Terry drew the dog's head from the side with crisp, effective pen strokes. "Your brother showed such potential," his mother said.

"The greatest dog that ever lived," Kyle shifted the subject.

"Lance was a comfort to me after you and Terry went away. That dog understood things like a person. Do you remember the night he died?"

"Oh yes," Kyle said. Christmas holidays, his final year at college, he stomped in after a long, snowy drive from Missoula. "Lance is sick," his mother said, and Kyle found the wonder dog trembling on his rug in the brothers' old bedroom upstairs. Lance rolled his eyes, looked up at Kyle and thumped his tail.

"You should have called," Kyle said to his mother.

"You were on the road."

"What about the veterinarian?"

"He was here. He said there's nothing to do."

Kyle stroked his dog's head. Lance seemed to sense that something important impended and his eyes held a depth, a vital question. "Where is the other one?" they seemed to ask. "When is he coming?" Kyle understood; Lance wanted to see Terry again.

It had pleased Lance to wait on the sidewalk in front of the Judith Theater when Kyle and Terry went to movies with other kids. One night the boys left the theater by a rear exit and walked home; no Lance, so Terry ran back downtown. Lance jumped up from the sidewalk where he had waited all along.

"I thought he might die this afternoon," his mother said. "I think he waited for you."

And for the other one too, Kyle thought. He waited for the other one too.

"It's all right, Lance." He stroked his dog's head. He was just a black and white sheepdog. "It's all right, Lance." Kyle held him as he died. He left the house afterward to walk in the snow because he did not want his mother to see him cry.

The next morning Kyle wrapped Lance in his old rug and drove the airport road to above Casino Creek. He carried Lance down through the snow to a knoll above the beaver dams where they camped summers when Terry was alive. Kyle liked it that you could not see town or houses from here. He chose a spot with a view of the Spirit Mountains, laid his dog gently down and dug a grave in the frozen ground.

He ruffed Lance's head, he wrapped him in his blanket. It hurt Kyle to cover his dog with dirt, to leave him there in the cold. It hurt him worse than anything, except when his brother died. It hurt him now to remember as he slowed for the stop-lights of Great Falls.

Kyle started early this morning to drive from Cut Bank to Cheyenne. He lingered late at the barricades last night and, with police still permissive, wandered over to the Indian side. There he met and talked with a former student at the University of Montana, Wayne Chappell.

Chappell, in his early twenties, seemed one of today's young Indians caught between. He owned a book store-pinball machine emporium in Browning that did not make money. Now he marked time at the barricades and tried to think of a better way. He and Kyle discussed not so much the current conflict, but rather the legacy of Lewis and Clark.

"Their significance is not the civilization that followed them," Chappell said. "It's the civilization they destroyed." This was not a new idea – Kyle already intended to bend his explorer articles in this direction – but skinny, pock-marked Chappell took the thought and pushed it further.

Consider, he said, the smallpox carried by white men that virtually wiped out whole tribes. Lewis and Clark spent their first winter, 1803-1804, with the Mandans of North Dakota. The smallpox epidemic of 1837, triggered by later white explorers, killed all but 31 Mandans out of a population of 16,000. Chappell ticked off the numbers.

He named white schools where Indian kids were punished if they spoke their own language. He talked of land grabs, of dis-crimination. Then, surprising Kyle, he said this: "We might have been just as bad if we had won. We tortured, we killed. Maybe our time was running out anyway."

What? Kyle pondered Chappell's comments as he wheeled into a fast food place on Tenth Avenue in Great Falls. Power corrupts? As simple as that? Could be, considering all the empires that have come and gone. He emerged carrying a cheeseburger and a vanilla milkshake and drove Route 89 south up and over the Big Belt Mountains.

He studied terrain today. He mentally walked ridge lines. It seemed to Kyle that after several weeks back he saw his surroundings in a fresher, tactile way. His terrain awareness genes had kicked in.

Clouds spread like feathers across the sky. The land south of White Sulphur Springs appeared abandoned, but, as if tagged with yellow flags, he noted fenceposts, the eroding bed of the old Jawbone Railroad, other scattered reminders of economic man. An abandoned Gothic church and unpainted houses lent a morose dignity to the old railroad junction of Ringling. Sixteen Mile Creek wandered through high grass – sixteen miles to where? Ahead, in the south, the peaks of the Absaroka-Beartooth massif climbed the sky.

Ginny Foster sounded throaty and come-hither on the telephone yesterday. He did not call her last night because she asked him not to telephone her at home. He stopped on a hill with a view and punched the number of the Mod Shop on his cell phone. "I'm driving to Cheyenne to talk to Sylvia Bright Angel. Salmon arranged it. What are your plans?"

"My helper, Marta, says she'll mind the store if I attend the clothing show in Seattle. Harley and his lads departed last night. They play at Iowa State Saturday and next Friday night at Sacramento State in California."

"Nine days on the road, you said. Long time away from classes."

"Harley's idea. They're unbeaten, you know, and he thinks if they win these two they've got a shot at a perfect season. He wants that. He wants his team inured to the climate of California."

"You're the one who told me about Sylvia Bright Angel. Want to come? It might help having another woman there when I talk to the girl."

"How long away?"

"Two nights. Maybe three. I'm on my way to Livingston. You could meet me there." Livingston, gateway to Yellowstone Park and Wyoming, was about 30 miles from Ginny's store in Bozeman.

"You and me? Well, mister, we're moving right along here, aren't we?"

"Just a couple of crazy kids," Kyle said.

"I'll meet you at the old railroad station in Livingston and leave my car there. What do you say to that?"

"Excellent."

"Give me an hour." Kyle did not expect this, and when he and Ginny began to kid about her coming he did not think she would do it. But now, suddenly, it seemed the most natural thing in the world.

He burst into song: "Breaking rocks in the hot sun; I fought the law, and the law won..." He admired the Crazy Mountains. Razor-ridges crested at 11,000 feet and broke to deep, tumbled-rock canyons. He and Glenda Lodermeier hiked and camped up there when they lived in Bozeman. Kyle wondered if Glenda ever thought of that now.

He crossed a bridge, glimpsed shiny ribbons in a white-rock bed, the Yellowstone River, water level as usual lowest in autumn. He turned off Route 89 onto Interstate 90, drove a few miles west, chose an exit and crossed the Yellowstone again.

Railroad men created Livingston in 1882 to service the Northern Pacific's steam engines before they chugged up and over 5,600-foot Bozeman Pass. Here, at the edge of town, the Yellowstone River makes a dramatic bend from north to east. William Clark and some of his guys camped here in 1806. They felled trees, hacked out dugout canoes and floated east to meet Meriwether Lewis at the lonely junction of the Yellowstone and the Missouri that Kyle visited two weeks ago.

He took pictures of the river, mountains looming behind. He bought two bottles of California cabernet sauvignon and pulled in at the old railroad station just before Ginny arrived. "Olla," she said. She wore jeans and a sweater of colored squares, the two brightest colors over her breasts.

She flung a red suitcase into his car, touched his shirt. "Nice choice for autumn. What is that, mauve?"

"I think of it more as plum," Kyle said. "What is mauve, anyway?"

"You don't need to know."

They rode south down the Paradise Valley, both talking at once, jagged mountains rising on each side. First on one side of the highway, then the other, clear and sparkling, the Yellowstone River tumbled north from its origins in Wyoming.

"Do you think your assistant suspects?" Kyle asked.

"Marta's not dumb. She saw me stroking the telephone. But I think she approves. I listened on the radio on my way here to Congressman Eldon Lauder criticize Blackfoot Indians for 'living the high life on welfare.'"

"I missed that. I know he continues to call for the bulldozing of the road barricades, even though he helped put them up again when those five guys pleaded not guilty."

"He and that judge are old friends," Ginny said. "Did I tell you? Every election Eldon Lauder proposes subsidies for ranchers and self sufficiency for Indians. Describes himself as a 'poor up-country farmer.' Last year he collected three-hundred and some thousand dollars in federal agricultural subsidies."

"You know that for a fact?"

"I tore out the clipping from the newspaper. I brought it along. Aren't you glad I came?"

"I am. I am glad. Where is Mr. Lauder from originally? Has he alway been a rancher?"

"Grew up hard in Miles City. Earned a scholarship to Montana State. Worked as a janitor, graduated in agriculture. Started small, kept buying land. Got elected to Congress. Nice story. Too bad he's such a prick."

"Tell me about Jeb Small," Kyle said.

"Comes from money. Law graduate at the university in Missoula. Always knows where the cameras are. Our next Governor. Doesn't play the hayseed like Eldon. Nimble hands."

"You speak from experience?"

"In my case," Ginny said, "the barricade did not come down."

Kyle laughed. "Tell me about your marriage," Ginny said.

They had only touched on this before, Kyle remembered. Now he described Glenda Lodermeier, her pointy nose, her cocky walk.

"You got divorced. She broke her leg skiing and the doctor married her. She must have been a looker," Ginny said. Driving south through Montana's magnificent Paradise Valley, she talked of boys she dated in high school and college. Tall for her age, she said, she sought strong, independent personalities.

"Do we rank Harley as strong and independent?"

"Yes and no. For example, if the Bobcats lose at Iowa State tomorrow, he'll call me after the game. That's not strong. If they win, he won't call, he'll be fine with the guys. That's independent."

"If it were the other way around, if he called when they won but silently bore the pain when they lost, that might suggest inner strength?"

"I don't know," Ginny said. She crossed and uncrossed her legs. "I'm confused."

Kyle laughed. "Will you speak with him during our trip?"

"When either of us travels, we try to talk every other night at seven o'clock. It's my turn to call him Sunday."

"Two days of reckless freedom first," Kyle said.

"Like skipping school, huh?" Ginny stretched and smoothed her hair. They drove a street dotted with motels in Gardiner, self-described as the only year-round entrance to Yellowstone Park. Beyond the stone Gateway Arch, dedicated by President Theodore Roosevelt in 1903, they saw a coyote posed in the sage-brush, one foot in the air.

Little traffic moved in Yellowstone this late in the season. Orderly clouds, white stripes on a vast, blue flag, shadowed the white terraces of Mammoth Hot Springs. Elk as tall as pickup trucks browsed the lawns of military row houses where park personnel lived.

They just missed an eruption at Old Faithful. The Inn looked the same, a Hansel and Gretel heap of struts and logs, but the summer crowds had gone. Kyle noted forest fire damage, but nothing like the devastation he remembered after the runaway forest fires of 1988. Fresh, green pines surrounded old charred, shattered stumps.

They passed Yellowstone Lake and the Two Ocean Plateau and parked to watch the Grand Teton, prince of Wyoming mountains, pull moisture from the wind. A cloud formed, tried to cling to the peak, ripped free, disintegrated in drier air. This happened again and again.

A strand of gold hung in the western sky above trendy Jackson. Mountains ringed the place. Designer shops contrasted with wooden sidewalks and cowboy bars.

Ginny nodded toward a motel with yellow and red marigolds in window boxes. "I want that one," she said.

# # #

CHAPTER 18

"I'll open some wine," Kyle announced. He took a corkscrew from his suitcase, stabbed at the bottle several times, finally got the cork free. He sat on the bed in their motel room, she on a chair, and they clinked plastic glasses.

"Well, here we are," she said.

They kissed. She got up and sat on the bed beside him. They kissed again.

They looked at each other. "Maybe we should go to supper first," Kyle said. "Assuage that hunger."

"Decompress. Yes. That's a good idea."

They held hands walking down the street, something Kyle seldom did. He hardly noticed his surroundings. They both ordered steaks.

"I don't usually eat steak," Ginny said. "You think about it: it's heavy, it's greasy."

"You're right. I don't usually order steak either."

Their food came and they attacked with enthusiasm. Aware that half a bottle of wine awaited in their room, he ordered a Scotch and water, she a vodka martini.

"I skied here once," Ginny said. "Did you ever? It's a big mountain."

"I mostly skied Big Sky and Bridger. Meant to try this place, never did. You and Harley came here?"

"I was with two other women, also married. We picked up some guys. Regretted it. Made an escape. How long do you think you've got before your newspaper calls you back to Washington?"

"It depends on what happens up at the barricades. If there's violence..."

"Then it's a bigger story. You could say that Eldon Lauder and the others who stir things up help keep you around. Professionally, they do you a favor."

Kyle thought about it, nodded. "Yes. Well said. I'm going to ask for more bread. You want dessert or anything?"

"Not tonight." Ginny said.

The bread came. Kyle looked at her. "That's a provocative sweater."

"Glad you like it."

Neither ordered dessert or coffee. He put forth a credit card and calculated a tip. They walked back to their motel, not holding hands this time, not talking much. The Wyoming sky sparkled with stars.

They sat on the bed in their room. He poured the remainder of the wine, almost filling two plastic glasses. He tripped when he stood to pull off his pants. Ginny laughed and began to remove her clothes.

Kyle heard a sound outside, a man's voice, and he imagined Harley Hawkins standing at a blackboard somewhere in Iowa diagramming football plays,

Ginny touched him between the legs. He lifted himself on his arms the better to look at her. He kissed her neck, her throat. A motorcycle roared by outside and Kyle thought, someday we all die.

He kissed her breasts. He ran his fingers up and down the inside of her legs, feeling above and below her panty line. Would he or wouldn't he? He remembered that sometimes she liked to lie on top.

The wiry hair of her muff agitated his penis. He felt her fingernails on his back. "Splendid Ginny." He pushed at her with his erection.

She lifted one leg, then the other, majestically, a drawbridge slowly opening. She wrapped them around him. "Come on in," she said.

Twice more that night they came together, hardly speaking. Her long body and her height excited him. Sometimes women seemed so small. Not this one. She was all there.

Kyle rose early, splashed cold water on his face, shaved. He opened the door and looked outside. Frost whitened the ground and a wind as cold as a glacier's breath swept down from the mountains.

"October in the Rocky Mountains," he said. He telephoned Sylvia Bright Angel at her home in Cheyenne.

"Problem," the young woman said. "There's an emergency at the hospital. I must postpone until tomorrow morning." The original plan was to meet at her house this afternoon.

"What if they need you again tomorrow? I don't have a lot of time."

"Tomorrow for sure. The other nurse will be back."

"You heard," he said to Ginny.

"Good. Now we don't have to rush, rush today."

"Well, it is a weekend. If I'm in Cut Bank I might go on a picnic."

"I originally intended to go to Seattle, remember? If you're worried about what's happening up at the roadblocks, why don't you call Edgar Ware? Or Salmon. He's plugged into things."

"Did you take a course in journalism up there at Northern Montana?" Kyle began with Salmon, and since it was Saturday called him at home.

"Yes, I'm in Jackson, Wyoming. Expect to see the nurse tomorrow. Anything happening at the barricades?" Kyle did not mention Ginny's presence.

"Just talked with a friend in Cut Bank," Salmon said. "Dirty looks. No shooting. Give me your cell phone number again. I'll call if I hear of something untoward."

Ginny pocketed a Chamber of Commerce blurb from the motel lobby and read it in the car: "Fur trappers, 'the mountain men of legend,' gathered in this valley in the 1820s and 1830s for their annual summer rendezvous. One who especially praised this area was named David Jackson..."

"That clears that up," Kyle said.

They drove south and a herd of horses raced them through a grassy canyon. Route 191 burst from shadow into a sunlit ocean of grass and sand. In the east, the Wind River Range lined the horizon.

They listened to radio news. Kyle telephoned his newspaper in Washington and affirmed his existence to an assistant editor. Dust swirled down a street half a football field wide in Pinedale, Wyoming. A poster on a wooden fence announced an annual Green River Mountain Man Rendezvous and Plains Indian Encampment, this one apparently held last July.

A concrete bridge spanned the Big Sandy River in lonely Farson, a town of maybe 200. "The Oregon Trail branched here," Kyle said, "one fork to California, the other to Oregon. We've got time. Let's look for it."

He parked in front of a wooden structure housing a restaurant below and an apartment above. "Where can we find the Oregon Trail?" he asked the waitress inside.

"Al," she called toward the kitchen, "where can these people find the Oregon Trail?"

"Take the road toward South Pass," a voice sounded.

"What about the junction where the trail branched?" Ginny asked.

"Don't know about that."

"Anybody ever call it the Holy Road?" Kyle asked.

"You're the first," the voice in the kitchen replied.

Kyle and Ginny walked across open prairie to the crumbly banks of the Big Sandy River looking for the old Oregon Trail. A lone cottonwood shed yellow leaves. "A lot of wagons passed here between 1840 and the 1860s," Kyle said. "John Unruh Jr. wrote in *The Plains Across* that so many people set forth on the Oregon Trail from Missouri in 1852 that wagon teams traveled twelve abreast. Entrepreneurs operated ferries at river crossings, and charged one to five dollars a wagon. Brigham Young complained, in 1857, of whites 'shooting at every Indian they could see.' Then in the 1860s came the railroads."

"You do your research."

"I love this stuff."

They drove east on Route 28 and stopped at a tourist marker. A distinct east-west swath about 100 feet wide crossed the prairie next to the highway, its surface a foot or two below the surrounding ground. Excited, they hopped out to see.

A sign said that this section of the Oregon Trail traversed 25 waterless miles – from the Sweetwater River to the Big Sandy – and in the process crossed the Continental Divide. Books say that even today South Pass, elevation 7,550 feet, remains the easiest route through the Rocky Mountains.

Kyle and Ginny drove on, climbing gradually, stopping occasionally to study a historical map. "It appears the Oregon Trail passed a little to our south," Kyle said. "Now if we can find a road that leads in that direction..."

"I'll look. You drive," Ginny said.

They tracked a gravel lane that led south to a cluster of weathered buildings, the remains of the old mining town of South Pass City. "We're looking for the Oregon Trail," Kyle said to a gray-haired woman seated on a porch.

"Can't find it now," the woman said. "Wind blows pretty hard up here."

They scrambled up a hill to study the situation. Level grassland stretched east-west several miles away, the logical route for a wagon trail, but they saw no road to take them there. Ginny pointed to the sky, where black clouds blotted mountain crests and rushed toward them.

They drove east through an area of tumbled red rock and snowflakes skittered on the wind. Route 28 crossed South Pass, began to loop downward and the snow turned to rain. Kyle wished they had time to drive to Independence Rock, the pioneer landmark, but they did not. They swung south instead toward Interstate 80, Laramie and Cheyenne.

The sun shook free and a rainbow glistened above brown mountains. "Let's try for the football scores on the radio," Ginny said.

Montana State beat Iowa State 27-14. The University of Montana also won. Both Montana teams, the Grizzlies and the Bobcats, remained undefeated.

Kyle bought a bottle of peppermint schnapps in Rawlins. They stopped to eat near Laramie and made Cheyenne an hour after dark. "Sign us in as "Mr. and Mrs. Increase Mather," Ginny said. Kyle laughed but wrote, "Kyle Hansen," on the motel ledger. He went for ice while Ginny lay on the bed turning pages in a booklet that listed this motel chain's locations around the country.

"What's the nickname of Indiana?" she asked when he returned.

"The Hoosier State."

"Too easy. What about Utah?"

"Land of Opportunity," Kyle said.

"You're SO wrong. Utah is the Beehive State."

"Probably everybody knows that but me," Kyle said. He shed his clothes and slid in beside her.

"To tell you the truth, I wondered at my readiness to come on this trip with you," Ginny said. "Do you want to know what I decided? I think it's because you will leave us soon. You're 'safe.' I can do things with you I might not want to risk with someone local."

"Whatever the reason, I'm pleased," Kyle said.

He traced with dancing fingers hoops of fire about her breasts. They rocked together, kissing, touching. Kyle lay on his back afterward, wondering at the the human body. He pictured his nerve-endings flushed and happy, shaking hands all around.

# # #

CHAPTER 19

Kyle awoke Sunday morning in a Monday mood. Yesterday he played tourist, today he returned to business. He needed to hit a homerun with Sylvia Bright Angel to justify this trip. Then he must hustle back to the barricades in northern Montana.

"Professional. But not intimidating." He studied the few clothes he had brought. "I'll wear my brown corduroys and white shirt."

"I brought a leather skirt," Ginny said. "I could wear that over a white turtleneck and strappy, black shoes. What do you think?"

"Let's see how it looks."

Exaggeratedly, Ginny modeled for him. Kyle laughed. "You look pretty racy."

She eyed herself in the mirror. "You're right. I'll put this away for tonight and change to my jeans."

She grabbed a tourist brochure in the motel lobby and read from it at breakfast. "'Before the Union Pacific arrived in 1867 this area was called Crow Creek Crossing. A railroad survey crew named it Cheyenne after the local Indian tribe. Most of the railroad workers were former Confederate soldiers. In 1869

Wyoming Territory became the first political entity in the world to allow women to vote.' Are you writing this down?"

"I'm recording it up here." Kyle tapped his head.

He telephoned Sylvia Bright Angel for directions to her home. It turned colder and it began to snow. "Salmon and I played football against the University of Wyoming in Laramie," Kyle said. "It was November and it snowed that day too."

He described it for Ginny as they drove across Cheyenne. Wyoming had a six-foot-five, all-conference end named Jones and Kyle's assignment on defense was to "obstruct" him at the line of scrimmage before he ran downfield to catch passes. Jones fixed him with yellow eyes. Play after play they slammed into each other. Jones caught passes, but did not run wild. Late in the game, as snow began to cover the field, Wyoming led by two touchdowns. People in the stands began to leave. Montana's defense trotted back into position after a running play and a looming shape hurtled at Kyle from behind.

"I knew instinctively that it was Jones. I turned just in time to save my knees. The game was already decided. He knocked me down from behind and the referees didn't even notice. I hopped right up. Next play and the play after that we beat at each other's faces with our elbows."

"So, he popped you illegally," Ginny said. "It happens. I'm a coach's wife. I don't harbor illusions."

Kyle started to say more, decided not to. Jones was black and of another tribe, and it seemed to him now, looking back on that day, that in the fury the two of them shared pulsed man's bloody history.

"There's the state capitol," Ginny said.

They found the address, a small house near Frontier Park on the west side of Cheyenne. A car and a soft drink delivery truck nudged each other in the driveway. Kyle and Ginny stepped through new snow to a porch where wind chimes tinkled. A long-haired, blond, young man opened the door. He wore a Denver Broncos sweatshirt. "You're the reporters? I'm Leroy Rader."

A svelte young woman in denim skirt, yellow t-shirt and white running shoes waited in a room with a television, a couch and several chairs. Her black hair, parted in the middle and combed tightly back, bunched below her ears and spread to tumble in shiny waves. Sylvia Bright Angel introduced herself. Leroy Rader sat beside her on the couch and held her hand.

"I represent a newspaper in Washington D. C.," Kyle began, "though, as Salmon Thirdkill probably mentioned, I grew up in Hightown in Central Montana. Salmon and I played football at the university. This is my friend, Virginia Foster, from Bozeman."

"I understand you're from Browning," Ginny said to the nurse. "I was raised on the High Line, not far from there."

"Salmon probably told you that we came to talk about Rudy Ottens," Kyle said. "Did you work for Mr. Ottens?"

"I cooked at his ranch one summer when I lived in Bozeman," Sylvia Bright Angel said.

"How old were you?"

"Nineteen."

"What happened?"

"I got pregnant."

"Ottens?" Kyle tried to maintain his neighborly tone.

The nurse looked at her boyfriend, and though Rader hardly spoke, Kyle felt the two young people as very much together. The young man played a role in the conversation whether he spoke or not. He nodded ever so slightly at Sylvia Bright Angel. "Yes," she said.

Ginny leaned forward, sympathetic. "Did you have the baby?"

The young woman hesitated. A dog barked outside. "Mr. Ottens paid for an abortion."

"Who performed it?" Ginny asked.

"A doctor in Bozeman," Sylvia Bright Angel said.

"Abortion is legal in Montana," Rader said. "I guess you know that."

"Do you see any connection between your relationship with Rudy Ottens and what recently happened to his cattle?" Kyle asked.

"He was married and had children of his own and I don't think of my time with him as a 'relationship'," the young nurse said.

"How would you describe it?" Kyle asked.

"He raped me."

The chimes tinkled on the porch. "He raped you?" Ginny said.

"Yes."

"Where did it happen?"

"In a separate building where I slept."

"You told police?" Kyle asked. Sylvia Bright Angel shook her head.

"Why not?"

"Mr. Ottens told me not to."

"He threatened you?"

"He said no one would believe me."

"Ah." It seemed they all leaned back and exhaled at once. "Did you tell anyone what happened?" Kyle asked.

"I told my cousin in Browning."

"Browning," Kyle said. "That's close to Rudy Ottens' ranch."

"I wanted someone to know just in case," Sylvia Bright Angel said. "I didn't want people to think I slept with him willingly. But I owe Mr. Ottens too. He paid my way through nursing school."

"How did that happen?"

"He knew I wanted to go, so he paid my way. For two years. I don't want you to use my name in any of your stories."

"I'm trying to show that someone killed Rudy Ottens' cattle for a reason," Kyle said. "I'm trying to show that he's not just an innocent rancher set upon by murdering fiends."

"I don't care what you're trying to show, I don't want you to use my name. That's why I agreed to talk to you. If you write that Rudy Ottens got an Indian girl pregnant, everybody around Browning will know it was me."

The snow had melted on their muddy rental car when Kyle and Ginny walked outside. He drove a few blocks and, since it was Sunday, called Jack Leventhal at home. Kyle told him what Sylvia Bright Angel had said. "I promised her we would not use her name."

"She says he raped her but she did not report it to police," the national editor said. "Robin Hood Indians avenge her. Good interview. I think we can find a way to write it without actually using her name. I guess you'd better get back to Montana. Take a day off when you can."

"I don't see how you could suggest rape without giving her away," Ginny said.

"Unless somebody else breaks the story first. I like it that someone's out there avenging Indians who other people wronged. I like it morally. I like it journalistically. It's a natural."

Kyle felt better about coming. He stopped at the Visitors and Convention Bureau, Ginny collected brochures, and they turned north on Interstate 25. It was 300 miles to Montana, 200 more to Livingston where Ginny had left her car, 300 after that to Cut Bank.

"Can't make Livingston until late tonight," Kyle said. "Want to stop somewhere, stay over? Salmon said he'll call if something happens at the barricades."

"I'm in no hurry," Ginny said. "I can call Harley from anywhere."

She pondered maps while Kyle drove. "Ten Sleep," she said, "don't you like that? Here's a town called Ten Sleep." It began to rain and gray mist enveloped the Bighorn Mountains.

"I remember Ten Sleep from when we lived in Thermopolis. Mountains, national forest signs and not a tree in sight. Cloud Peak's over there somewhere. I always wanted to climb Cloud Peak."

"Hello!" Ginny said. "There's a turnoff ahead to the Fetterman Battlefield."

"Let's take a look," Kyle said. It's another place where the Indians won."

They rolled off interstate to an intersection featuring two road signs. One route led to a visitors' center at Fetterman Battlefield, the other to a hill where the last soldiers died. They chose the second, and followed it to an obelisk atop a lonely knoll.

Wyoming flatness spread away to the east. Slopes climbed in the west and clouds shrouded mountains beyond. Kyle parked, he and Ginny donned rain parkas, and they trudged up the open, grassy slope of Lodge Trail Ridge. The climb took longer than expected, as usual out here. From on top the ridge their car looked like a tin toy below.

"There,"Ginny said. West, toward the mountains, they saw the brown, grassy outline of old building foundations. She read from a brochure: "'The Army built Fort Phil Kearny and filled it with soldiers to guard the fledgling Bozeman Trail. Captain William Fetterman boasted to other officers that with fifty men he could ride through the entire Sioux nation.'"

"So," Kyle said. "We know where this is going."

"'December 21, 1866, dawned clear and cold. A team of wood-cutters escorted by soldiers left the fort to cut firewood.'"

"Still there." Kyle pointed. "Trees not far from the old fort."

"'...Crazy Horse, then in his 20's, and other Sioux shot from a distance and feigned an attack. Fetterman took the bait and with eighty soldiers galloped forth. There was shouting among the soldiers, much arm pointing,' – that's a quote from a book by Mari Sandoz." She read again, "'Fetterman had distinct orders not to pursue beyond Lodge Trail Ridge, but Crazy Horse stopped, feigned injury, and the soldiers rushed on.'"

"Yes. Yes." Kyle tried to imagine the scene.

"'The Sioux and Cheyenne waited in ambush. The Sioux had often fought these strangers from the East. The Cheyennes wanted revenge for Sand Creek in Colorado, where, two years earlier, soldiers under Colonel John M. Chivington massacred more than one hundred Indian women and children. Some of the cavalrymen carved out dead woman's vaginas and wore them as trophies on their saddle horns.'"

Ginny, paused, shook her head, continued: "'Some of the waiting Indians carried guns. Others tied pieces of buffalo horn into their bows to make them shoot arrows harder. Sioux Chief Red Cloud nodded, a warrior waved his lance, the Indians charged. They killed the foot soldiers first. The troopers on horses fled down the hill' – the one we just climbed – 'and bunched together on the knoll where the monument now stands. Toward the end Fetterman and another officer put pistols to each other's heads and pulled the triggers. All eighty-one soldiers died.'"

"That happened right about where we're standing," Kyle said. "If it weren't for Custer ten years later, today we'd see paintings of Fetterman's Last Stand on barroom walls."

"'Afterward the government abandoned Fort Phil Kearny and Indians burned it to the ground. The Fetterman fight symbolized the only war – Red Cloud's War – that the United States Army lost to Native Americans.'"

They took a last sweeping look, lifted coat collars against the cold and started down the hill. An old Chevrolet nosed around a curve in the road below and parked near the obelisk. A man in a buckskin jacket jumped out and looked directly up at them. He raised a lance, a skinny Indian lance, and swung it back and forth so that the feathers at one end splayed out in the wind. He got back in his car and drove away.

"What the hell," Kyle said. "Do you suppose the Chamber of Commerce pays him to do that?"

"He probably does it just for visiting journalists."

Kyle muttered. He didn't like puzzles you could not solve. He wanted to believe in holy roads and ghost dances and ultimate retributions, but he did not. He and Ginny drove north again toward Montana.

They stopped for the night in a motel in Sheridan, Wyoming. He would drive fast tomorrow, Kyle thought, all the way to Cut Bank. Today was Sunday. He showered while Ginny telephoned her husband with his football team in California.

Kyle emerged from the bathroom. "Everything okay?"

"Harley and his team fly on to Sacramento tomorrow for next Saturday's game. He's got new restaurants to try. He's happy his team won yesterday. He didn't even ask where I was."

She changed to her leather skirt and white turtleneck and they drove to a restaurant on Sheridan's main street. A hostess showed them to a table. "We're having fun, aren't we?" Ginny said.

During the meal they each ordered glasses of two different wines. No dessert, though. "Iron discipline," Kyle said. Instead, they returned to their motel and swam in its heated indoor pool.

Two Indian boys, fully dressed, wandered in from the lobby. "I wish WE had a pool like this," one of them said, loud enough for Kyle and Ginny to hear.

"I wanted to say, 'We're on YOUR side,'" Ginny said afterward. A lamp illuminated their bed, and Kyle noticed a scratch on her arm.

"How did you do that?"

"I fell playing tennis. Look here under my chin. When I was little I jumped off a diving board and hit the concrete edge of a swimming pool." She tilted her head, showed Kyle the scar.

"How old were you?"

"Eight. I rode my bicycle to the doctor's office."

"Brave Ginny. I wonder what would have happened if we had met back then."

"Nothing. Maybe if we sat next to each other in college."

They lay on top of the bed covers and watched a weather forecast on television. "Ever been to Italy?" Ginny asked.

"No. You?"

"No."

Kyle thought, make sure tonight, somewhere during the evening, that she lies on top. The time came. So moist, so hot; he entered easily, almost without effort. He rolled beneath. Would she lie on him or sit up? She shook her hair in his face and rose to a sitting position. This was good, he thought. He could look at her. She could look at him. He could touch her breasts.

"Will you come back to see me after you return to Washington?"

"Will you want me to?"

Ginny did not answer. We had better get going here, Kyle thought. He feared he might slip out. He lifted, lifted again. She began to move. Up. Down. She had definitely done this before.

# # #

CHAPTER 20

A skim of white coated the ground in the morning, snow diamonds in the sunshine. Kyle Hansen and Ginny Foster drove north beneath an endless autumn sky.

Kyle stopped to telephone Salmon Thirdkill. "Talked to Sylvia Bright Angel. She says Rudy Ottens raped her, paid for an abortion and then financed her two years in nursing school. So now we've got a villain, a benefactor and a motive for Indians, presumably, to do bad things to Ottens' cattle."

"Whoa," Salmon said. "That's a lot all at once."

"What thinkest thou?"

Just sit on this, OK? Let me ask around."

Kyle and Ginny drove north. An announcer on the car radio talked about the baseball World Series, recently ended. "Dad used to tell a story about Ty Cobb," Kyle said. "If Terry and I heard it once, we heard it forty times. 'Cobb's getting old,' Dad began. 'It's the Detroit Tigers against the White Sox at Comiskey Field in Chicago. Cobb makes outs his first three times at bat and the Chicago fans love it. They're yelling at him, cursing him. Eighth inning, score tied, a runner on second, Cobb comes to bat again. The pitcher throws at his head and knocks him down.'"

Ginny pointed. A herd of antelope lifted their heads on the prairie to watch them pass. "Beautiful," she said. "On with the story."

"'The pitcher knocks Cobb down. The crowd loves it. Cobb gets up, dusts himself off, holds the bat with his hands apart the way he did. Next pitch, he lines a shot into left field. It's in the gap; it's a two-base hit for most players. Cobb's picking up speed rounding second base. He slides into third, spikes flashing in the sun, and in one smooth motion comes up on his feet, sweeps off his hat and bows to the crowd. Ty Cobb,' Dad always said then. 'Ty Cobb.'"

Ginny smiled. "Okay," she said.

"Terry and I calculated Dad would have been two years old if he saw Cobb play when he said he did. No matter. He's in a graveyard in Wyoming. Terry's beneath a headstone on a hill in Montana. No matter."

They passed the exit to the Little Bighorn Battlefield. "The car wants to turn, but we don't have time," Kyle said. They listened to the news. Someone who called himself "Wovoka" predicted more cattle killings in letters to the editors of several Montana newspapers.

"Wovoka's the Indian shaman who originated the ghost dance, I guess you know," Kyle said.

"The college library in Bozeman carries most of the Montana newspapers. You could stop and look at the letters to the editor. I'll call ahead, if you like." Ginny punched a number on her cell phone.

"Jonathan, please." She spoke to Jonathan in Bozeman as they drove past Billings, with its 80,000 inhabitants Montana's biggest city.

"Terry called Billings 'The Streets of Laredo,'" Kyle said. "Billings has those dust-dry summers."

They fell silent along the Yellowstone River. The Crazy Mountains took shape and on their left the Beartooth-Absaroka massif poked at the sky.

"Got time for food? I'll make you something."

"I'll grab something along the way," Kyle said. "I will stop at the library, though. You say I should ask for Jonathan?"

"I'll meet you there," Ginny said.

Kyle delivered her to her car in Livingston and they drove in tandem over Bozeman Pass. The first view of the Gallatin Valley did not disappoint. Mountain range succeeded mountain range, endless. Ginny turned off toward her house; Kyle drove on to the college library he remembered from Glenda's days as a student here.

He liked libraries, especially this one, a gleaming edifice of brick and glass. He liked gymnasiums and wine stores too, but libraries were special.

"Hansen?" A tall, young lad handed him a sheath of newspapers. "Courtesy of Miss Foster." The kid grinned.

Wovoka's letters to the editors, ornately written, spoke of retribution. "Beware the robes of power," read one. "A moment's satisfaction, a lifetime of regret," read another. The prevailing theme: revenge. More bovines must die. Kyle copied the letters, at ten cents a pop, on a library machine.

He heard a stir, the sound of clicking heels. Ginny had changed to a high-necked blouse and a long skirt. Hair up, wisps unraveling, she reminded Kyle of a photo in a homesteader's cabin.

"Nourishment," she said. She handed Kyle a big, red apple and some coconut cookies.

"Well thank you, Ginny."

"Get what you need?"

"Made copies. Letters rife with retribution."

"Retribution for what?"

"That's for us to decipher."

"Two heads are better at deciphering than one. I hope we talk again soon. I enjoyed the trip, Kyle." He kissed her behind a bookshelf. She'll make a performance of leaving, he thought. He watched. Her head popped out two rows down. She made a face, she bared a leg.

Kyle crunched on his apple as he wheeled out on the interstate. Why did a man in a buckskin jacket wave a lance at him and Ginny at the Fetterman Battlefield? Who was Wovoka, and why was he angry? Might as well ask why, on his first day back in Montana, fate pointed him straight to Ginny Foster.

Kyle glanced toward the Bridgers and a strange sight held him; a waterfall, a huge, gray waterfall tumbled silent in the sky. He rubbed his eyes and looked again; the waterfall transformed itself into a cloud, spilling like water through a gap in the mountains.

He drove 300 miles to Cut Bank and dined at a restaurant frequented by reporters. The situation remained tense, they said, with Indians and law officers facing each other across seven road barricades in northern Montana. Lately, lacking violence, the ladies and gentlemen of the media scrambled for sidebar stories.

Someone painted a red arrow and a hand closed against a forehead on a rock at a highway pulloff near Three Forks, and a reporter for the Great Falls Tribune asked a professor at Montana State what the drawings meant. She told Kyle the result.

"Three rocks piled atop each other suggest, 'Hey, come look,' and a red arrow signifies war. A right hand held against a forehead and rotated counterclockwise represents the Plains Indians sign for anger or madness. I find this interesting because Native Americans considered the white mans' calculated assault on their culture as a madness, a wrong that must be revenged."

"Probably just college kids having fun," another reporter said. "Now everyone and their uncle will babble about red war arrows and right hands rotated counterclockwise."

Kyle laughed, and he did not mention the three rocks piled atop each other when next he spoke with National Editor Jack Leventhal. "I talked to Edgar Ware on the Indian side and Lars Bjornson in the Governor's office and the sticking point remains the same. The Blackfeet want the five locals who beat up the two Indian kids hit with a face-saving jail sentence. State officials and politicians want the Indians to open the roads first, then negotiate. Unofficially, they think the Indians will give in when the weather turns cold."

Kyle and his newspaper sat on Sylvia Bright Angel's story. Ginny Foster had suggested one possibility: since the young woman was under age when Rudy Ottens allegedly raped her, the statute of limitations did not apply and she could legally bring criminal charges or a public civil suit. But that would take the case public, and thus far she had not.

"You could quote unnamed sources as saying that Rudy Ottens 'abused' an Indian girl," Leventhal said. "Then you could find someone to say police believe other Indians killed his cows in retaliation."

"She thinks if we do that, people will know it's her. Then I cheated on my promise."

"Okay, let it ride for now. Kyle, I may want you back in Washington in a week or so. Meanwhile, try and polish your Lewis and Clark series."

"I'm doing that, Jack. I'm halfway through."

"Good. We won't run them until late November or early December. We'll spot them about a month in advance of the actual start of the bicentennial."

Kyle sat in his motel room and replayed the conversation. Obviously his national editor wanted him to pen a piece saying Indians massacred cattle to avenge Sylvia Bright Angel. Should he? After all, he remained here at his newspaper's expense.

He called Salmon Thirdkill. "Well, did you talk to her?"

"I did. Not yet. Okay?"

"If I don't come up with something dramatic my newspaper might call me back to Washington."

"Frankly, I'm surprised you are here this long."

Kyle reached Ginny Foster at home that night, the first time he had telephoned her there. "Harley comes home after Saturday's game in Sacramento, right? Any chance you might drive up here for a night or two before then?"

"Where are you?"

"I'm in Cut Bank. It's just a two-hour drive from Havre."

"I know where Cut Bank is," Ginny said. "I was born there. What are you doing?"

"I'm trying to finish my Lewis and Clark series. Say Salmon and Judy invite you? How about that? Say a Save the Land committee meets in Havre, something you and Judy ought to attend?"

"Better. That I can explain to Harley."

Kyle called Salmon Thirdkill. "Onrushing time, Captain Courage. Might you and Judy invite Ginny Foster up between now and Saturday when Harley returns to Bozeman?"

"Ginny? What? She's willing?"

"She rode with me on my trip to see Sylvia Bright Angel."

Silence. "You rascal. We invite her, she stays with you?"

"Yes. And we drive to your house for dinner."

Salmon pledged to produce an invitation. Kyle drove to the Route 2 barricade and poked around. He returned to his motel and typed another two pages on Lewis and Clark. He telephoned his mother in California, something he did maybe once a month. She asked intelligent questions, and recently he told her about Ginny. "This one sounds different," she said.

"In what way, Mother?"

"You finally found a tall one," she said.

He couldn't concentrate. He got up and wandered outside. A cone of light glowed across the plains from the east and grew in intensity. Kyle watched the prairie give birth to a quivering, red moon. It clung for a moment, as if reluctant to leave mother earth, and burst free.

# # #

CHAPTER 21

Ginny Foster swung an airline carry-on suitcase from her car Thursday afternoon, plopped on the bed in Kyle Hansen's motel room in Cut Bank and kicked off her shoes. She wore jeans and a sweater and big, yellow sunglasses. Her hair spilled across her face.

She'll fling it back now, Kyle thought. He waited and she did, but a rogue strand or two still tickled one cheek. She'll try to blow that back too, he thought, but it won't work, and she'll give her head another toss. He watched. She did.

"I tend to forget that you used to live in this town," Kyle said.

"We moved away years ago, but I don't want to run into people I knew. 'Where's Harley?' they will ask. 'Who is this strange man you're with?'"

"You'll say, 'Just someone I used to know.'"

"That will catch their interest. When do I get to see the barricade?"

"We'll go in the morning. I just left there two hours ago."

"Do you file a story every day?"

"I try to. Lacking violence, I try to talk to both sides and include lots of quotes."

"Who did you quote today?"

"Lars Bjornson said the Governor wants to settle, but that every time he or Jeb Small nudge the five yahoos toward jail, Eldon Lauder and his friends nudge them away. Edgar Ware said it's getting cold camping out. He says his guys want to go back to ranching and pumping gas and sleeping with their girlfriends."

"You wrote that in your story?"

"I smooth it out. I made everyone sound dedicated."

"There are real issues here," Ginny said. "I hope the Blackfeet don't compromise too easily."

"Salmon thinks Edgar won't cave. Edgar still feels double crossed from last time."

"I hope to meet some of these people tomorrow. Now about dinner..."

"You pick a restaurant."

"I suggest we don't go out to a restaurant tonight. I suggest we order pizza."

"That works for me," Kyle said. "I purchased a robust, red wine."

An ad for a local pizzeria lay at hand. He phoned and ordered medium size, half mushroom for Ginny, half pepperoni for himself, and a Greek salad. A kid arrived with plastic forks, salad in a plastic dish, and pizza in the usual square cardboard container. Kyle glanced outside as the kid left. Snowflakes swirled in the wind.

"It's snowing," he said. He opened the wine. They clinked plastic glasses.

"I feel warm and fuzzy," Ginny said. "Harley called last night and I told him I returned early from Seattle and Judy invited me to Havre. I told him I'd come home Saturday and cook him supper."

Kyle visualized Ginny and Harley at table. "You never cooked me supper."

"You never bought me jewelry." She picked up a book. "*My Life As An Indian*. What's this?"

"It's by a man named J. W. Schultz who came west in the eighteen-sixties and married a Blackfoot woman. White settlers made it hard for her, so the two of them moved to the Blackfoot Reservation. She died. Read the last paragraph."

Ginny read aloud: "'By day I think about her, at night I dream of her. I wish I had that faith which teaches us that we will meet again on the other shore. But all looks very dark to me.'" She shook her head. "Serious stuff," she said.

"He makes you see the West before the crowds."

"I notice you wrote your name and a date inside the cover," Ginny said. "Do you do that when you finish?"

"If I like the book. Yes."

"I do that too."

"Great minds," Kyle said. "You look good, Ginny."

"I feel good," she said.

Kyle poured more wine, draining the bottle. "My editor might call me back to Washington soon," he said.

"We know that's coming. Maybe it adds to the intensity."

"Of our relationship?"

"No, the weather," she said, Ginnyesque. "Of course, our relationship."

They ate. Each visited the bathroom. They took off their clothes. Ginny's big toenail jabbed Kyle's leg. They kissed and her hair spilled across her face. She laughed and tried to sit astride him, but he wrestled her down.

They took their time and lay close afterwards. The bed trembled as trucks rumbled by on the highway outside.

"There are always trucks rumbling by Montana motels," Ginny said.

"In New York it's sirens."

"How do you know about New York?"

"I know more than you think," Kyle said. "I've walked the Great White Way."

Ginny peeked out later. "It stopped snowing."

"Good. I'm not ready for winter yet."

They watched late night television. They drove in gray morning to the barricade on the highway outside town.

Two tent cities sprawled on the prairie, Indians west of stacked hay bales, journalists and lawmen east. Several tents sagged as if abandoned and the smell of portable potties rose from the land.

Ginny fell into conversation with a woman reporter in a sheepskin coat and a big, furry hat. Kyle showed his press pass and asked permission from a sheriff's deputy to stroll over to the Blackfoot side. "Me too," Ginny said. "I want to come too."

The deputy eyed her, shook his head, and motioned them both through.

Kyle looked for Edgar Ware. "He usually shows up around noon," a young Indian said. He and several others, including Wayne Chappell, the former University of Montana student Kyle had interviewed several days before, stood in a circle shifting their feet and warming their hands over a fire.

The tribal council supplied them with food and pocket money, one said. Yes, damn right, they would shoot if anybody tried to charge their barricade. They postured a little for Ginny, Kyle thought.

Seeking provocative quotes, he asked their opinion of Congressman Eldon Lauder, who at a press conference yesterday again advocated the use of bulldozers to rip the barricades away.

"Let him talk. He might wake up to some kind of surprise," Wayne Chappell said.

"A surprise?"

"You know..." Chappell cocked a finger and sighted as if ready to pull a trigger. An older Indian, standing near, overheard, stepped between and nudged Chappell away. Kyle thought he detected a quick look of warning.

# # #

CHAPTER 22

"Hello down there!" The voice came from above. Ginny Foster had scampered up steps made of wooden boxes and stood atop the hay bale barricade next to an Indian holding a rifle. She said something to the man and the man smiled. She picked her way back down.

Kyle's cell phone jangled. It was Salmon Thirdkill. "Stop by my school on your way to dinner tonight?"

Kyle calculated. First they drive over 100 miles to Salmon's school, then turn around and drive back to Havre, where Judy would serve them dinner. Then he and Ginny continue on back to Cut Bank. It meant a long evening on the road.

"Sure," he said. Salmon had tipped him to more than one good news story, and tonight he had questions to ask.

"I'll expect you about three. Look for me on the football field."

Kyle Hansen and Ginny Foster drove east across Montana's High Line. Brown prairie stretched away to distant hills, color-less beneath a gray autumn sky. The Bearpaw Mountains dominated the almost-roadless country to the south, a country little changed from the days of Lewis and Clark. It took them over two hours to reach Hays Lodgepole High School on the desolate Fort Belknap Indian Reservation.

Salmon Thirdkill, school principal, wore a "Thunder Birds" sweatshirt over a white shirt and wielded a football blocking dummy on an austere practice field. "Pound it! That's the way the big boys do it. Yes! You, Yellow Tail." He chattered, slapped shoulders, leaped about.

He looked up, saw Kyle and Ginny, winked in recognition, and as he did one of the big kids jolted him backward. "Ouch!" Salmon pretended to stagger. He introduced the football coach, a dark, young man, hair coiled in a pony-tail, to the visitors. "Who's next?" Kyle asked him.

"Winifred Saturday," the coach said.

"Played basketball there my younger days in Hightown," Kyle said.

"They still use the same little gym," the coach said.

"Roy had the bandbox," Kyle said. "If you got any arc on your shot, the basketball hit the ceiling."

"Don't get him started." Salmon tugged Kyle away. "Come inside, you two, and admire my school."

They approached the entrance and it seemed to Kyle, looking up at the rushing sky, that the building actually leaned into the wind. A girl passed in the hallway inside and Salmon patted her on the head. "Can't make 'em go home," he boomed.

Two boys about thirteen followed a young Indian woman into Salmon's office. The bigger boy had made fun of the smaller one's clothes, the teacher said, and the two fought in the hall. Salmon studied the accused instigator. "Gary, you're now our arbitrator on style?"

"What?"

"I mean if you're the one who decides what people ought to wear around here, maybe you should give us a list, 'this is okay, this isn't,' that kind of thing. What's Vern wearing that doesn't meet your standards?"

"Look at his pants."

"What's wrong with his pants?"

"They're too short."

"I had a pair of those," Salmon said. "Those are Prussian paratrooper pants."

The smaller kid studied his trousers, frayed, faded, too short by inches. He glanced at Salmon, his eyes questioning. "Looking good, Vern," Salmon assured him. "Looking good."

The teacher and the boys left. "Well, Salmon, finally we get to observe you in an educational environment," Ginny said.

Salmon stared out a window at a bicycle rack, a brown lawn and a yellow school bus. "Feels like home," he said. He showed them a framed photo of kids in football uniforms and a bushy-haired man. "Here's when I played football in Browning. That's me, with the big helmet. I was a sophomore. Coach looks Indian but he's not. Don Milne was his name."

Kyle leaned close the better to see the pictures on the walls. "Coach Milne is in a lot of them."

"He had four daughters, one right after another," Salmon said. "Naturally, being a coach, he wanted a son. In class one day he tapped me on the left side of the chest. 'Boy's solid here,' he said. 'Some people' – he tapped me again – 'right here they're hollow.' I didn't understand what he meant until years later. Coach tapped me right over the heart."

"Ah, yes," Kyle said.

"Another time I'm horsing around with some of the guys before class, Coach says, 'Thirdkill, you always attract flies.' It's a funny thing to say; it's like he wanted to tell me he thought I was something special. I didn't figure all this out until a lot later. Freshman year, basketball, he moved two other players up to B Squad so I could be high scorer on the freshman team. Sophomore year he played me on the B Squad instead of varsity and I was high scorer again."

"Building your confidence," Ginny said.

"I think so. He started me at center my junior year in basketball and my senior year, the year you guys had the powerhouse team in Hightown, we clobbered everybody in our league. Coach did the same in football; he brought me along gradual, didn't play me at first-team halfback until my junior year. I got voted all-state. My last year – his team, the team he built – we won everything. I made all-state again and the university offered me an athletic scholarship."

"Where's Coach Milne now?" Kyle asked.

"They fired him after my senior year. He wasn't an Indian himself, you know, and some fathers complained he didn't play their sons enough. Someone accused him of sleeping with the girls' basketball coach on a road trip."

"Did he?" Ginny asked.

"Don't know, don't care," Salmon said. "The thing is, they fired him. He got a job coaching at another school. Didn't do well." He glanced at his watch. "Well. I'll call Judy and tell her we're coming."

Kyle took a last look at the pictures. They walked outside. "Any action at the barricades?" Salmon asked.

"Someone shot at a police pottie," Kyle said. "Deputies shot back and an Indian kid got wounded in the arm. Salmon, who is this 'Wovoka' who writes letters to the editor saying more cows must die? Is it Edgar Ware?"

"Doubt it. Why don't you call him and ask him?"

"Something else: today at the Cut Bank barricade one of the young guys suggested some kind of Indian retaliation against Congressman Eldon Lauder."

Salmon looked surprised. "I haven't heard anything about that. Come on, we need to make tracks. Judy's got a faculty meeting at Havre High School tonight after dinner ."

Ginny strode ahead of them to the parking lot. She wore hiker boots and it struck Kyle how neatly the heels had worn. They did not tilt in either direction as they did on most people. Her steps landed precisely, concisely balanced.

They followed Salmon in his car. "We won't stay late," Kyle said. Already he rationed his remaining hours with Ginny.

Judy Thirdkill, already dressed for her faculty meeting later, greeted them at the door in Havre. She hugged Kyle and eyed her former college roommate. "Harley comes back when?"

"Saturday," Ginny said. "They play in Sacramento Friday night."

"He knows you're here?"

"I told him I'm visiting you and Salmon, and that we've got a Save the Land committee meeting."

"That's right; we do." Judy nodded briskly. "We'll meet right here at the dinner table tonight."

Judy served dinner. Salmon poured Scotch. "Have you talked to Sylvia Bright Angel?" Kyle asked him.

"Soon, Salmon said. "Soon."

With Ginny embellishing, Kyle again related what the nurse told them, the rape, the abortion. "My newspaper wants to use the story," he explained to Judy.

"I heard rumors that Ottens chased her around," Salmon said. "Maybe it's fitting somebody killed his cows."

"The question is," Kyle said to Judy, "is do we use her name in a story?"

"I take it she doesn't want you to," Judy said.

"At least if Kyle did it, he could do it diplomatically," Ginny said. "If somebody else gets on to the story, who knows?"

"I'll call Miss Bright Angel and speak with her," Salmon said. "I told you, I remember her from back in Browning."

"And you traveled with Kyle to see her in Cheyenne," Judy said to Ginny.

"Spur of the moment. Harley was away. We did some sight-seeing in Wyoming. Did you know Indians used to call the Oregon trail the Holy Road? Kyle and I looked for ruts."

"I'm cursed," Kyle said to Salmon. "I can't get that sign you and I saw on the Chief Joseph Battlefield out of my mind. 'Follow the Holy Road.' What does it mean? Did you ever find out who put it there?"

"Some things we aren't meant to know," Salmon said. "Like against Utah State our senior year, when Ardo McCullough threw the pass and it hit the bird. And why Rudy Ottens raped a girl and then paid her way to nursing school."

"Guilt," Judy said. She jumped up. "I'm late for my meeting."

"We'll clean up," Ginny said. She accompanied her friend to the door.

Salmon leaned toward Kyle and spoke softly. "Does Harley know?"

"Ginny doesn't think so."

"Surely he suspects."

"That could be."

"I'll follow this situation with interest," Salmon said.

"That coach of your's, the one who got fired, what finally happened to him?" Kyle asked.

"He ended up teaching civics at an elementary school in North Dakota. He died of cancer a few years ago."

"I'm sorry to hear that."

"I wish I had written him. I had the chance, but I didn't. I wish I had thanked him."

"You don't think about those things when you're young," Kyle said.

"Yeah, sure." Salmon looked away. "Sports can break your heart," he said.

# # #

CHAPTER 23

Harley Hawkins' Montana State football team won its Friday night football game in California and remained unbeaten. Kyle Hansen and Ginny Foster, in bed together, listened to the last quarter on the radio.

"You know, Ginny, you could do well in Washington D. C.," Kyle said.

"You think so? Doing what?"

"Something that combines clothing and politics."

She crossed her ankles over his. "A well-dressed lobbyist?"

"Anything," he said. "You're capable of anything."

"And what about you? I see you as a crack reporter or editor for a Montana newspaper."

"I did that. I reported for the *Bozeman Chronicle*. That's not to say I would not consider Billings, Great Falls, Missoula."

"I should think so. I know you like the mountains."

"You might change your mind and want to come East," Kyle said.

"Harder for me to go there than for you to come here," Ginny said.

They stretched side by side. Kyle liked to lie full length beside or on on top of her, legs and arms intertwined. Slowly, gradually they drove toward coitus, in a motel in Cut Bank, Montana. The wind gusted outside, windows rattled. "I'll miss you," he said.

Around midnight, Ginny faded to sleep. Kyle lay thinking. What had he accomplished? What did he want? Kids? What kind of career?

He remembered when in the eighth grade, age 13, just moved to Hightown, Montana, from Thermopolis, Wyoming, he discovered girls. Overnight they became exciting. He wanted to feel them, to kiss them. All around the same thing happened to other kids. Seventh and eighth graders held parties, invented games to touch each other.

Kyle and Terry lived close to the junior high, grades six through eight, and rode their bikes to school. They wheeled in, leaped off. Eighth grader Kyle strode the halls, contender for king of the hill. He dated a girl three doors down the street, got comfortable with her, and moved up to Lois, one of the seventh grade cheerleaders. He gave Lois a ring.

He asked out DeeDee Johnson, queen of the seventh grade girls, and necked with her in the balcony of the Judith Theater. Lois heard about it and dramatically flung away his ring. Kyle continued to date DeeDee. Anything seemed possible.

A week before he began his freshman year in high school Kyle got his front two teeth knocked out broomstick sword fighting with another boy. For weeks – forever – while a dentist measured and ordered a plate with two false teeth to fill the embarrassing void, Kyle Hansen began high school, self conscious, trying not to to smile.

The best looking freshman girls dated upperclassmen who descended upon them like hungry lions. Kyle descended from lord of the manor in eighth grade to nothing kid, a little guy in a school filled with bigger and older boys, some of whom even drove cars. DeeDee, now a buxom eighth grader, dated high school sophomores and juniors. Kyle's social descent seemed breathtaking.

He, gap-toothed during his crucial early weeks in the Big Time, sought solace in sports. It took him two or three years, he realized now, to really regain social confidence. Meanwhile athletics became his outlet. There, in football and basketball, he began his advance.

He married soon after college and in two years divorced. Lately, glancing back, his marriage seemed but an episode. Then, last week in the "in Memoriam" section of a Montana newspaper, Kyle read this, from a husband grieving for his wife a few years dead:

"To love you, my wife, is to daydream of you often, to think of you so much, and miss you so terribly.

"To love you is to remember joyfully the days you made so memorable, the moments that will live forever in my heart, the dreams we hoped for, the feelings we had for each other.

"To love you is to miss the warmth of your arms, the sweetness of your kisses, the friendliness of your smile, the loving sound in your voice, and the happiness we shared.

"To love you is to realize that life without you is no life at all. That's a little of what it's like to have been in love with you.

"Thank you for being my wife." Here the man signed his name.

Kyle Hansen, his 36th birthday not far ahead, wanted to experience a relationship like that.

And now there was Ginny Foster.

They breakfasted, the two of them, at a diner. They kissed and Ginny waved as she drove away, returning to her clothing store and her husband.

Kyle retired to a motel room and worked to finish the fourth and final article of his Lewis and Clark series. He revised and rewrote over the next few days, seeking that perfect melding of fact and flow, and winged his final version away to his newspaper.

Salmon Thirdkill talked with Sylvia Bright Angel and then with Kyle, who talked in turn with Jack Leventhal. They agreed to imply in a story that Rudy Ottens wronged an Indian girl and that his cattle suffered accordingly, without using Sylvia Bright Angel's name.

Kyle spoke with her again on the telephone and found her poised and unexcited. "If, or maybe I should say 'when' somebody does use my name, I will hold a press conference and tell the whole story." Kyle learned later that Salmon Thirdkill now acted as her behind the scenes advisor.

He drove to the barricades every day. He jogged on the prairie for exercise. Ambitious, "auditioning," as he liked to think, for higher status on the national desk or maybe even a future media job in Montana, he pursued other ideas for feature articles.

Kyle talked with Indians leaders in Montana, Wyoming and South Dakota and wrote about unemployment on Indian reservations. He did a piece on an Eastern foundation that sought to buy up Montana land and substitute buffalos for cows. He tried to analyze why so few high school graduates on Indian reservations continued on to college. The Herald printed his articles and Ginny Foster saw to it, via the internet, that they also reached the eyes of Montana news editors.

November advanced. Whenever a settlement appeared near in the standoff between the Blackfeet and Montana legal authorities something seemed to happen to screw things up again.

Random crazies shot up an elk herd on the Blackfoot Reservation. Witnesses said four white men opened up with automatic rifles, killed eight or nine elk, wounded several more, and drove away leaving beer cans and dead animals scattered on the ground.

Shooting erupted at the road barricade west of Cut Bank. Kyle heard popping sounds and a sheriff's deputy sprinted toward him. Puffs of smoke drifted from behind hay bales. "Christ!" the lawman yelled, racing by. Others began shooting. Edgar Ware appeared on the barricade, angry. "Stop it! Stop it!"

An Indian and a deputy sheriff got wounded. Each side blamed the other for shooting first.

Salmon Thirdkill called Kyle on his cell phone. "You heard?"

"Heard what?"

"Remember Clinton Mosby, the rancher near Bozeman who criticized Ginny after her slide show? I hear he's organizing a vigilante group."

"Vigilantes?" These had a bloody and a checkered past in Montana. "What for?"

"Inflict pain. Take revenge. Mosby claims he's lost a sheep or two."

"You think he means to bring his vigilantes here to the barricades?"

"No, no. That's small stuff. Mosby doesn't give a shit about that. It's politics. Methinks the man wants to run for office."

"What will they do? Wear hoods and gallop around the country?"

"Ask Mosby," Salmon said. "You're the reporter."

"Thanks, Salmon; I'll call him."

"Who?" the rancher asked.

"Kyle Hansen, *Washington Herald.*"

"Fact is, I do intend to announce the formation of a Ranchers Safety Committee."

"When will you do that?"

"Tuesday morning at the Baxter Hotel in Bozeman."

"Ranchers Safety Committee: would it be correct to call them vigilantes?"

"That's our model. It worked before in Montana."

"Why vigilantes? What will you do?"

"We ranchers have seen our cattle butchered. We've watched haystacks burn. We've seen horses limp home maimed. If designated law authorities cannot protect us, we will protect ourselves." It sounded as if Mosby read from a script.

"What haystacks? What horses maimed? You blame Indians?" Kyle flung questions.

"Ask me Tuesday at the press conference."

Kyle telephoned Jack Leventhal. "Hooded demons." The national editor rolled the words. "Okay, forget about coming home just yet. See if you can get pictures."

Gunfire erupted at another barricade, on Route 89 north of Dupuyer, and an Indian boy died, hit in the throat. Kyle rewrote an earlier story, leading this time with the death. Federal agents, still nearby, arrived quickly. Blackfoot Chairman Edgar Ware and State Attorney General Jeb Small conferred by telephone and agreed to separate all combatants with wider no-man's zones.

Governor Otto Cloninger demanded immediate peace talks. That afternoon and into evening fresh faces arrived to join the journalists' contingent at the Cut Bank barricade.

Kyle telephoned Ginny Foster at her clothing store in Bozeman. She knew about Mosby's upcoming press conference. "I want to go too," she said.

Kyle drove south on a Monday, windshield wipers clicking, a day in advance. Cold rain fell and it snowed in the mountains. He ought to work the weather into his stories more, he thought. He played with sentences: "Winter crept down those mighty slopes that promised so much but rewarded only effort," stuff like that.

The sun burst free near Helena. Kyle rolled into Bozeman mid afternoon and parked in front of the The Mod Shop. A young woman he did not know worked in the window. Kyle watched as she undressed a mannequin. She removed a short skirt, a filmy blouse, black underwear. She wrested a fishing rod from the silent mannequin's hand.

Kyle rapped on the glass and made a show of clapping. The young woman smiled and bowed.

He entered and spotted Ginny amid softy woolies in great colors wearing a t-shirt lettered, "Women: You Can't Beat Them." She encouraged a customer who tried on a dress before a mirror. The customer purchased. Ginny, talking, touching, accompanied her to the door. "Olla," she said to Kyle. She tapped a pencil against her teeth. "I'll introduce you to Marta."

They stepped out on the sidewalk and watched the assistant in the window reclothe the mannequin in a black cocktail dress. She cocked the mannequin's right arm and fixed in her hand a basketball.

"No football this year," Ginny said. "We're letting her go straight from fishing to basketball."

The young lady emerged. Her blonde hair looked freshly cropped, a bug had bitten the back of her neck. Ginny introduced Kyle to Marta Hollinger.

A customer entered; Marta took her in tow. Too strong for most of the guys she meets, Kyle thought. Needs a bigger town.

"Where are you staying?"

"The GranTree Inn." Kyle named one of the larger local motels. "My room's in back."

"Think I can sneak into the press conference tomorrow?" Ginny asked.

"Easily. You could also sneak into my room."

"We'll see," Ginny said."

The late autumn sun etched every shadow on Main Street. Kyle gazed up at the ridge line of the Bridger Mountains and wanted suddenly to hike, to do something physical. He touched Ginny on her arm. "How about a walk, right now?"

"I can get away for an hour or two."

Ginny told Marta she'd be back by five and changed to a pair of hiker boots she kept at hand. "Have fun." Marta flashed them both a look.

They drove past the lumberyards and the railroad tracks to the base of a steep mountain at the south end of the Bridger Range. An eroded trail led from a parking area up a bare, open slope to the Montana State "M."

Ginny climbed fast. Kyle tried to climb faster. They dueled for about a third of the way and stopped, gasping.

"It's steeper now than when I lived here before," Kyle said.

"Ha," Ginny said.

"Mountains look the same though." The Spanish Peaks, tipped with snow, gleamed in the sun. Autumn's last reds and yellows brightened the courses of streams across the Gallatin Valley.

An ambulance passed on the interstate, red light flashing. "Even on sunny days people die," Ginny said.

They climbed to the whitewashed rocks of the "M," the stones rough and as rippled as some medieval ruin. The University of Montana, 286 miles away in Missoula, also sported an "M" not unlike this one. Every autumn at both schools freshmen lugged brooms and buckets of whitewash up their respective hills.

Kyle nodded toward the football stadium on the Montana State campus. "Where do you sit at games?"

"First row, with the assistant coaches' wives."

"Like an army base; commanding officer's wife surrounded by lesser spouses."

"It's not unlike that."

"Tell me about Clinton Mosby," Kyle said.

"I see him at basketball games; roly poly, little eyes; his ranch nudges up against the Bridgers. His wife committed suicide. She was an alcoholic. His son's back East, hardly ever comes home. The old man's got his sorrows."

"Jesus, now I'm sympathetic to him."

"He savages my Save The Land programs," Ginny said, "but sometimes I feel sorry for him too. I think he concocted this vigilante thing just to have something to do."

"He's serious, you think?"

"He's swearing in charter members. You'll see some of them tomorrow. After that? Where do you go from here?"

"I want to write about the men who slaughtered the elk on the Blackoot Reservation."

"What about the five guys who beat up the Indian kids at the bar in Dupuyer? Why not interview them? Maybe it's the same guys who shot the elk."

"Well done, Ginny. Good idea."

"Macho madness," Ginny said. "The Chronicle quoted a psychiatrist who said that during times of stress men swap their penises for guns."

Kyle laughed. "I'd like to use that in a story."

"Feel free." Ginny flung her hair back, the familiar gesture.

"I started Joseph Conrad's *An Outcast of the Islands*. The hero says, 'I did all this. What more have you done? That was my life. What has been yours?'" Kyle spread his arms as if to take in all of creation.

"It's the journey, not the destination." Ginny grinned. She nudged a rock and it clattered down the mountain.

They descended, drove to town. "Press conference starts at ten in the morning," he said. "If I don't see you tonight, and it appears I won't, I'll meet you at your store, nine-forty-five."

Ginny leaned against his car. "I'd like to get you and Harley together. Only that once, in Helena, did I see you side by side."

Kyle looked at her, surprised. "Why do you want to do that?"

"It might be helpful. I could prod and compare."

"You're serious"

"You wouldn't object?"

"Not if it's important to you. We'd better do it soon, though, before my time runneth out."

"Interesting, so far it seems like something always happens to keep you here," Ginny said.

# # #

CHAPTER 24

About sixty years old, bulky as a gone-to-seed wrestler, Clinton Mosby glared from a dais in a second-story banquet room in Bozeman's Baxter Hotel. He wore a big hat and two-tone cowboy boots. Other men similarly dressed sat behind him, and about fifteen reporters occupied two rows of metal folding chairs.

A man in a business suit moved among the journalists distributing statistics extolling the importance of ranching to the American economy. Everybody, including Mosby, watched this man. One of the ranchers on stage coughed and crossed his legs. Kyle recognized Rudy Ottens.

Mosby began: "Ladies and gentlemen of the media, I need not describe for you the depredations of ranchers' property since vandals took it upon themselves to blockade roads in and out of the Montana's Blackfoot Reservation. We have suffered cattle killed, fences cut, horses maimed. We resolve, therefore, to do what we must to protect ourselves."

Silence. "Does that mean shoot to kill?" a reporter asked.

"We will do what is necessary," Mosby intoned.

Not bad, thought Kyle. He expected Mosby to wave the bloody flag, to go for the easy headline, and, happily for these assembled journalists, he did. But the man also exhibited a certain wounded decorum.

Kyle rose. "Mr. Mosby, could you read us the names of the founding members of the Ranchers Safety Committee?"

"I'd be happy to." Kyle counted fourteen, including Rudy Ottens.

"Do you term yourself 'vigilantes?'" Kyle recognized the voice of this questioner; it was Ginny Foster. They earlier separated at the door and he turned to look. She stood framed against the rear wall of the room, fetching in white turtleneck and leather skirt. Men on either side exchanged a glance.

"Greetings, Mrs. Hawkins. Vigilantes? No, we do not object to the term."

A woman reporter from the Billings Gazette asked, "Mr. Mosby, do your vigilantes imitate the Montana originals, who in the 1860's lynched suspected outlaws in the gold camps?"

Mosby smiled. "Let me read you a quote from one of those early bringers of justice, Thomas J. Dimsdale: 'There is not now – and there never has been – one upright citizen of Montana who has a particle of fear of being hanged by the Vigilance Committee.'"

"Non-upright citizens should fear hanging?" the reporter shot back.

"I think I made my meaning clear."

Kyle made a note that Mosby's hat cast a hangman's noose shadow on the wall behind him. "So you will hang cattle killers," someone said.

"We hope that will not be necessary. We hope that our very existence will serve as a deterrent."

Questions abounded: how could vigilantes guard an entire state? How decide whose ranches to protect? Did vigilantes intend to cooperate with police?

"What if it's not Indians?" Kyle asked. "What if it's Scottish Presbyterians killing steers? Would you hang them too?"

Mosby hesitated. "Well, anyone...Certainly we would deal with everyone the same."

Ginny Foster circulated among the crowd when the press conference ended. "First they've got to catch them," Kyle heard her say. He looked for a quiet corner to use his cell phone.

"I don't want to engage the man in a pissing contest," Edgar Ware responded from his ranch on the Blackfoot Reservation. "Between you and me, we want this whole thing settled. Our wives want us home. We need gas and groceries and winter's coming. I spoke with Jeb Small today; I think we will meet soon." Ware sounded weary.

"Can I say that in a story?"

"You can say we're willing to compromise."

Kyle sought out Ginny. "Do you think your friend Jonathan at the library can find the book by Thomas J. Dimsdale that Mosby mentioned?"

"I'll wager he can." Ginny retired to one corner with her cell phone, Kyle to another with his. He tried unsuccessfully to reach State Attorney General Jeb Small in Helena. He did get through to Lars Bjornson, Governor Cloninger's press secretary.

"I know. We heard. Just say that the Governor deplores anyone taking the law into their own hands."

Ginny motioned. "The book is called *Vigilantes of Montana* and Jonathan will hold it for you."

"Thanks so much, Ginny. You coming to the library?"

"I think not. Today I sell clothes. Why don't you call me at the Mod Shop whenever you make new plans."

"I shall." He kissed her furtively in an alcove of the old Baxter Hotel. She'll put on a show leaving, Kyle thought. She stepped out on the sidewalk and he idled behind. She stopped and posed at a parking meter, one arm behind her head. She ran a lazy hand along her leather skirt.

Kyle thumbed through newspapers from around the state at the Montana State College Library. A letter to the editor in the Lewistown News Argus caught his eye:

"A MATTER OF TIME

Anticipate appropriate retaliation against those twin pillars of pestilence, Eldon Lauder and Clinton Mosby." It was signed, "Wovoka."

Jonathan appeared with Thomas Dimsdale's *Vigilantes of Montana* and Kyle asked, "While we're at it, do you have anything on Wovoka and the ghost dance?"

"I think I know what you want. I'll get it for you."

Two books to read, and nothing else to do this Tuesday afternoon but drive 300 miles back to Cut Bank. Kyle found a table in a corner. "Swift and terrible retribution is the only preventive of crime, while society is organizing in the Far West," Dimsdale began. High-spirited, eye-witness accounts of 1863 and 1864 lynchings by vigilantes followed. Dispassionately, in the time-honored manner of executioners safe from harm themselves, the author spun his tales.

Suspected murderer Club Foot George, a noose around his neck, jumped off his box without waiting for it to be kicked from beneath him. Boone Helm watched a friend swing and observed, "Kick away, old fellow; I'll be in hell with you in a minute."

"Frank Parrish requested to have a handkerchief tied over his face... He seemed serious and quiet, but refused to confess anything more, and was launched into eternity." Another doomed man's wife fought to save her husband, but the vigilantes, local citizens, dragged her away.

"...Peace, order and prosperity are the results of the conduct of the Vigilantes," Dimsdale concluded.

It struck Kyle that the vigilantes thoroughly enjoyed themselves, as in those pictures of smiling bystanders at Southern lynchings in the 1920s. Well, why not? During the 1991 and 2003 U. S. invasions of Iraq, American television presented live pictures of bombs falling on Arab cities as virtual sports events.

Now, Wovoka. Kyle poured another cup of coffee and turned pages in another frayed, old volume, *The Ghost Dance Religion* by Richard Mooney.

The U. S. Government in 1890 hired Mooney, a self-described "ethnologist," to investigate a new Indian rite, the ghost dance, that spread across the West. Where did this dance originate, and why did it frighten so many soldiers and settlers?

Mooney traced the ghost dance to a man named Jack Wilson, a Paiute Indian six feet tall, about 35 years old, who grew to adulthood in the Mason Valley of Nevada near today's Carson City.

"His native valley, from which he has never wandered, is a narrow strip of level sage prairie some thirty miles in length, walled in by the giant Sierras, their sides torn and gashed by volcanic convulsions and dark with gloomy forests of pine, their towering summits white with everlasting snows, and roofed over by a cloudless sky whose blue infinitude the mind instinctively seeks to penetrate to far-off worlds beyond..."

Kyle imagined what today's editors at The Herald would do with a sentence like that. He read on.

A total eclipse on January 1, 1889, "When the sun died," introduced Jack Wilson to the supernatural. Wilson adopted the name, Wovoka, and experienced his defining vision. Indians must dance from right to left following the course of the sun. They must dance in a circle and observe certain purifying rituals. Do these things, preached Wovoka, and your dead relatives will return and live again. The buffalo will reappear and darken the plains. The white man, bringer of troubles, will vanish from your world.

This last alarmed white settlers and politicians. They called for the army, for soldiers and guns, and the Seventh Cavalry, General George Custer's old command, rode toward South Dakota.

Indians rejoiced at Wovoka's promises, this new hope, born, wrote Mooney, "of the intolerable stresses laid upon them by poverty and oppression."

Mooney traveled in South Dakota that autumn of 1890 and watched the men, women and children of the Sioux dance in a circle holding hands. They chanted, "Father, I come; Mother, I come; Brother, I come; Father, give us back our arrows." They sang: "The whole world is coming, A nation is coming, a nation is coming, The eagle has brought the message to the tribe. The father says so, the father says so. Over the whole earth they are coming. The buffalo are coming, the buffalo are coming, The crow has brought the message to the tribe, The father says so, the father says so."

Kyle got up and wandered for a few minutes. There are many spirits scattered across the West, he thought. His spine tingled.

He circled his table twice more, sat down and returned to the book.

The United States Army ordered Salmon Thirdkill's old tribe, the Sioux, already penned in reservations, not to dance the ghost dance again. The Sioux did not trust the soldiers and several hundred of them fled toward the Badlands to the south. On a raw December day in 1890, along a creek called Wounded Knee, troopers of the Seventh Cavalry set up machine guns on a hill and massacred by actual count more than one hundred and fifty Native Americans, most of them, as usual, women and children.

The magic of the ghost dance, Mooney wrote, also died that day. Wovoka himself lingered on, scarcely remembered, until 1932. Now, more than 70 years after his death, letter writers in Montana revived his name.

Kyle started for Cut Bank. He waited on Route 287 between Three Forks and Helena, motor idling, while a line of cattle crossed the road. Two boys on horseback, aware of motorists watching, chased a calf or two and made shows of copiously spitting.

Snow streaked the peaks of the mountains. Every night the sun set a minute or two earlier and slid a notch or two further south. The evening sky shaded from blue to black and in the west a slash of red backlighted the long line of the Rocky Mountains.

Kyle thought of Ginny. He thought of Mona in Missoula and his brother and the great dog. He reached his motel in Cut Bank around ten at night and turned the television to a pro basketball game. Up and down the floor they ran. Kyle watched a few minutes, realized that he did not care who won, and turned to a news channel.

# # #

CHAPTER 25

Kyle Hansen rolled over and looked out his motel window Wednesday morning in Cut Bank. He wanted to interview the five men who beat up the two Indian boys in Dupuyer. He hoped to track down the elk shooters. He wondered how long would it take Clinton Mosby's vigilantes to commit an atrocity.

The waitress at a restaurant down the street automatically set before him his usual breakfast, two bowls of cereal, wheat bread toast with butter and grape jelly, coffee, orange juice. "Who's reputation will you destroy today?" she asked.

"Today I take on offshore cartels," Kyle jested in return. He tipped her two dollars, returned to his motel and sought to contact the five Dupuyer assailants by telephone. Ginny had suggested this, yes, but he would have come around to it anyway, he told himself.

He reached three of the five. Two said yes and Kyle set up interviews for tonight. The other man told him to kiss off.

Kyle studied his road map. Why not ask the good people of Dupuyer, a hamlet so small his road atlas did not even bother to list its population, their opinion of all this? After all, it was events at their doorsteps that launched the road barricades and all that followed.

Kyle drove 35 miles of gravel backroad to a square building with blinking beer signs, Dupuyer's Ranger Bar. The Rocky Mountain Front loomed in the west. A cold wind blew from the north. South and east brown prairie grass whipped in the wind.

Two old-timers sat along the bar at ten-thirty in the morning. Kyle identified himself as a reporter and mentioned the incident of six weeks ago. "You saw it?" he asked the young bartender. He felt easier starting with him.

"Standing right here."

"What kicked it off, anyway?"

"The usual. Somebody mouthed off."

"Who? The two kids?"

"Listen, you going to quote me on this?"

"I'd like to."

"I didn't hear who said what. All of a sudden I saw two kids on the floor."

One of the older men, tufted eyebrows, tipped back his cowboy hat. "Those boys asked for it," he said

"One of them almost broke the glass in the cigaret machine," the second man said. "Said he didn't get his change." This man wore a plaid jacket and combed his white hair straight back.

"That made the five men angry?"

"Earlier that day somebody shot out the tires on their truck," the second man said.

"You think the two kids did that?"

"Listen mister, I don't know."

Kyle ordered a draft beer. "You think those five might have been the ones who shot the elk on the reservation the other day?" He wanted to interview the elk-shooters too, but no one seemed to know their names.

"Different crowd," the bartender said. "The five in here that night were older."

"How do you know that?"

"Newspaper said the elk hunters looked young, college age, almost kids themselves."

"If the newspapers know what they look like, I wonder they haven't been arrested," Kyle said.

"Whoever it was killed Mr. Ottens' cows ain't been arrested either," the man in the cowboy hat said.

"Mind if I take some pictures," Kyle asked the bartender. "Give your place some publicity?"

"We could use that." The bartender grinned at the others, draped a towel over one arm and patted back his hair.

Kyle focused on a sign over the cash register that read, "My job is so secret, even I don't know what I'm doing." He photographed the Ranger Bar from inside and outside.

He ought to get back to Cut Bank, but the historical marker he intended to visit weeks ago, near where Meriwether Lewis and his men killed two Blackfeet on July 26, 1806, awaited just up Route 89. Kyle decided, what the hell, go take a look.

He drove there and read the sign beside the road. He had already described this incident in his Bicentennial series, but it did seem a historical irony that now a Blackfoot road barricade blocked modern Highway 89 just a few miles away.

He glanced westward at the ramparts of the Continental Divide. He prepared to go. Something held him. What? The mountains, he realized. Ginny was right. He didn't want to leave the mountains.

Kyle laughed. He drove back to Cut Bank and his cell phone rang. "Where are you?" asked Jack Leventhal.

"Just got back to my motel."

"Turn your television to the cable news."

Kyle saw live pictures of bloodied cows, throats cut, sprawled across a barren ridge. "...alarmed Montana officials note that this is the second such incident..."

Leventhal waited on the telephone. "The ranch is near Virginia City and the camera crew is from the Butte television station. They got there fast. How far is this from you?"

"Virginia City?" Kyle had to stop and think. "Five or six hours. I missed the early part of the news report. Has anybody established a connection between this cattle killing and the previous one?"

"That's for you to find out," Leventhal said.

Kyle's phone rang again. "I want to cancel our appointment to talk." It was one of the men involved in the incident at the bar in Dupuyer.

"Why?"

"Thought the better of it, you might say."

Kyle guessed the other man would also call and cancel, but he did not wait to find out. He packed his overnight bag, reserved one of the last available rooms at a motel in Virginia City and headed south.

In Montana if they caught you speeding on the Interstate, they fined you maybe $5. It's like they WANTED you to go fast. Kyle did. Every 30 minutes he heard on the radio, "...nine cattle belonging to Madison County rancher Edmund Purcell..."

He stopped for coffee. He called Lars Bjornson in Helena. "The Governor offers a twenty-thousand dollar reward for information leading to the conviction of anyone who kills livestock," Lars said.

"Just cattle? What about elk killers?"

Lars paid no attention. "This morning near Lame Deer some idiot shot two horses belonging to a Native American rancher."

"Maybe it was the vigilantes," Kyle said.

"That's your surmise, not mine. That's why Governor Cloninger warns people against taking the law into their own hands."

Kyle called Edgar Ware and this time actually reached him. "Ever hear of a man named Edmund Purcell?"

"Have now. Hadn't before. No, I don't know who did it."

"Edgar, are you the Wovoka who sends these threatening letters to the editor to newspapers around the state?"

"Give me a break. Besides, you think I would tell you if I was?"

The Madison River rustled in moonlight between treeless banks. Kyle stopped for a sandwich in Ennis and telephoned Salmon Thirdkill in Havre. "Captain Courage, who's killing these cows?"

"I don't know," Salmon said. "And I never heard of this Purcell guy. Did you talk to Edgar Ware?"

"He said he's never heard of Edmund Purcell either. I asked him if he was Wovoka."

"What did he say?"

"He kind of chuckled."

"Edgar's clever," Salmon said.

Route 287 labored up a long slope from Ennis into the foothills of the Tobacco Root Mountains. State police manned a checkpoint. No reporters would be allowed to visit the Purcell ranch until morning. Kyle continued on and checked into his motel in Virginia City around midnight.

He arose early and followed a police cruiser along a gravel road in a procession of cars. They bumped over a cattle guard and parked near a bleak ranch house sheltered by a jut of rimrock. Kyle leaped from his car, feeling himself a wily veteran among these fresh media faces.

A TV satellite dish perched on a pedestal near the house pointed south. Kyle noted a parched lawn and fresh firewood and kindling stacked behind the frost-seared remains of last summer's vegetable garden. Mud-tracked flagstones approached a sagging porch. Play fair, Kyle told himself. Nobody ever said ranching was easy.

He plodded with other reporters up an open ridge to where nine dead cows lay scattered on the ground. It appeared the executioner or executioners selected the biggest and fattest and cut their throats, and that these fell to their knees before they died.

A young deputy demonstrated this theory for a woman reporter. He rolled upside down, kicked his legs in the air and abruptly lay still.

"Okay, Bobby, that's enough," an older lawman said.

Kyle took pictures of these carefully bred, genetically engineered meat machines. He understood the rancher's anger, and yet he felt no emotion himself. He would regret the death of a wild predator like a wolf or a cougar, he knew. A million years of intelligence blazed in a wolf's eyes. But he saw only dullness, at best a flickering capacity for surprise, in the eyes of other cows grazing nearby.

He looked for trampled grass, for signs of dancing, but on this rocky ground you could not tell. He approached the rancher, Edmund Purcell. "Nine? Why nine?"

Purcell glanced across a vast valley at the Madison Range, removed his hat and scratched his head. He wore the requisite denim pants and jacket. His gray hair looked well cared for, his hat perfectly creased.

"Maybe the tenth got away."

"Who do you think did it?"

"Somebody who knew my layout," Purcell said.

"You've hired Indians?"

"Sheriff asked me that; my wife's working up a list. Sure I've hired Indians. Man gives me an honest day's work, I don't care who he is, he gets no trouble from me."

"Maybe somebody held a grudge," Kyle said.

Purcell fixed him with a stare. "Maybe they just got the wrong ranch."

Someone announced that Purcell would take questions at a press conference on his front porch. Reporters drifted back down the hill to the house. Plump clouds floated, fecund, Eastern. Unusual in arid Montana, especially this late in the year, globules of moisture clung to Kyle's skin.

"How many cows do you graze on national forest land?" Kyle asked Purcell after the press conference began.

"A hundred and fifty maybe," the rancher said.

"How much do you pay for grazing right?" asked a woman reporter.

"How much do we pay? The going rate."

"How much is the going rate?"

"I don't know, how much is it, Cal?" Purcell lobbed the query to his ranch foreman.

"It's the fair rate," Cal said.

"When those steers were calves, we carried them in from the cold," Purcell said. "We tended them, we nursed them along."

"What do live cattle sell for these days?" the woman reporter asked.

"About seventy cents a pound, little lady."

"So when you ship a live cow to a slaughterhouse, a fifteen-hundred pound steer brings, say, eleven-hundred dollars?"

"I suppose that's about right," Purcell said.

"If live coyotes brought seventy cents a pound, maybe you'd bring their pups in from the cold."

Kyle laughed and looked at the woman reporter more closely. Young, she wore her hair in braids. But she was old enough to know that ranchers had reigned politically supreme in the Mountain West for a long time, and that they grazed their cattle for pennies on public land.

Kyle sidled closer. "Buy you dinner in Virginia City," he said.

"Well thank you, but I'm going back to Helena with my group."

Another celibate night. Kyle wanted to call Ginny Foster, but she would have closed her store by now. He descended a dusty road to Virginia City.

It always seemed to him on high school football and basketball trips that a special loneliness afflicted southwestern Montana. The light looked different. Ranches and little towns huddled defenseless. Seated with his laptop beneath a streetlight on a park bench in Virginia City, Kyle tried to incorporate this mood of loneliness into his news story. Above, from the east, a depthless blue-black crept across the sky.

Kyle strolled up one side of Virginia City's central street and down the other. Cars with out-of-state license plates nudged wooden sidewalks. Artsy-craftsy buildings flanked directions to a boot hill, and he thought he heard a banjo. These days Montana's original boom town mined tourists instead of gold.

E. M. Forster wrote, in *A Passage to India*, "Most of life is so dull there is nothing to be said about it." Kyle sipped soup in a diner among a busload of oldsters. He wondered what Ginny Foster looked like in a bikini.

A deputy sheriff stomped in and Kyle listened as the man conferred with another lawman. A park ranger at the Big Hole Battlefield reported seeing "incriminating drawings." Kyle sought an angle, any angle, to distinguish his story from all the others in newspapers tomorrow, and he identified himself to the deputy sheriff. "Why incriminating?" he asked.

"Park ranger found paintings of a beaver and nine upended cows the afternoon before Purcell's herd got hit. Nine died, you know. And Purcell did run his herd in the Beaverhead National Forest."

Kyle called his newspaper and suggested to an assistant editor that someone thumbed their nose at authority and announced mayhem in advance. "I'll drive over there and take a look," he said.

"I'll put the rewrite man on," the editor said. "Before you go, give him what you've got."

Kyle liked driving in the night. There would be motels ahead. It was cold, he turned on the heater and he peered at old buildings in the darkness as he passed through the resurrected ghost towns of Ruby Gulch and Alder. Snug in his warm cocoon of a car, he drifted into reverie.

He had done stupid things in his life. He had caused pain. Alone in Montana night, Kyle Hansen reveled in the luxury of his former badness. Vanity. Vanity. He had liked to think of himself in his early years as a Johnny Appleseed of the heart. He scattered tears, yes, but layered a legacy the richer for his coming.

Things change. Matched now against the solidity of Ginny Foster, knowing he approached 40, the old hedonism did not cut it anymore.

Kyle got a motel room in Dillon, sipped a Scotch and water and gazed at pictures of homesteader cabins on the walls. The next morning, at breakfast he saw the words REVENGE and REVEALED emblazoned in a headline on the front page of the *Bozeman Chronicle*. Gingerly, he read the story.

Chronicle reporters tracked two Indians who had filed legal complaints against rancher Edmund Purcell to a wheat-harvesting crew in Kansas. The pair accused Purcell of cheating them of hundreds of dollars in wages, thus establishing a tentative motive for yesterday's cattle killing.

And this: "A potential revenge motif also emerged in the slaying earlier this fall of cattle belonging to Big Timber area rancher Rudy Ottens. Medical records reveal that a Bozeman doctor performed an abortion two years ago on a young Indian woman, Sylvia Bright Angel, who worked for Ottens as a cook. An affidavit identifies the father as Ottens himself..."

The two former ranch hands had alibis; witnesses observed them in Kansas the night Purcell's cattle died in Montana. And no one believed that Sylvia Bright Angel cut the throats of ten of Rudy Ottens' steers. Still, Kyle had to admit, the Chronicle reporters had aced him twice in one day. They did an excellent job.

Speaking later to Jack Leventhal, he sought to shift the focus ahead instead of behind. "The new news is that somebody's roaming around Montana hitting on ranchers who once upon a time wronged an Indian. Any Indian. Whoever killed Purcell's cows thumbed his nose at authority and telegraphed his intentions in advance. That's where this story is heading. I hope to get some leads on that tomorrow."

Leventhal sighed. "I can't keep you there forever, Kyle."

"I know."

# # #

CHAPTER 26

Kyle Hansen drove into a wide mountain valley of haystacks and barbed-wire fences. National TV continued to leap onto this second cattle killing, parading shots of bloody steers, jagged peaks, taciturn cowboys. He had left that scene and driven 90 miles shadowed on his left by the Continental Divide, with Idaho just over on the other side.

Rain sotted his windshield. Probably it snowed up high. Kyle remembered driving through this valley years ago in a blizzard and seeing moose huddled in ditches along the road. At forty below zero, they lost their fear of man.

He parked at the Big Hole Battlefield Visitor Center, on a hill above the Big Hole River. His was only the second car. He identified himself as a reporter to a National Park Service ranger, who walked him down into the woods to a white boulder surrounded by pines. "Voila," she said.

Someone had painted a red beaver a foot high and twice as long, its tail fanned behind, on the boulder's flat surface. Next to this the artist depicted nine ostensibly dead cows with splashes of red around their necks. The oily, crimson color, whatever it was, appeared to have permeated the very surface of the rock.

The ranger, young and pigtailed, crisp in her green uniform, pointed with a stick. "No, not homemade colors; it's basic paint store stuff. Note they outlined the beaver and the cows in black. One motion, one line. They drew the beaver's tail cross-hatched, odd, and as on the cows they drew two legs instead of four." She made a little hop and viewed from another angle. "Early-era cave drawings of animals look just this way."

"Any theory who did it?"

"Came to work two days ago, there it was."

Kyle jotted notes. "And that?" A modern, metal-tipped arrow protruded from a cleft in the rock.

"See? It points toward the tree blazes."

"Tree blazes. Why tree blazes?"

"Someone having fun, someone with imagination. Three blazes, in Indian lore, simply mean 'pay attention.'"

Kyle took pictures of the drawings and the blazes, three sticky, yellowish cuts hacked into a large pine. Periodically the ranger glanced up the hill, in case new sightseers arrived. "A beaver. Nine bloody cows, the same number later found killed on Beaverhead National Forest land. It appears to me that whoever painted these pictures knew exactly what would happen," the young ranger said.

"I have to agree with you." Kyle looked around. "While I'm here, where's the battle site?"

"It's all around. You know the story?"

"I read Alvin Josephy's book," Kyle said. In the summer of 1877, after federal troops hounded them from their ancestral home in Oregon, Chief Joseph and his band of Nez Perce paused here to camp and U. S. Army troops under Colonel John Gibbon and a ragtag posse of white civilians crept up in the night and attacked at dawn. They clubbed or shot 60 Nez Perce to death, as usual most of them women and children.

The Nez Perce men rallied and chased the soldiers and the civilian posse back across the river. The braves pinned them there all day while surviving members of their families made their escape. The Indians found whiskey bottles strewn on the ground where the soldiers had camped. "We thought some got killed by being drunk," Yellow Wolf said years later.

The Nez Perce fought on for several more months while continuing to move east and north trying to reach Canada. Army troops surrounded them on their final battlefield near the Bearpaws, the site Kyle walked in September with Salmon Thirdkill.

A bus rolled in up at the visitor's center. A crowd of school children clattered down the hill.

Kyle drove away into the mists. He may have missed some nugget of aftermath at Edmund Purcell's ranch today, but he had a new wrinkle – the rock paintings as teaser warnings – to play with in his next cattle killing story.

He wanted to approach Jeb Small next, and the Governor and other politicians, to prod them about the slowness of their efforts to make peace with the Blackfeet.

Missoula was not that far away. He still kept the phone number of Mona, the restaurant hostess, and he stopped in Butte to call.

"I remember," she said, "you're the journalism major."

"What's it been, seven weeks? I'm in Butte and I wanted to say hello."

"Thanks for calling, Kyle. I think maybe I worked out 'my problem.'"

"Way to go. Who's the guy?"

"A grad student. He works part-time as a bartender. I found a phonograph needle that works."

Kyle laughed. Now he was off the hook. "So, you'll stick with him?"

"Actually, no. Now I'm curious about other men."

Hmmm. Kyle considered. Don't risk it, he thought. If you do, sure as hell she'll revert.

He listened to the radio news, driving north through the mountains. Harley Hawkins' Montana State Bobcats demolished Northern Arizona today 41-7 and remained undefeated. The University of Montana, Kyle's old school, also won for the eighth straight time. The two Montana schools stood alone atop the Big Sky Conference standings and Kyle sensed an epic taking shape. Two weeks from now the Bobcats and Grizzlies finished their seasons against each other.

He called Salmon Thirdkill. "I want you to know, Salmon, I did not use Sylvia Bright Angel's name in any of my stories. She did tell me, though, that she might hold a press conference."

"No," Salmon said. "She won't. Why remind people? I advised against it."

Kyle checked into the Vigilante Hotel with its lingering aura of Ginny Foster. He could not locate Attorney General Jeb Small, the state's point man in the peace negotiations, on this Saturday night, but he did reach the Governor's spokesman, Lars Bjornson.

"This might interest you," Lars said. "The Gallatin County Sheriff assigns deputies to patrol Clinton Mosby's ranch in the Gallatin Valley."

"Someone threatens the leader of the vigilantes?" Kyle liked the bird-chases-cat twist of this.

"We hear that more Wovoka letters to the editor will surface in the Sunday papers tomorrow, naming Clinton Mosby as prime target."

"Does anybody take this Wovoka seriously?"

"We do," Lars said.

"Well, that's good enough for me." Kyle called the Washington Herald and told an assistant editor that tomorrow, Sunday, his normal day off, he intended to drive to Bozeman to research a possible story. "I'll do it on my own time," he said.

"Where? Yeah, sure," the editor said.

Kyle dreamed that night of the Blackfoot River. It was May, as always, and the water ran high with snowmelt. He, Terry and the others camped north of a bridge and in the morning, in the rapids below the bridge, he watched his brother drown.

He awoke in a hotel room in Helena and it took him a while to realize where he was. Must be proximity, he thought. He did not have these dreams in Washington.

He bought the Sunday papers. "Vigilantes who play with fire..." one Wovoka letter began. Another paraphrased Andrew

Marvell: "... for at my back I always hear, armed revengers drawing near..." Wovoka ought to ease off, Kyle thought. Now he just stirs up sympathy for Indian-bashers. He took a chance and called Ginny at home.

"A hike? Where?"

"Sheriff's deputies guard Clinton Mosby's ranch. There's a trail along the Bridgers above his place I used to walk when I lived there."

"A Sunday stroll?"

"Yes. Maybe I'll take some pictures, see where somebody might try to sneak in if they wanted to get at Mosby's cattle."

Ginny called back ten minutes later. "Harley wants to come."

"Why?"

"He says I'm different lately."

"Are you different?"

"I'm happier. He's suspicious."

"Okay," Kyle said, "bring him along." If this was competition, and she the prize, he wanted to play.

"We'll have fun," Ginny said. "Marta and I climbed to Lava Lake from Gallatin Canyon last week and I've never seen the mountain ashes so brilliantly orange. She'll mind the store. She usually does on Sunday. Meet you at the Mod Shop."

It was warm for November and Kyle drove to Bozeman in khaki shorts and hiker boots. A soft sun cast long November shadows. Harley waited in his car in front of the Mod Shop. They did not shake hands. "The women are inside," he said.

Kyle entered, followed by Harley, and greeted Ginny and Marta Hollinger. "Pack a lunch?" Harley asked.

"I thought I'd stop and buy something to take along."

"No need for everybody to wait while you go shopping," Harley said. "Ginny made enough for all of us."

"That's right. There is enough," Ginny said.

"If Harley doesn't eat it all," Marta said.

"He might. He likes my sandwiches," Ginny said. They bantered, Kyle shifted his feet. Ginny cuffed Harley on the shoulder. What's going on? She and Harley seemed so together, so casually cocky, that Kyle decided, in self defense, to flirt with Marta.

"You lived in Alaska, right? Ten men for every woman."

"Loners and losers," Marta said.

"'Loners and losers.'" Kyle savored the phrase. "I would have thought, 'adventuresome.'"

"Long nights," Marta said. "Don't misunderstand. I did meet men I liked."

Ginny moved toward the door. "Have a good time," Marta said. The three hikers piled into a sports utility vehicle with COACH license plates. Harley, at the wheel, donned a pair of rakish sun glasses. Kyle sat in the back seat. They roared out of town past the parking lot at the base of the "M" and through a notch in the mountains into Bridger Canyon.

The canyon widened. Green meadows and wood fences flashed by. "Reminds me of the Virginia horse country," Kyle said.

"They don't have 'hills' like this in Virginia," Harley said.

Ginny turned to glance at him and finally Kyle sensed something like awareness in her eyes. "You said you hiked the Bridgers when you lived in Bozeman?"

"Sacajawea, Hardscrabble," Kyle named two of the higher peaks. "The ridge trail north of Ross Pass passes just above Clinton Mosby's ranch."

"What's the problem with Clinton Mosby?" Harley asked.

Kyle started to say, "Ginny didn't tell you?" and changed his mind. "There's talk that somebody might try to retaliate against him for organizing vigilantes."

Harley considered. "What did you do when you lived in Bozeman?" he asked.

"I worked at the Chronicle, my first reporting job."

Harley nodded. "Do you feel pressure as a reporter," he asked, "when you write your stories, to support the political views of whoever owns your newspaper?"

"Well...yes," Kyle said, surprised at the question. "But happily, in Washington at least, mine and the owners' politics seem to coincide."

"If they didn't?"

"I'd probably have to bend," Kyle said. "But I knew where they stood politically before I applied for the job."

"Liberal."

"I suppose."

Pastures gave way to pines. Streams sparked in the sun. Harley turned left onto a logging road and they looped, curved and climbed toward the high ridge of the Bridgers.

They entered a clearcut wasteland of stumps and slash piles. Kyle glimpsed far below the road they had followed up Bridger Canyon and, dead ahead, centered like a gunsight, Ross Pass.

They parked, stepped out into coolness. Rags of cloud disintegrated in the wind and Ross Peak blazed suddenly with light. The sun raced toward them and struck the car with an almost audible pop.

Ginny smoothed a U. S. Forest Service map, vintage 1984, and traced with her finger a hiking trail, shown in red, along the Bridger ridge. "This the one you mean?"

"That's it." Kyle pointed to a spot on the opposite, western side, hemmed by close-hatched altitude lines. "Dry Canyon." He slid his finger a half-inch further west. "Clinton Mosby's ranch."

A gust of wind tore at the map and the three of them wrestled a mass of flapping paper high on a logged-over mountain slope in Montana. Harley won. "I'll fold it," he said.

They sipped from water bottles, slid into daypacks and climbed a footpath up onto the open tundra of U-shaped Ross Pass. It seemed to Kyle that every few steps the wind blew stronger and another hundred miles hove into view. Ginny, in front, halted at a wooden stake that marked the top of the trail.

They stood beneath a hard, blue sky in a niche on the high ridge of the Bridger Mountains. Other mountain ranges rolled away in every direction, separated by long, wide valleys. Kyle spotted one break in these barriers, a gap in the east between the Crazies and the Absarokas, and beyond this aperture he glimpsed the Great Plains, endless, shading away into brown distance.

Ross Peak jutted on their right, a massif of red-yellow rock lit by the sun. They walked a new path, a trail that followed the high ridge of the mountains, around and under its cliffs. A knob appeared on their left and, as if an identical urge possessed them, the three of them bolted from the trail and through a thicket toward this protuberance. Kyle, in front, extended a hand to Ginny. She winced as he pulled. "Sore rotator cuff," the coach's wife said.

Harley shook his head as if Kyle had just fumbled at the goal line. "Never pull sideways like that," he admonished. "Here's the way to do it." He demonstrated in slow motion, as if instructing a child.

Ginny pointed. Kyle looked down and saw a green meadow and cattle grazing along a stream.

He took pictures. If something untoward occurred here, he wanted these photos in the bank. He drew a map on a notepad, indicating with arrows places where he thought intruders might sneak in. "Done," he said. "Anybody hungry?"

"I'm guessing there's a better view a little further on," Harley said, and so they walked maybe another fifty yards and sat on a rock. The view was not as good as the one they had left.

"Good sandwich, Ginny." Kyle praised his peanut butter and honey on wheat bread.

"Ham and cheese; mine's better than good," Harley said.

Ginny passed a bottle of apple juice and Kyle drank deeply. Harley only sipped. "Best to save some for other people," he said.

Jesus Christ, Kyle thought. He's a deliberate pain in the ass. Doesn't Ginny notice?

They chewed their food. Harley glanced at his watch. "Got to get back for football practice."

"You're practicing on Sunday?" Ginny asked.

"Quarterbacks and ends. Want them to catch and throw." They started back along the ridge and Ginny dropped behind. Harley moved up next to Kyle. "Coming to the game next Saturday?"

"If I'm in town. If I'm still around."

"How long do you think you will be around?"

"I suppose until the barricades come down and the roads reopen."

"Friend of mine says he saw you and Ginny in Cut Bank. Says he saw you holding hands and walking down the street. Ginny told me she visited Judy and Salmon in Havre."

"That's right. The three of them drove to Cut Bank from Havre so Ginny could see her old home town and we all had dinner together."

"Hansen, I can't play wounded soldier here because I've fooled around a few times myself. Comes a time, though, when people have to decide. If you're serious about Ginny you ought to say so. If you're not, you ought to leave her alone."

"She's a grown girl," Kyle said. "Seems to me it's up to her to decide who she sees and who she doesn't."

"Listen," – Harley jumped ahead and faced him – "I'm telling you to butt out."

Kyle looked at his old coach and it was autumn and they stood on a football field. He recalled the sting of sweat, the green grass. He saw the horses along Casino Creek raise their heads. "You know what I want?" he said.

"What do you want?"

"I want Ginny to divorce you and move to Washington."

"You're a wise-ass bastard, you know that. You're just like your brother."

Kyle shoved Harley and knocked him off balance. Harley recovered, swung at Kyle and missed. Ginny rushed between. "Look at those woods down there," she said. "Anybody could walk onto that ranch and kill fifty cows if they wanted to."

Single file, Ginny in the middle, they hiked back toward Harley's car. Both men had time to think. Harley, within grasp of a rare undefeated season, did not need an incident now. Kyle, involved in covering a potential career-advancing story, did not need one either.

Ginny did most of the talking on the ride back to town. Harley dropped them in front of the Mod Shop. "Remember what I said." He looked at Kyle and roared away.

"What did you two talk about?" Ginny asked.

"You. He wants me to leave you alone."

"What did you say?"

"I suggested you divorce him and move to Washington."

"Well. See how we're clearing the air. That's what happens when we get the two of you together."

"And now you go home and sleep with him tonight." Kyle hopped in his car, petulant, turned the key and started the engine.

Ginny rose on tiptoe, as if to physically block him from leaving. "Judy Thirdkill called last night. She's pregnant, after eleven years of trying."

Kyle turned off the motor. "This is good. I bet Salmon's pleased."

"Takes all the credit. Listen, I know I forced the issue today. Harley and I quarreled last night. I used the 'D' word. We slept in separate rooms. He's not dumb. He knows I didn't drive all the way to Cut Bank to discuss animal husbandry with Judy and Salmon."

"You used the 'D' word? Divorce?"

"I did."

"Well good."

"Yes," Ginny said, "but what do I do now?"

# # #

CHAPTER 27

Lars Bjornson left a message on Kyle's cell phone. "Governor Otto Cloninger announces a press conference for tomorrow in Helena at which he will introduce Blackfoot Tribal Chairman Edgar Ware and Montana Attorney General Jeb Small, who the Governor expects will each offer proposals leading to a final settlement of the impasse between the Blackfeet and the State of Montana."

Kyle listened to the message again. A settlement. He tried to decide whether he should feel happy or sad. He drove toward Helena and heard the news repeated on the radio. He stopped for gas and called Ginny.

"This could be it. Back to Washington. What's going on with you?"

"I looked at an apartment in Bozeman today. I think Harley and I have about worn out our relationship. You must come see me before you go."

"An apartment; that's good," Kyle said. "I'll try and get there soon."

He drove west toward Helena, surrounded by mountains. He asked for a high floor in the Vigilante Hotel, made phone calls, and headed for the bar. He wanted to talk, sample opinions. Other journalists began to arrive and Kyle recognized faces and moved from group to group. Some ordered second drinks, thirds. They reveled, these men and women of the media, in working far from supervision. But stories die, freedom ends. It struck Kyle that most of these ink-stained wretches were ready to go home.

Later in his room he leafed through books he had accumulated. He saw that he had underlined the farewell remarks of the defeated Indian leader, Black Hawk, July 4, 1838, in Wisconsin:

"A few snows ago I was fighting against the white people; perhaps I was wrong; let it be forgotten. I loved my towns and corn fields on the Red Rock River; it was a beautiful country. I fought for it, but now it is yours...I was once a warrior, but now I am poor...I loved to look upon the Mississippi. I have looked upon it from a child. My home has always been upon its banks...I will say no more."

Kyle wondered again, as he had so often on this trip, from whence the eloquence of these dead and gone Native Americans?

He turned to a television news channel and watched today's talking heads present America's ongoing invasions of Iraq and Afghanistan as contests in which we, the good team, occasionally of necessity forfeited a player or two. But not to worry, these "experts" suggested, every day we eliminate more players on the other side.

At breakfast Monday Kyle read the letters to the editor in the Helena Independent Record. Crucifixion for cow-killers, one self-described pious person suggested. Ginny would appreciate the irony, he thought. The more Christian and God-fearing the writers claimed to be, the more savage their letters sounded.

The press conference began exactly at noon in a conference room in the state capitol building. Governor Otto Cloninger, as sad-eyed as Kyle remembered him, greeted members of the media. "We hope you enjoyed your stay with us." A former wheat farmer, never a rancher, he viewed from a "Will it rain or won't it rain?" perspective, Kyle thought. He actually seemed to care about people.

Attorney General Jeb Small ascended the lectern. "If the Blackfeet open the roads," he said, "the State of Montana will not prosecute any of the involved individuals."

"What about cattle killers?" several voices asked at once.

"If they walk in within a grace period that we will determine, they are free to go. We consider this a major concession."

Edgar Ware rose: "If Attorney General Small is serious about what he just said, we, the Blackfeet, withdraw our demand for jail terms for anyone on the other side. This includes the five men who assaulted the two Indian boys and others who illegally killed elk on our reservation."

Kyle jabbed at his notepad, as surprised as everyone else. Both men offered more than expected. He understood that they floated these proposals as trial balloons to put pressure on die-hards on both sides, and that this was far from a done deal. But this took political courage. This was a big step.

Kyle spoke with Edgar Ware afterward. "Now can you tell me if you knew who was involved in the 'operations' against Rudy Ottens and Edmund Purcell?"

"I can't," Ware said, "because I don't know."

Kyle tried another approach. "My editor wonders if the Blackfeet conducted Native-American para-military, cow-killer training camps in the hills." Jack Leventhal had indeed suggested this.

Ware grinned. "Once Sioux Crazy Dog warriors drove stakes in the ground and tied themselves to them with thongs. Either you won or you died, though friends might gallop to your res-cue and jerk up the stakes. Suicide fighters led charges in the old days. Today? Who needs training camps? Lots of our guys served in the military."

"You think Vietnam vets killed those cattle?"

"Give me a break, Kyle. What I'm saying is I think it was young men tired of no jobs and no futures. And as we now know, there was also an element of revenge."

They shook hands. Ware left. Kyle drove north to photograph the final destruction of road barricades, fully aware that some weeks ago he did the same thing only to see the hay bales rise again. This agreement looked more secure.

He probably would return to Washington soon. The city might seem strange to him at first, the traffic, the noise, and then in a week or two he'd feel as if he'd never left. But now there was Ginny.

It occurred to Kyle that he had not congratulated father-to-be Salmon Thirdkill, so he pulled off the road and telephoned him at his school. "A baby in the basket. Well done, Captain Courage."

"Thank you, Wandering Journalist. I was about to call. I watched the press conference on TV."

Kyle detected something in his tone. "Yes, Salmon?"

"Some of the young guys do not feel good about this. They still want to hit Eldon Lauder."

"Bad timing, don't you think? Seems to me Edgar and the others want to declare victory and go home. Besides, it's Clinton Mosby's ranch the guys with badges are protecting."

Salmon waited before replying. "Exactly."

"Oh, Christ, Salmon. This is crazy. You really think something will happen?"

"That's the talk."

"When?"

"A day or two."

"It doesn't make sense. It's against the interests of the Blackfeet. They are tired of all this."

"I know," Salmon said. "I agree. But there are people who hold a grudge."

"Tell me again where Lauder lives." A strike at the Indian-bashing Congressman would make a hell of a story.

"He's out in the flats sixty miles east of the Little Bighorn Battlefield. You could go through your old home town on the way. You can still find teepee rings up in the Spirit Mountains, did you know that? You ought to hike that ridge along the top."

"I'm not going to spend a lot of time on this, Salmon. You hear anything different, you let me know?"

"Instantaneously, what with the miracle of modern communication. If you get over to the eastern part of the state, visit Bear Butte in South Dakota. It's not far from the state line. Climb to the summit, the sacred center. That's where we Sioux went for visions."

"Visions? You think it will work for me?"

"Worth a try. And from there it's not far to Wounded Knee."

"Wounded Knee? What do I do at Wounded Knee?"

"Stop your car, turn off the ignition and walk up to the mass grave. Two of my great-grandfathers are buried there."

"Four years in college; you never told me that."

"I never told you a lot of things."

Kyle telephoned Jack Leventhal and repeated what Salmon said. "The other reporters head back to the barricades. But actual peace is probably at least several days away. I mean, we don't know if both sides will accept the terms. In the meantime, which is a better story, waiting for hay bales to fall or a violent attack on a United States Congressman's ranch?"

"That's a loaded, hypothetical question," Leventhal said.

"I could arrive at Lauder's ranch tomorrow. At worst, I interview him, get his views on the peace settlement. That could be interesting. Then I come back here."

"I wish I was a reporter again," Leventhal said. "Dashing here, dashing there. From what I hear of Congressman Lauder, he makes news just sitting in his kitchen. Great names these guys have. Eldon Lauder. Clinton Mosby and his Vigilantes: sounds like a rock band, doesn't it?"

Kyle laughed. He signed off and studied his Montana map. It looked quicker to drive east via Twodot instead of through Hightown.

He sang as he approached this way station in the wild: "I climbed up the Rockies; I swam down the Snake, spent winters trapping in the Missouri Breaks. This ain't the first time I've been in a jam; I'm from Twodot, Montana, and I don't give a damn..."

He and various college friends once drove meaningful miles to Twodot's lone saloon to hear Hank Williams Jr. sing this song. He stopped, looked inside. The bar still functioned, but the old jukebox was gone.

Kyle stayed at a motel in Billings. He talked to Ginny. She moved into her new apartment soon. Meanwhile Harley bunked at the home of an assistant coach.

Kyle rose early Tuesday and hurtled east on the interstate. Filament clouds speckled a pale sky. Smoke plumes drifted across the Yellowstone Valley and Kyle played with the thought, my god, Indians attack the settlers! Then he remembered that this time of year farmers burned summer's dried grass to clear their irrigation ditches.

Eldon Lauder's place lay out in the wilds east of the Little Bighorn Battlefield, with two narrow Indian reservations, the Crow and the Northern Cheyenne, between.

Kyle called Salmon Thirdkill. "I'm approaching the Little Bighorn Battlefield. You still think something might happen?"

"If it does, you're there. I wouldn't just drive up to to the ranch gate and announce you're waiting for the fireworks, though."

"I'll stop at the Custer Battlefield. I always like wandering those hills. I'll find a motel. I'll call Eldon Lauder and request an interview."

Kyle saw against the sky the familiar white monument. He wheeled up the hill from the interstate, entered the visitor's center and read a short treatise on the life of General George Custer.

Custer first killed Indians in 1868 on a cold November day much like this one when he led soldiers against a camp of Cheyennes on the Washita River in today's Oklahoma. His men massacred more than 100 people and, with winter coming, shot the survivors' horses and burned their food, teepees and clothing.

In 1874, in violation of a government treaty, Custer and 1,000 soldiers rode onto Sioux lands in South Dakota and found gold "from the grassroots down." Miners followed. The Indians lost the Black Hills.

On June 25, 1876, an Arapaho brave remembered "Yellow Hair," as they called Custer, on his hands and knees on this bare ridge amid the smoke of battle. "He had been shot through the side and there was blood coming from his mouth...Four soldiers were sitting up around him but they were all badly wounded... The Indians closed in and I did not see him anymore."

Watching from across the valley, Black Elk, a boy of 13, saw "a big dust," and horses coming out of it with empty saddles.

Sitting Bull said years later that Custer laughed at the end. "You mean he cried out," a newspaper reporter prompted.

"No, he laughed," the old chief said. "He had fired his last shot."

Kyle walked outside to the bare ridge and just stood there a while. He tried to imagine the dust, the noise, the warriors on their horses. He went back inside and jotted in his note book a potential story lead in case something did happen at Lauder's ranch. He noticed someone jogging up the circular drive from the highway, an Indian boy in his teens. The boy's head bobbed from side to side and his shoulders sagged, but he kept coming.

The kid cut across the prairie in a shortcut, ran into the visitor's center and spoke excitedly to a woman at the concession stand. She – his mother? older sister? – looked like the woman who sold Kyle the book *Cheyenne Memories* when he visited here in September.

The boy's chest heaved. He struggled to catch his breath. Kyle walked over. "Did something happen?"

The kid just shook his head. Kyle looked at the woman. She smiled and made a motion as if slitting her throat.

Kyle ran to his car and turned on the radio.

# # #

CHAPTER 28

Kyle Hansen drove Route 212 straight east. Fragments of Indian lore churned in his mind. Crazy Horse, when pursued, ran his horse downhill and slowed to a walk on the uphill side. The young men of the Sioux rode ahead to kindle fires when they moved camp in winter, so the rest of their people could travel from fire to fire. If a Cheyenne murdered another Cheyenne, members of the tribe's military society rode the culprit across four rivers or four ridges and abandoned him. Four rivers or four ridges; Kyle liked that.

Eleven of Eldon Lauder's cattle died, their throats slashed, amid trees about two miles from his ranch house. The congress-man, who had called the Blackfeet welfare cheats and impeded attempts by the state to settle their grievances, was home, had been home for several days. It was dark and cold and a state trooper stopped Kyle on a lonely road south of Ashland. "Do you live around here?"

"No, but I'm originally from Montana."

"Sorry, sir. Residents get in, non-residents don't."

Kyle got a room in a motel in Broadus and called around for background and reaction. "We will not let this incident torpedo our peace talks," Edgar Ware said. Jeb Small said, in a statement released to the media: "We condemn violence and will press ahead with our agreement."

Off the record, Lars Bjornson admitted to complications. How do you drop charges against the perpetrators of two cattle killings if you press charges against the perpetrators of a third, especially if it turned out some of the same people were involved?

Shootings occurred in Montana and Wyoming. Someone torched a barn. Cowboy-Indian fights erupted at bars.

Kyle wrote for his newspaper: "Acts of violence boiled today across the high plains of Montana and Wyoming. Some compared it to 1988, the summer of the forest fires, when for days smoke from the blazes darkened the land..." It struck him that now he penned Montana versions of his old Fear Stalks the Streets of Washington stories.

He followed other cars up a gravel road early on a cold November morning and parked in front of a ranch house ringed with trucks and cars. Three times now he had repeated this process.

The dead cattle lay along a little stream beneath wind-tilted pines and leafless cottonwoods. Their bodies looked pale against the ground, their throats seemingly merely nicked, not ax-blade gory as radio and TV reports led one to believe.

Kyle took pictures, recalling as he did the white headstones on the Custer Battlefield. He found remnants of a circle stomped in the grass, and other reporters noticed it too.

He called Jack Leventhal. "They ghost danced? Sure, go with it," the national editor said. "Wing us your blood-drenched account. Talk to Lauder. We'll get statements from the two Montana Senators."

That afternoon, on the same porch where he posed for pictures holding a hunting rifle during previous campaigns, Rep. Eldon Lauder presided at a press conference. His opinions carried weight; Montana, because of its sparse population, was one of seven states to hold only one seat in the House of Representatives.

The others included Alaska, Delaware, North Dakota, South Dakota, Vermont and Wyoming. Populous California, by contrast, reveled with 53.

Why you? Reporters sought to light the congressman's fuse.

"I've always been a plain-spoken man. Sometimes you pay a price for that." Lauder's gray hair stirred gently across his forehead.

"Do you think your comments about Indians, such as them 'living the high life on welfare,' might have contributed to this?" Kyle asked.

Lauder seemed not to hear. "You cannot protect every living creature from fanatical terrorists, as we in this country so sadly know," he said.

"How did the intruder or intruders get in?" a reporter asked.

"Look around. It's wide-open country."

"Do you suspect anyone from the two Montana Indian reservations nearby?" Everyone, including Lauder, seemed to take it for granted that the evildoers must be Native Americans.

The Sheriff of Powder River County fielded this one. "Our information suggests that the intruders entered from South Dakota."

"What information?"

"I cannot reveal that to you. As you know, there are three Indian reservations nearby in South Dakota, Standing Rock, Cheyenne River and Pine Ridge. We're looking in that direction."

Kyle circulated, seeking the origin of the South Dakota rumors.

"Heard it from a deputy sheriff," one reporter said.

"Which deputy sheriff?"

"Can't say for sure."

"Which reservation?"

"Pine Ridge." This reluctantly. Reporters like to cradle their secrets.

Kyle began to write a story for his newspaper sitting in his rented car near a manure pile. Noting a surge of reporters into a back door of the ranch house, he jumped out and followed. Congressman Lauder held sway in the kitchen, sipping a beer.

"You've been pretty hard on the Indians," someone said.

"No matter what I do, they'll never vote for me anyway."

"How do you urge self sufficiency for Indians and every year collect yourself, what is it, three-hundred thousand dollars in agricultural subsidies?" Kyle asked.

"Please." Lauder waited for a ripple of chuckles to subside. "The check comes in the mail," he said, to more laughter. "Okay, consider other groups the government subsidizes: defense, the elderly, Wall Street. So we in Montana get a little back too. I'm a farmer and a rancher. The government sends checks to me and other farmers and ranchers and the money flows into the Montana economy. I'm just doing my job. That's why the voters keep sending me to Washington."

Kyle stepped outside to telephone his newspaper. "Lauder's here and holding court. Deputy sheriff says the cow-killers came from the Pine Ridge Reservation in South Dakota. That's not far."

"I'm guessing you want to go there," Jack Leventhal said.

"The thought occurs."

"Tomorrow?"

"Right now."

Kyle extricated his car from a clutter of vehicles, returned to Route 212, crossed the Powder River and drove east. Twice police cars in search of cow killers pulled him over. He took a motel room in Belle Fourche, South Dakota, the first town of size. It was late and his muscles twitched from weariness.

It pleased him Thursday morning to look out and see brightness. More than most people, Kyle responded to weather. He liked to feel the sun on his face. He stepped outside and away in the south dark shapes rose. Kyle realized he looked at the long line of the Black Hills.

Where was Bear Butte, the magic mountain Salmon mentioned? It showed on his map as a few miles north of Sturgis, a town half an hour down the interstate. Kyle pulled off for gas when he got to this town, but could see only a non-descript, scrub-piney protuberance where Bear Butte was supposed to be. He asked the gas station attendant.

"Yep, that's Bear Butte all right."

What had he expected? Misted escarpments? He sped east along Interstate 90, the Black Hills shouldering ever closer on his right. Slopes darkened by pines, they resembled a long, high plateau more than hills or mountains, though Kyle knew summits jutted up there, topped by 7,242-foot Harney Peak.

Something clicked from his recent reading. In 1855 troops led by a General William S. Harney shot and clubbed to death 86 Indians, mostly women and children, in their camp on the Bluewater River. In response, admiring white settlers named a mountain after him.

That puts a few dead cows in perspective, Kyle thought.

He stopped at a rest area and called Ginny Foster at her shop in Bozeman. She had heard, of course, of Eldon Lauder's diminished herd. "I'm in South Dakota. Police think the culprits came from here."

"I doubt anyone will step forward and confess. If I were with you, I would want to visit Mount Rushmore."

"I don't have globs of time. I'll also miss Wind Cave National Park and the dancehall floozies in Deadwood."

"They legalized gambling in Deadwood," Ginny said. "Did you know that?"

"If I didn't I would have guessed, from the billboards along the road. What's the news in Montana? Any road barricades tumbled down?"

"Not yet. There's anger that someone – read 'Indians' – tried to embarrass Eldon Lauder, but the betting is the agreement will hold."

"You know, I'm starting to hope it does. There are other stories. There's you. I think I'm getting stale chasing this one around."

"Let's frolic, whatever happens. Not my new apartment – Harley drives by every now and then. Pick a neutral site and let me know."

Kyle drove through Rapid City and followed potholed, cracked Route 44 southeast toward the badlands. The sun glinted off the hood of his car, the land undulated in molten brown waves. Red and yellow earth castles reared above a curling stream. Spectacular, and nobody here to see it. Alone in space, Kyle Hansen traversed the back country of Badlands National Park.

He studied his map and realized why so few cars: most people entered Badlands National Park the easy way, driving a loop from the Interstate further north.

An isolated visitors' center appeared, lost in vastness. Kyle left the south end of Badlands National Park and entered the Pine Ridge Indian Reservation. Two roads to Wounded Knee presented themselves, and both looked equally lost and deserted. Kyle chose the western route because, according to a brochure he picked up at the visitors' center, it passed the closest to Crazy Horse's grave.

Crazy Horse died in 1877, a year after Custer, shot and killed by Indian police sent by whites to arrest him. His mother and father wrapped him in a buffalo robe, carried him on a horse travois into the hills and left his body on a scaffold so his spirit could fly to the sky. Legend says they never returned to the spot or gave directions to anyone. Kyle drove south, eying lonely hills that rippled away into distance. Crazy Horse lay out there somewhere.

Dorothy Johnson in her story *Scars of Honor* described the land where dead Indians go: "The place is neither heaven nor hell, but just like earth, with plenty of fighting and buffalo and horses, and tall peaked lodges to live in, and everybody there who has gone before." If he ever adopted a religion, Kyle thought, this was the one for him.

His road followed Wounded Knee Creek, topped a hill and descended on the far side to ragtag houses and a flat, open place. A big, crudely-lettered sign told the story. Here on December 29, 1890, a sad thing had happened.

Dance, Wovoka had said, and the white man will disappear; the buffalo will return. By 1890, Crazy Horse had been dead thirteen years and most Indians had been forced onto reservations. Whites accused Sitting Bull of promoting this new ghost dance and sent Indian policemen to pull the old chief from his bed and kill him.

Learning of this, another Sioux chief, Big Foot, fled with his band of 400 Sioux toward the hoped-for safety of the Pine Ridge Agency. The Seventh Calvary, Custer's old command, rode to stop them.

Kyle gazed up at the hill where Captain John Forsyth set up four Hotchkiss repeating guns. Forsyth told the Sioux they must go to prison and ordered them to surrender their arms. Warriors stacked their rifles. A shot sounded. Soldiers manning the Hotchkiss guns, an early version of today's machine guns, opened fire on the assembled crowd below.

One woman, Blue Whirlwind, took fourteen bullets. Soldiers chased Indian kids into ditches and shot and stabbed them. Witnesses said women raised their arms to try and shelter the children and soldiers killed them too. In one case, a soldier swinging his rifle broke a woman's arm, then broke her other arm, and left her to die. Between 150 and 200 Sioux died. It began to snow and the bodies froze.

Kyle walked up the hill to the mass grave where Salmon Thirdkill's great grandfathers lay. Stone markers cast shadows toward the north and someone had scattered flowers that faded in the November cold.

Black Elk wrote years later: "I did not know then how much was ended. When I look back now from this high hill of my old age I can still see the butchered women and children lying heaped and scattered all along the crooked gulch as plain as I when I saw them with eyes still young. And I can see that something else died there in the bloody mud, and was buried in the blizzard. A people's dream died there. It was a beautiful dream... The nation's hoop is broken and scattered. The center is gone..."

Kyle looked around at the brown hills. He wanted to do or say something appropriate, but could think of nothing. On the flats below a second car pulled in next to his. As Kyle walked down the hill a man walked up, a white man like him. Their eyes met; they didn't speak.

Kyle saw an Oregon license plate on the man's car. He liked the stranger for driving here, far from the main roads, and for silently climbing this hill. He looked back and saw the man standing alone.

Kyle had contacted a teacher in this area when he wrote his feature article on the low number of reservation Indian students going on to college. He telephoned the man's school and asked for him now.

"Gone," someone said.

"Where?"

"He had a car accident."

Kyle drove past a broken structure that a sign identified as a museum. It appeared to have been abandoned years ago. Further on along this rutted road he saw a hovel. It looked inhabited and he stopped and knocked.

An Indian woman opened the door. She held a baby. Kyle intended to discuss Eldon Lauder's cows, to ask gentle but leading questions, but as he stood there looking at the woman with her child all that seemed irrelevant somehow.

He asked, just to say something, "The museum, when does it open?"

The woman stared at him. "Not soon," she said.

\# \# \#

CHAPTER 29

Kyle Hansen drove toward the town of Pine Ridge in South Dakota, intending to talk with the locals, when he heard on the radio that Montana Governor Cloninger offered a $50,000 reward for information leading to the conviction of whoever killed Eldon Lauder's cows. An extensive manhunt was said to be underway.

He called Jack Leventhal. "I think I should go back to Montana." Leventhal agreed.

Kyle launched north into a vastness of yellow grass on one of the loneliest roads he had ever driven. He wanted to cross a bare ridge that Indians called The Thieves' Road after General George Custer, who rode this way in 1874. Lewis and Clark passed in 1804 and 1806, but it was probably too late to weave this landscape into his explorer series.

He spotted no old wagon ruts along this curve of earth between the Missouri River and the Black Hills. At Mud Butte he turned west toward Newell. The sun sank low. Kyle felt those old weary blues.

He topped another hill and the sun seemed to bounce on the western horizon. He rubbed his eyes. In the south, across the prairie, a strange, dark shape rose. This isolated eminence reared abruptly off the prairie, well apart from the Black Hills beyond. Its north slope, the side Kyle faced, climbed dark in shadow and black with trees, a ghostly island in an ocean of grass.

The view held him. Kyle stopped, took pictures. He expected the magic to fade as he drove closer but instead the mountain loomed ever more mysterious. He studied his map again. This morning, seen from the south, the summit he now viewed appeared as a nodule without distinction. But now he saw it from the north, the direction from which generations of Plains Indians probably approached. Kyle realized he saw Bear Butte, really saw it, for the first time.

He drove closer. On its steep, north side, a fork of the Belle Fourche River eroded the base of the mountain cleanly away. Thus, seen from the north, Bear Butte climbed abruptly and dramatically from the prairie. On its southern side, bare and brown with grass, all sense of isolation and mystery vanished. No surprise, then, that the mountain appeared so ordinary from that direction.

It grew dark. Kyle felt at the edge of vital discovery. He decided to stay the night in Sturgis and climb Bear Butte in the morning.

He read that night everything he could find about Bear Butte. Crazy Horse was born near its slopes. Scattered bands of Sioux camped annually in its shadow. On top of Bear Butte, Sweet Medicine, the Moses of the Cheyennes, received the tribe's Four Sacred Arrows. Kiowas, Arapahos and other tribes quested here from across the West to seek magic of their own. Generations of individual Indians climbed the summit to fast and await their personal visions.

Kyle awoke Friday to a blue-sky November day. He drove twelve miles up an approach road to a parking lot and a visitor's center. The State of South Dakota now preserved Bear Butte as a state park and had constructed a mile and a half hiking trail to the summit.

Kyle saw a volcanic peak sliced flat at the top, connected to a lesser peak by a long, sheer ridge. He read on a bulletin board

Black Elk's tribute to Crazy Horse: "It does not matter where his body lies; there the grass is growing. But where his spirit is, that would be a good place to be."

He started up the mountain.

Wait. He wanted to do this as the vision-seekers did. He retraced his steps, took a long drink, and left his water bottle and lunch sandwich in his car. He climbed again, carrying only an extra jacket for warmth.

Cliffs jutted in cold sunshine. Trees tilted precariously. Climbing Bear Butte must have once involved much agility and effort, but now wooden railings and switchbacks gentled a trail for modern man.

It was still steep. A half mile up a dirt path sliced off to the left. Further on, he paused to look back. The path he passed led out to a spur of open rock and an old Indian knelt there. Kyle watched as the old man bowed and raised his arms to the sun.

Kyle was moved, shaken. He had not expected this.

Vestiges of old trails snaked through rocks and trees, each with its faded-footprint stories to tell. Kyle smelled the odor of burning wood, rounded another switchback and saw teepees in a meadow below. People gathered down there around smoking campfires. He had read Indians still camped here, but he had not expected to see so many.

His trail zigzagged up to the mountain's backbone ridge and suddenly the world opened. The Black Hills defined the horizon to the south. North and east yellow-brown plains, wavy in the sun, shaded to infinity. Ahead the summit of Bear Butte jutted upward, ringed with heavy pines, dark against the sky.

We respect today those who resisted, Kyle thought. Admirers still pilgrimage the way-stations of Crazy Horse's life. We read the words of Chief Joseph. Following the Custer battle, Sitting Bull stuck a note on a stick on the prairie for Colonel Nelson A. Miles to find: "I want to know what you are doing traveling this road. You scare all the buffalo away. I want to hunt this place. I want you to turn back from here. If you don't I will fight you again."

Kyle climbed steps onto a wooden platform on the bare-rock summit of Bear Butte. Hawks circled. A chipmunk darted from hiding place to hiding place. Wafers of cloud drifted over Wyoming to the west, puffballs in an otherwise cobalt sky. The air smelled of pines, of woodsmoke and of cured, brown grass.

Kyle spread his arms. The clean line of the Black Hills looked tame and safe compared to the lost, wild infinity of the plains.

Patience, he thought. I must learn patience.

A blond young couple climbed the steps to the platform. "Some view!" the young man said.

"Sure is." They left, Kyle stayed. He decided to think of this as a day off from work. Other visitors arrived and departed. The sun warmed as it climbed the sky.

A family munched cookies and drank from water bottles and Kyle thought of the food and water he left in his car. He would leave soon, he told himself. But the shadow of the guardrail crept across the platform and he did not go. He saw something move down in the trees. He watched. He did not see it again.

An hour might pass between visitors, or fifteen minutes. Some were Indians, most were not. Kyle talked if they wanted to talk. The dark shadow of Bear Butte moved further and further across the prairie.

He ought to call his office. He ought to descend. The sun set around five o'clock this late in the year and as it slid toward the Black Hills the flow of visitors ceased. Ignoring a sign that warned against it, Kyle stepped off the wooden platform onto the bare rock of the mountain. He took one step to his left, then another. Tentative at first, then surer, he sought a rhythm. He faced a sun become huge in a translucent sky. He thought of his brother drowned in the Blackfoot River. He thought of the great dog Lance asleep on his hill.

Kyle Hansen danced the ghost dance on Bear Butte in the rays of the dying sun. "Let me see my brother again," he asked the mountain. "Forgive me those I may have hurt. Forgive me the bad I may have done."

The sun touched the horizon and dropped until only a glowing point remained. The sky flashed and the silhouette of the

Black Hills hardened. Yellow, red and then purple-orange tinted the clouds above Wyoming. Kyle Hansen shivered in the creeping cold.

He thought back over his nearly three months in Montana. Ginny Foster. Salmon Thirdkill. Salmon took him to his first Indian battlefield. Salmon told him of the Old North Trail.

Wovoka was Salmon Thirdkill, Kyle realized. Salmon Thirdkill was Wovoka. It was Salmon who chose the rancher targets and arranged the killing of cows. His friend, his wife now pregnant, faced grave danger.

It was almost dark. Kyle realized he was hungry and thirsty. He started down the mountain.

He had climbed Bear Butte, and he had received his vision.

# # #

CHAPTER 30

Kyle descended to his car, drank from his water bottle, ate a peanut butter and jelly sandwich and drove into Montana, stopping only for coffee. He made Miles City at about ten, got a motel room and telephoned Salmon Thirdkill at his home in Havre.

"Captain Courage, I think I know the identity of Wovoka and I'd like to drive up and discuss this with you."

"When would you like to do that?"

"Tomorrow. You'll be home? I'm in Miles City now."

"Come ahead," Salmon said.

Kyle informed his newspaper that he thought he knew who had organized the cattle killings, but that he needed time to confirm. If he was right, Salmon and others faced real risks. He stumbled into uncharted territory here.

He called Lars Bjornson to see if any suspects had been arrested in connection with Eldon Lauder's eleven dead cows.

"No," Lars said. "The real news is that Governor Cloninger may extend the state's amnesty offer to whoever bopped Lauder, if they walk in quickly and submit to minimum jail time."

"Can I write that in a story?"

"If you do, we'll deny it."

Kyle Hansen drove west toward the dark line of the Spirit Mountains, turned north and crossed a concrete bridge over the Missouri River. The wind shook his car and swirls of snow swept down from the Little Rockies.

Salmon Thirdkill stepped out the front door of his house in Havre before Kyle got out of his car.

"Judy knows," he said. "Talk to her. I'll bring in a load of firewood."

Kyle found her in the kitchen, kneading bread dough in a pan. He kissed her on the cheek. "Why's the flour so dark?" he asked.

"I use five cups of whole wheat to one of bleached." Judy scooped up the dough in her hands and slapped it into a buttered bowl. "Now we wait for it to rise." She dusted her arms and began to cry.

Salmon came in and hugged her. She pushed him off and then pulled him close and held him. "Fifty thousand dollar reward," she said. "I keep expecting someone pounding on the door."

"It's starting to snow," Salmon said. "I'll start a crackling fire."

Kyle watched his friend stack logs in the living room fireplace and ignite a conflagration. Judy entered and stared at the flames. "I suggest the Blackfeet just tear down the barricades and announce that they've won. Let the state pay the ranchers for the cows. Let everyone forgive and forget and go home." A bell dinged in the kitchen and she hopped up. Salmon followed her into the kitchen. Kyle heard the pop-crackle of ice and his friend returned with Scotch and water in tumblers.

"Ottens, Purcell, Lauder?" Kyle asked. "All three?"

Salmon nodded. "We hit the first two before I knew Judy was pregnant. I didn't want to do Lauder after she told me, but the guys prodded me into it. Judy overheard me on the phone talking tactics; I had to confess." He sounded relieved. "It took you a while to figure it out, though."

"It came to me on top of Bear Butte," Kyle said. "Who actually swung the knives? Did somebody really dance?"

"Young guys. They love this stuff. Like the old days, stealing horses. We had plenty of volunteers. Two or three wanted to dance so I thought, 'What the hell.' We had a good ride. Now the problem is getting off without getting hurt. You climbed Bear Butte?"

"You told me to, so I did. Were you there yourself at any of the actual throat-cuttings?"

"No. I picked the targets, I wrote the letters. I lined up cars, brought the guys together. I organized, I'd guess you say, like back in college."

"Lars Bjornson told me last night that the state may extend its amnesty offer to whoever hit Lauder's ranch."

"You serious? Cattle killers too?"

"Yes. There's a catch, though."

"Judy, come in here," Salmon called. "I want you to hear this." She entered, wiping her hands.

"Tell her," Salmon said. Kyle repeated his conversation with Lars Bjornson.

"Including Lauder? He specifically mentioned that?"

"He did. But whoever's involved must surrender soon, and do at least minimum jail time."

"You've got to go for it, Salmon," Judy said.

"It's not official yet," Kyle said. "They'll try and line up political support. It's to Salmon's advantage that the Lewis and Clark Bicentennial begins in January. What's that, six weeks away? The state wants its roads open. It wants the tourists back."

"Salmon, if there's any opening you must try for it," Judy said. "Please take this opportunity."

"When and if it's official," Salmon said. "I need to see or hear the Governor or Jeb Small say it."

"It might help, politically, if someone on the Indian side takes the barricades down first," Kyle said.

"Edgar," Salmon said.

"He could offer to open all the roads in return for across-the-boards amnesty," Kyle said. "With conditions, of course, for those who did the Lauder job."

Salmon stroked his chin. "He's probably home right now."

They heard him speaking on the telephone in another room. "I don't care if he has to go to jail," Judy said. "I just don't want him killed."

Salmon returned. "Edgar says they'll knock down barricades, they'll pledge allegiance, they'll drive at the posted speed limits, they'll give up smoking, if the state makes a decent offer. He says he will tell this to the Governor."

"Well. We're advancing," Kyle said.

Salmon grinned at Judy. "You see? There's hope."

She tried to smile. "Remember, it's not just the two of us now," she said.

Salmon patted her tummy. "Can you hear me in there? Listen to your mother. Your's mother's always right." He jumped up and strode around. "Kyle climbed Bear Butte," he said to Judy.

"I tried to dance the ghost dance all alone up there on top."

"Did you make a wish?"

"Two or three, I guess."

"Don't tell, if you want anything to happen."

"I drove to Wounded Knee. I saw the mass grave."

"I had my own vision while you were away," Salmon said. "We've got eleven tribes and seven reservations in this state. Native Americans constitute seven per cent of the population of Montana. What we want to do is get every damn one of us over 21 registered to vote."

Judy stroked Salmon's hair. "At last," she said to Kyle, "a legal outlet for his energy."

"Judy's involved," Salmon said. "It's called Montana Women Vote. The idea is to get women to register and to get more of them to run for office. Ginny Foster's a mover in this too."

The fire popped. Kyle looked out a window at the falling snow. It felt good sitting here. It reminded him of driving home from Yellowstone Park with his family, under that red Wyoming sky.

"I'll go make dinner," Judy said.

Salmon waited until she was in the kitchen. "It's a long shot, isn't it?" he said softly to Kyle.

"Worth trying," Kyle said. "If things break right..."

They sat quietly staring at the fire. "Wouldn't it be great to be back in junior high school again, "Salmon said. "Just starting to play football. Just starting to play basketball. Have it all ahead of you, all those games..."

"That would be good," Kyle said.

"Montana and Montana State both won again today," Salmon said. "I guess you heard."

"Yes. I'm happy for our old team."

Salmon glanced at his watch. "Time for the news." He snapped on the TV and an announcer led with today's top story, a car crash in front of a school in Shelby. Salmon and Kyle exchanged a glance. No names yet. The cattle-killers had safely navigated another day.

# # #

CHAPTER 31

"The Governor has to know that if he offers amnesty the people who cut the throats of those cattle will personally come in and surrender," Lars Bjornson said. Kyle Hansen spoke with him from Salmon Thirdkill's house on Sunday morning. Several inches of fresh snow fluffed the ground outside.

Kyle telephoned Montana Attorney General Jeb Small at his home and sought to convey the impression of a settlement gaining speed. It helped, Kyle realized, that he represented a big Eastern newspaper. Otherwise some of these state officials might not answer his weekend phone calls.

"I'm ready to go public," Small said, "but I need to know when, where and how many people will surrender."

"Edgar Ware says he'll work that out with the Governor."

"Why not have him work it out with me? I'm the state's chief legal officer."

"I'll call you back," Kyle said. He turned to Salmon. "Would you walk in with flashbulbs flashing?"

"What do you think, Judy?"

"God, yes. It's much better than the alternatives."

Edgar Ware called. "I informed the Governor this morning that if the state bargains in good faith we pull the road barricades down."

"When did Edgar find out you were Wovoka?" Kyle asked Salmon.

"Oh, hell, he's known for a long time."

More phone calls and several hours later Lars Bjornson agreed to act as surrender coordinator. "Where is this Wovoka? When can I speak to him?"

"If you drive to Havre right now," Kyle said, "I think we can track him down."

"Where do I meet you?" Kyle named a drugstore downtown. Judy left for an exercise walk with her neighbor across the street.

Salmon stared out a window. "At least everybody's forgotten about Sylvia Bright Angel," he said.

Lars Bjornson drove the 200 miles from Helena to Havre in less than three hours. Kyle met him at the drug store and led him to Salmon's house. Lars and Salmon shook hands. "I don't think we played basketball against each other in high school," Lars said. "We knew better than to schedule Browning. I competed against your friend here, though."

"Lars was the Helena team's floor general," Kyle said. "Newspapers called him 'the crafty little left hander.'"

"Left handers were always 'crafty,'" Salmon said. "If you were right handed, I guess they figured you lacked imagination."

They laughed. They talked sports. Judy entered, offered coffee around. Salmon cleared his throat. "If, for example, I were involved, however obliquely, in any of the cattle killings..."

And so they thrashed it out. Lars explained the Governor's clemency offer. Salmon confessed his behind the scenes role.

"Will you do it?" Lars asked. "Will you walk in?"

"How about the younger guys?"

"Them too, of course."

Salmon looked at Judy. "I'm naked once my name is out there," he said. She nodded as if to say, "I understand, but this is the best way."

"Let's do it quick," Lars said, "before someone in the Lauder or Mosby crowd gets a chance to screw it up. Day after tomorrow?"

"Tuesday? I think I can convince the others by then."

"You realize," Lars said, "you should expect short jail terms, two or three months maybe."

"Can we have that in writing? The 'short,' I mean."

"That could be difficult. Let me work on that. I want to say something else. If you don't accept, I don't reveal your name. Any names. But remember, if police track you and the others down, you could go to prison for years."

Salmon looked at Judy. "Do it," she said.

"It would make it easier for us," Salmon said, "if Jeb Small or the Governor made statements specifically spelling out terms."

"I think that's doable," Lars said.

"Stipulating that no one will be handcuffed or anything like that?"

"That's fair," Lars said. They shook hands all around. Lars drove away.

"Okay if I tell my newspaper the general details?" Kyle asked Salmon. "No names. Just alert them as to what might happen."

"What do you think, Judy?"

"Don't say anything you don't have to."

Kyle spoke on the telephone with Jack Leventhal. "The cattle killers might surrender. Could be dramatic. No story now. I'm alerting you it could happen."

"When might that be?"

"Hopefully Tuesday."

"You know the people involved?"

"Some. Yes."

"Good story. Get pictures at the surrender," the editor said.

"I'll need some old football shots," Kyle said to Salmon. "What about Boy Scouts? Were you ever prom king?"

"I ought to sell my tale to the highest bidder. Isn't that's the way it's done these days?"

"You'll have that chance," Judy said. "Later on."

Salmon and Kyle walked outside. It had stopped snowing and a fitful sun peeked through. "Where now?" Salmon asked.

"In the best of all possible worlds I'd rendezvous with Ginny Foster. She left Harley, did I tell you?"

"You're serious?"

"I am."

"I'm surprised. Intelligent girl."

"I'll see you in Helena Tuesday," Kyle said. "I may call you now and then. You've got my cell phone number. Act naturally, huh, Salmon."

"I'll eat my eggs and toast and go to my school Monday just like always."

Kyle stopped along the road to telephone Ginny and tell her what had happened. "I've a day or two," he said.

"Where do you suggest?"

"Harlowton. Close to Bozeman and close to Helena."

"I can do that."

# # #

CHAPTER 32

Kyle reached Harlowton first. It was dark and cold. He heard a vehicle crunch gravel and peeked out a window and saw a tall person step from a car. That's a fine-looking woman, Kyle thought. He looked again and realized it was Ginny Foster.

"I feel violated," she said, "somebody stole my checkbook and wrote checks all over Billings. Bassinger's called and wanted to know where to send the birdcage. No damage, thank you, I stopped payment. In my next life I come back as a reporter." She wore an orange blouse and a brown skirt and she sat on the bed and crossed her legs. She laughed and touched his arm. "Got something to drink?"

"Schnapps. I'll go for ice."

All of a sudden they were kissing. He stroked above and below her panty line. She twined her long legs around him. The heavens opened, the Red Sea parted. Kyle felt he had waited months and ridden hard miles for this.

Wind pounded at the windows and Kyle felt the cold silhouette of mountains outside. Ginny smoothed a pillow. "I've been chaste for a while. I won't ask about you."

"Oh, sure, I've had all kinds of adventures."

"Is this the room where you first scored with Glenda Lodermeier?"

"You know, it could be."

Hungry, they decided to walk downtown. "Look what our cars did while we were in there," Ginny said. It appeared the two vehicles had eased together and touched.

"They're from Twodot, Montana," Kyle said, "and they don't give a damn."

They strolled Central Avenue past Schenk's Saddlery to the Graves Hotel, a sandstone building overlooking the Musselshell River. "Nineteen-o-Eight," Ginny read a date chiseled in stone. A rising moon fingered the peaks of the Crazy Mountains.

"Scotch with a ditch," Kyle asked the waitress, western for Scotch and water. Ginny ordered a martini. Kyle filled her in on the details of Salmon Thirdkill versus the State of Montana.

"Salmon can be a bastard," Ginny said. "It bothers me he virtually led a guerilla movement and never told Judy."

"It just got out of hand," Kyle said. "He didn't know until a week or two ago she was pregnant."

"Well, a wry smile did crease my face when I heard what they did to Eldon Lauder. I heard Lauder speak on abortion, did I tell you? He talked about the 'sacredness of life.' I stood up and said, 'Good, oppose war.' I used to think in high school that's what 'pro life' meant."

"That's funny. I used to think that too," Kyle said.

"I might run for the Montana Legislature," Ginny said. "Our Bozeman Democratic House representative retires next year. You've heard of Montana Women Vote?"

"Judy told me they want women candidates. What if you run and win? You win, and then you'll never want to leave. Next you'll want to run for governor."

"That's bad?" she asked.

"Maybe from my point of view."

"See? Already you're possessive. We can be together, my sweet, if you become a Montana journalist. I found a spiffy apartment near the Montana State campus. I moved my stuff."

"How's Harley taking it?"

"He's already telling everybody it was his idea."

Kyle smiled. "Acceptance is good," he said.

He filled Ginny in on the surrender talks. During dinner both he and Ginny sneaked peeks at the television over the bar. Nothing. No mention yet of a surrender or a settlement announcement.

They strolled through town and along a highway toward their motel. November night descended clear and cold and Kyle spotted chalky lines in the darkness. "Football field!" He scrambled down into a natural amphitheater.

"Did you ever play here?"

"Not in our league. We played the BIG SCHOOLS." Kyle saw bleachers and ghostly goalposts. He sprinted this way and that. "Whenever I see a football field, I want to run on it."

"What position did Terry play?"

"End. Like me in college. He was tall; he liked to reach up and grab those passes."

"Why didn't Harley like him?"

"Harley was just out of college himself, not much older than we were. Terry and Harley fixated on each other from the start. It was like they were rivals."

"Well, if Harley beats your old college team next Saturday, he gets his undefeated season. I wish him well. I owe him that."

"I don't wish him well," Kyle said. "The bastard broke my brother's arm."

They walked toward their motel and a dog rushed at them in a frenzy of barking. Kyle looked around for a stick or something with which to defend themselves. Ginny held out her hand. "Good dog," she said. The animal – a male, Kyle noticed – calmed and wagged its tail.

# # #

CHAPTER 33

Flat-bottomed clouds sailed the sky and the sun sliced through in sweeping, searchlight angles. Kyle Hansen eyed the jagged peaks of the Crazy Mountains. "Not much snow yet," he said. He and Ginny Foster breakfasted at a window table in downtown Harlowton.

"I'm worried about Salmon," Ginny said. "I'm worried about Judy."

"I worry too," Kyle said, "but I try to remain optimistic." Ginny honked, he honked; she turned south toward Bozeman, he west toward the Big Belt Mountains and Helena. Kyle stopped to urinate on a lonely hill. He pondered an abandoned ranch house and the long, dark line of the Spirit Mountains. He listened, as always, to the radio news.

A stockgrowers group offered an additional $10,000 reward, raising the ante from the Governor's previous $50,000, for information leading to the conviction of whoever killed Eldon Lauder's cattle. Kyle imagined Judy Thirdkill's thoughts when she heard this.

Why the delay? Jeb Small and the Governor should spell out their amnesty offers, Edgar Ware and the Blackfeet should tear

215

down the road barricades, but it seemed everybody waited for the other side to act first. All seemed so promising yesterday; today Kyle detected in the news, even in people's faces, a harder, a meaner tone.

He drove to Helena and into a raft of problems. Jeb Small complained he had not been adequately consulted, and seemed to resent the role of Lars Bjornson, the Governor's spokesman, as newly designated mediator. The Governor, instead of getting out front, sat in his office waiting for Small to commit. Edgar Ware held off opening the roads until either Small or the Governor publicly promised to forgive and forget.

It was Monday and the world and Jack Leventhal in Washington returned to work. Kyle sought to summarize for his national editor.

"Jesus Christ," Leventhal said. "I thought we had a cattle-killer educator ready to confess." Kyle, to add spice to the story, had already, without naming Salmon, mentioned a school connection.

"It will happen," Kyle said. "It will happen."

Meanwhile, the world wallowed in alarmist news. Across the seas, in Iraq, conditions worsened following the United States invasion earlier in the year. Republicans warned of future "terrorist" attacks. Democrats mostly went along, fearful of being accused of softness on national security.

In Montana, agitator-Congressman Eldon Lauder and vigilante leader Clinton Mosby leaped into the leadership vacuum. "Amnesty to murderers?" Lauder thundered. "I think not." "Crimes have been committed," Mosby orated. "The reputation of our state is at stake."

Kyle Hansen watched them perform on television. Then he heard: "...This just in: the Native American principal of Hays-Lodgepole High School, a former star athlete at the University of Montana, today stands accused..."

"Shit!" Someone had turned Salmon in, probably hoping to collect the $60,000 reward.

Kyle called Salmon's school: left for the day. He tried his house and got an answering machine. He telephoned Jack Leventhal in

Washington. "Our school principal's a fugitive. Somebody ratted on him. I just sent you pictures. I'll try to contact his wife. I'll find out what I can."

Kyle sprinted first to Lars Bjornson's office, not wanting to chance waiting on the phone. "It wasn't me," Lars said. "I don't know who. Troopers tried to arrest him, but they can't find him."

"Lars, radio's broadcasting his name as king of the cow-killers. What happened to amnesty?"

"Small didn't follow through. Maybe Eldon Lauder and the ranchers got to him."

"What about the Governor? You work for him. Where's he? I thought we had a deal."

"Governor Cloninger can and will exert pressure to get Thirdkill and the others shorter jail sentences. But he can't overturn the laws of this state."

"Jesus, Lars. 'Will exert pressure...' What the hell does that mean?"

"It means your friend's in trouble. I suggest you try to talk him into surrendering before a posse catches up with him."

"Come on. A posse?"

"Small issued a warrant for his arrest."

"Well Christ. That's great."

"Kyle, you know as well as I do; there's people out there who love to shoot first and explain later; Clinton Mosby's vigilantes, for example. Salmon's your friend. Tell him to surrender."

"Where is he? How can I tell him to surrender if I don't where he is?"

"His wife thinks he's headed up into the Spirit Mountains, over near Hightown."

"She's home? I just called there, got no answer."

"Try again. She asked if I knew where you were."

Kyle found an empty corridor and used his cell phone. "Judy, I'm in Helena. I just heard."

"They found his car. I think he went up Half Moon Canyon into the Spirit Mountains. They want to kill him, Kyle."

"Did he take his tent, his camper stuff?"

"I think so." Judy hesitated. "I think he took his rifle too."

"Do police know that?"

"I didn't tell them. He's got his cell phone, so maybe you can reach him. I'll try too."

"You want me to try to convince him to surrender?"

"Do it, Kyle."

"I'll try. I'll call you back." Kyle ran back to Lars Bjornson's office. "If he surrenders, the state throws him in jail for twenty years?"

"I think, with the Governor's help, we can whittle his sentence down to a lot less than that. Even so, prison certainly beats the alternatives. You talked to his wife? What did she say?"

"She doesn't know where he is. She wants him to surrender."

A television camera crew burst in. Kyle watched the circus unfold and wondered if he, as a reporter, had played a part in this. He had encouraged Salmon to seek amnesty. He influenced him to reveal his identity as Wovoka prematurely to Lars Bjornson. The more Kyle circled the situation, the more he felt himself implicated.

He thought back across the years to when his brother drowned on the Blackfoot River. He, Kyle, organized that adventure, and at the moment of crisis he did not risk himself, he did not dive into the water. What now?

He gazed from the steps of Montana's capitol building up at the Continental Divide. He saw snow up there, but also lots of open terrain. The weather warmed, it was not yet December,

and the Spirit Mountains did not rise as high as these. Hiking conditions might be good.

Salmon knew everyone looked for him, and Kyle understood his old football friend's sense of drama. He pictured him now, striding some wind-whipped ridge, a rifle slung across his back.

# # #

CHAPTER 34

"Where you headed?" a deer hunter asked.

"Up on the ridge."

"Don't fall off," the hunter said.

Kyle Hansen climbed through pine forest above the camp-ground at Emerald Lake. The police had found Salmon Thirdkill's car twenty miles east, in the trees near the entrance to Half Moon Canyon, and a posse, including members of Eldon Lauder's vigi-lantes, chased after him up that winding route. Already police blocked off that area, and probably soon would bar other access roads too. Kyle guessed he made it here just in time.

It was late November but the sun shone and he sweated as he climbed. He had often hiked in this area as a teenager and, though he never walked all of the top ridge, he had some idea where Salmon intended to go, and where he hoped to come out.

On his way here Kyle had purchased camping equipment in Hightown. "Expense it," Jack Leventhal said. The national edi-tor commiserated over Salmon's plight, but immediately saw the story possibilities. "I won't tell you to go up there," he said to Kyle, "but I won't tell you not to either."

Ginny Foster drove to Hightown to join her friend, Salmon's pregnant wife. Kyle talked to Ginny on the phone. "Damn Salmon," she said. "This is destroying Judy."

Recent warmth melted most of the early snow. The day continued to warm and Kyle emerged from wind-torn pines onto open rock and shed his jacket. A fisherman floated in a yellow raft on Emerald Lake, a lemon drop on a splash of blue. Beyond, the brown-yellow plains of Central Montana vanished into distance.

Kyle knew that lawmen, media and curiosity seekers converged on these mountains, indicated on maps as a smudge of green near the geographical center of Montana. He wanted to find Salmon before the posse did, and urge him to surrender. But, he recognized, other motives drove him too. In one scenario, that grew more vivid as he climbed, he imagined himself the author of a career-advancing, eye-witness story.

Ginny Foster took another tack on this: "The more journalists up there the better, so the vigilantes know someone is watching."

Kyle stopped on an open slope and tried to reach Salmon via cell phone. Again, no answer. But of course Salmon knew: if he responded, police might fix his location.

An isolated "island" range surrounded by prairie, the Spirit Mountains rose above 9,000 feet and extended east-west for 50 miles. Salmon started about in the middle. His route tracked a stream seven miles up wooded Half Moon Canyon and broke into the open on the top ridge of the mountains. Here it became a ridge trail, crossed a narrow rock formation called the Knife Blade, and proceeded west along the top. If Salmon walked that way, west, and he, Kyle, walked east, inevitably they must bump into each other.

Granted, Salmon could veer off north or south into any of a dozen lonely canyons. But law officers already patrolled the foothills on either side. Recognizing Salmon's affinity for the theatrical, the grand moment, Kyle guessed his old football teammate would stay high.

He drank from one of his two water bottles. He picked his way across rock slides. He topped a protruding spur of rock and directly ahead the massive summit ridge blocked the sky. He heard an explosive roar and a black helicopter burst into view. It skimmed close along the top, wheeled and hovered, and Kyle saw two faces staring down at him.

He stopped in mid-stride and stared back. Ten, fifteen seconds passed. The helicopter shot upward, wheeled, and in a rush darted on.

A helicopter might ferry armed men to the top of the mountain. But only two or three at a time, and they would need camping equipment and would remain captive to the weather. No, Kyle thought. They would surround Salmon, creep at him, wait him out.

Salmon had talked of camping in these mountains and of finding teepee rings up here, so Kyle assumed he knew the terrain. But if a helicopter swooped down on him? Salmon could hide under trees or overhanging rocks. He could walk in the woods below the crest and avoid obvious open stretches.

If pressed, he might unlimber his rifle and start firing.

Kyle's trail straightened and as if he stood on the deck of a tilting ship that slowly righted itself he strolled up on the summit ridge of the Spirit Mountains. Pine trees grew spaced as in a park, patches of dirty white snow in their shade. Vast views framed vast horizons. A trail sign on a weathered pole – "Half Moon Canyon" – pointed east.

The summit narrowed and the trail wandered out of trees into the open. Bare humps of mountain extended ahead, one rise like another, a gigantic elephant's back.

Kyle stopped to study things. On his left, north, the Hightown side, thickly timbered canyons formed, deepened, merged, and wound outward to disgorge onto the wheat fields of Central Montana. On his right, cliffs threaded by deer and mountain goat paths dropped steeply. Dryness ruled on this southern side, exposed in all seasons to the sun. Streams marked by lines of trees snaked out onto arid vastness and in a mile or two simply disappeared.

Kyle hiked steadily eastward along the summit ridge. The pale November sun declined. Saucer clouds drifted above the prairies at about the same level at which he walked. Far off, beyond the prairies, in every direction, dark mountain chains rose.

He searched for a place to set up his tent and second thoughts assailed him. The weather forecast mentioned snow, and he recalled a childhood fear of becoming hopelessly lost in the wild. If he did find Salmon, would his unexpected arrival help or hurt? Two trying to hide instead of one? Kyle knew his friend abominated prisons. Salmon fled on instinct, and it would be hard to talk him down.

He settled on a flat spot amid a scattering of stunted pines that lived their lives in the wind. He unrolled his sleeping bag and set up his tent. Dead limbs, perfect for burning, scattered the ground like buffalo bones. A flash of red spread the sky and a flaming crescent, a last point of sun, dropped behind the distant Castle Mountains.

Kyle sat on the ground and in fading light traced on a forest service map the summit trail he followed. Eight or nine miles more and he reached the Knife Blade. Salmon probably camped somewhere in that direction. Police with helicopters and high-powered rifles searched for him but now, as darkness came on, Kyle imagined Salmon preparing for night just as he did.

He decided to light a fire as a beacon to his friend, and an indication of clear conscience to possible enemies.

What if Salmon had already surrendered? Kyle took it as a good sign that he heard no shots, but that could also mean the chase was over. He had not considered this. The editors at the Washington Herald would know. He felt in his pack for his cell phone.

His fingers touched wet. Bad; a water bottle leaked. He shook the telephone, wiped it, tried a number. Nothing. He did this several times.

Well, this was great. He did not think to bring a portable radio. The darker it got the more Kyle felt alone. He saw snowfields on the Absarokas over 100 miles away, but on his own mountain ridge not a light, not another campfire. He tried the phone again and still it did not work.

Kyle counted mountain ranges and got to twelve. Fresh stars winked in the sky each time he looked. His fire grew hot and smelled of cedar. This would be a great spot to camp with Ginny on a summer night.

Maybe Salmon saw his campfire right now. That would be something, if his friend strolled in casual from the dark. Kyle wished he had brought some Scotch along.

The streets of Hightown glittered on the plains far below and across the Judith Basin the pinpoint lights of ranches winked alive one by one. Suddenly curious, Kyle strolled over the top of the ridge to see how things looked on the other side.

That splash of light must be Harlowton. That little place? Probably Judith Gap. But apart from these two towns all seemed undiscovered country over here; isolated ranch lights, miles and miles of darkness.

Kyle grilled pork chops, wearing a sock on his hand to protect it from the fire. He ate a carrot. He devoured coconut cookies. He had grabbed at a supermarket whatever food came to hand.

It was still early. Now he really wished he had brought some Scotch.

He walked away from his fire and stared upward, startled. He had never seen so many stars. The Milky Way circled immense, a mass of silver specks in a deep, dark stream.

Wind shivered along the top ridge and despite his campfire Kyle felt cold. He crawled into his tent, peeled off his outer clothing and slid into his sleeping bag. He looked at his watch.

Fourteen minutes past seven. His day had ended. Down in Hightown the evening barely began.

# # #

CHAPTER 35

Kyle slept fitfully, as on the night before a big game. He awoke at dawn to the sound of wind flapping his tent, dressed, crawled out and stood mesmerized at the sight of snowfields on the far Absorokas pink in early sun. Grayness smudged the northwest; feather clouds streaked the rest of sky. Once more, futilely, he tried his cell phone. He mixed powdered milk into water, fingers shaking, and poured it over sugared cereal.

He shouldered his pack and hiked east along the open summit, warming as he walked. Noise exploded behind and above and Kyle turned and saw the day's first helicopter fling itself along the ridge.

He looked up. Faces peered down. He waved. Someone waved back. By now they probably knew a reporter wandered up here. With a grinding noise, the helicopter shot away. They haven't found him yet, Kyle thought.

No matter how fast he walked, the top of the mountain bald ahead seemed to remain about a mile away. A strange sensation tingled his back and Kyle felt the presence of his brother Terry.

He stopped and looked around. His face burned. The wind felt alive.

Something had changed. The smudge in the northwest sky advanced toward him, transformed to black clouds sheared smooth across their bottoms. Dust and twigs whirled past. Dirty fragments at the clouds' forward edges tore off in the wind. Kyle wondered if Terry wanted to warn him about something.

Hurrying, he reached the top of the next bald and saw ahead a narrow bridge of rock. His shadow vanished. A corner of strangely lit sky dangled in the southeast and hung there, a wistful beacon, then grayness swallowed that too. An iron door closed. Onrushing gloom swallowed the low November sun.

The storm struck with a roar. Flung off balance, Kyle leaned against the wind to stand. Something stung his face and hurt his eyes. He had to turn away from the wind to see. My god. Snow blew in a level line across the ridge, a pure, level line.

The wind ripped at his backpack and Kyle flapped in the wind like a sail. Find shelter, he thought. He knew cliffs dropped on his right, so he angled the opposite way, directly into the gale. He saw something black, toppled toward it and realized he lay in the lee of a large rock. Snowflakes settled placidly on his clothes while a few feet above the storm's jet stream roared.

Good-bye helicopters, Kyle thought. Wherever Salmon was, he would know this. He would know too that now he left tracks in the snow. Kyle weighed pro against con and scored it a plus for his friend.

Mountains make their own weather. Storms blow in fast, they blow out fast. Kyle sat and waited. Already the wind abated, and between swirls of snow he saw maybe a half mile along the ridge.

He rose, averted his face from the wind and plodded east. Wind-driven snow hummed around him as might a swarm of bees. Along the lee, the south side of the ridge, sculptured drifts began to form.

The wind helped as well as hindered, for it scoured the ground in exposed places so that Kyle often walked on bare, broken rock. He hiked these gritty lanes for over an hour, jacket hood pulled low, warmed by his own movement. He saw a flat place ahead and beyond that the narrow arc of the rock bridge they called the Knife Blade.

Kyle had heard hikers talk of this high, tremulous spot, but he had never crossed it himself. Such was its width, people said, that on a summer day children might scamper across. But in bad weather, like today, you noticed the precipices, the thousand-foot drops on either side. Bad days like this, you thought about the rocks below.

He approached the narrow crossing. Salmon may have already passed over and fled down into a canyon and, if so, he had missed him. Kyle felt his tiredness now. Cold and doubt chipped away at his urge to help his friend. His right ankle hurt. He felt hungry. What was he doing up here anyway?

A thunderclap exploded amid the driving snow. Something darted across the Knife Blade toward him.

Salmon Thirdkill lunged by. "Come on!" he shouted.

Kyle scrambled after him. Shapes moved out on the rock. Crack! This second report rang sharp and close. Whoom! Salmon fired his own rifle almost in Kyle's ear. He turned and saw the shapes out on the Knife Blade tumble back.

"What the hell!" Kyle yelled. Together, as if choreographed, he and Salmon flung themselves behind a rock.

Salmon's eyes looked glazed. "What are you doing here?"

"Looking for you." Kyle stared at him, unbelieving. "Are you guys trying to hit each other?"

"Not me," Salmon said. "I don't know about them."

Kyle peered from their hiding place. Two forms appeared on the Knife Blade and the one in front slipped, cursed and fell several feet to a protruding ledge. The second tried to help him, and lost his balance too.

Salmon sighted his rifle, but did not shoot. Other forms appeared on the rocks, wind-blown apparitions. They hesitated, and when Salmon did not shoot, advanced again. Slipping, sliding, calling to each other, they came on. The man who fell cried out in pain when the others tried to pull him to his feet. One of his legs dangled strangely, and Kyle thought of the day Harley Hawkins broke his brother's arm. The others dragged him back and out of sight.

"That's the posse?"

"In the movies, maybe," Salmon said. "This crowd's mostly guys out for a good time. You can see. No one's wearing a uniform."

"Thirdkill!" a voice shouted. "Thirdkill!"

Salmon touched Kyle's shoulder and pushed him down. "Two of us now," he said. "They're wondering."

"Judy wants you to surrender."

"Can't," Salmon said.

"Why not?"

"I shot someone."

"Oh, shit," Kyle said.

"One of them hit me too."

Kyle didn't catch his meaning at first. "You got shot?"

"Yes, goddamn it," the high school principal said. He touched his left side.

"Is it bleeding?"

"I don't think so; not now."

"How bad?"

"Bullet nipped some skin and fat, the love handle." Salmon indicated a spot on his side just above his belt. "In, out. A scratch, as they say."

"What about the other guy?"

"Could be trouble," Salmon said. "I may have killed him."

# # #

CHAPTER 36

"That's not good," Kyle said.

"Tell me something I don't know." Salmon crouched in the falling snow, his coat, his hat, everything, frosted in white.

"If you don't surrender, what then?"

"Maybe like Sitting Bull I go to Canada."

"Give up. You've got a wife. You've got a kid on the way."

"They'll shoot me, Kyle. I don't like these guys and they don't like me."

"They won't shoot you with journalists all over the place. I'll talk to them. Maybe the guy you hit isn't dead."

"If he isn't dead, he's sorely wounded. I think I hit him in the chest."

Kyle shook his head. "At least let me try." He stood up, his arms held high. The wind whipped maelstroms of snow and the Knife Blade emerged and disappeared before him as a ship in a stormy sea.

"Truce," he yelled. "Truce!"

He heard a roar. Something metallic struck a rock and whined away with the sound of a buzz saw dying.

Kyle found himself on his hands and knees, huddled in the shelter of the rock. What had happened? "They don't know I'm a reporter," he said.

"Put on your press badge." Salmon's mouth curled at one end in a way that reminded Kyle of his dead brother.

Kyle looked around and tried to orient himself. Nothing happened today as he had imagined it. He had pictured, in one scenario, Salmon launching a wild, dramatic charge into the teeth of blazing guns and somehow surviving. But nothing about their circumstances struck him as romantic now. "Let's wait for somebody in a uniform," he said. "We'll tell him you want to surrender."

"You surrender. You're the reporter. They won't hurt you. I didn't ask you to come up here." Salmon looked through him and beyond him.

"You're hurt. How can you run?"

"What do you know about it, anyway?"

Huddled in the falling snow, Kyle Hansen experienced a moment of introspection. He had accumulated in his role as a journalist a fatty layer of immunity, but up here nobody cared where he went to college or how much money he made. Up here in the cold, wet and scared, Kyle glimpsed life as most men from the beginning of time had known it.

"Got to move," Salmon said.

Kyle hesitated. His friend had shot someone and he had a price on his head. Other men sought to capture or kill him. He, Kyle, had climbed up here supposedly to help, but as a reporter too. "I'll follow you," he said, more from guilt than conviction.

The wind blasted from the north and the snowdrift along the high ridge curved in the form of a breaking wave, a cornice forming. They followed this, seeking to walk on ground the wind had cleared. Kyle looked back but could see little. His world consisted of a few feet around him and a figure plodding ahead. Salmon's pace began to slow.

"How you doing?"

Salmon shook his head. "Let's take a break." They sat with their backs to a stand of pines.

"Where are we going?" Kyle asked.

"You'll see."

"You've got a plan? Tell me."

"All in good time," Salmon said.

"Why not tell me now? You think they might capture me and torture it out of me?"

Salmon stared into space. "I wish I hadn't shot that guy," he said.

"Ginny's driving over from Bozeman," Kyle said. "She and Judy might hike in behind you up Half Moon Canyon."

"You talked to Judy?" Now Salmon showed interest.

"She told me she wants you to surrender."

"I hope she doesn't try to follow me up here. She'll know better than that." He swung his hips, as if testing, and Kyle saw him wince.

"Did you bandage it?"

"I put some disinfectant on. I always carry a first aid kit in my pack."

"Disinfectant. Good," Kyle said. "That's something."

"I guess Judy's heard what I did." Salmon avoided Kyle's eyes.

"You mean that you shot somebody? I don't know. But from what you say, it sounds like self defense."

"I don't think the police and the courts will see it that way."

"A good attorney will," Kyle said.

Salmon lifted his arms, dropped them, did it again. "You got anything to eat?"

Kyle felt around in his pack and found a pop-top can he had grabbed at the supermarket. "Boston brown bread," he said. "I've never tried it before."

"It will be a first for both of us."

Kyle opened the can and broke off chunks. A miracle: this Boston brown bread tasted moist and plump, and they wolfed it down. Salmon produced two candy bars and they chewed these slowly, reflectively. "Can you see anybody behind us?" Salmon asked.

"No. Wait... No. Don't think so." Kyle imagined for a moment they came on a pleasure hike and would soon drive back to town.

A cramp gripped his right thigh. He straightened his leg; still it hurt.

"When did you talk to Judy?" Salmon asked.

"Right after she came home and found you gone."

"I don't know what she's doing here. She shouldn't be climbing in these mountains when she's pregnant."

"I think exercise is okay up until the sixth or seventh month," Kyle said. "We could call her if my goddamn cell phone worked. What about yours?"

"Lost it. Wouldn't use it anyway. It would just help them find us."

Kyle licked his fingers, still tasting the candy bar. "What now, Captain Courage?"

"Keep going. As long as it blows like this we don't have to worry about helicopters." He inserted one arm through his pack straps, then the other, rose to his feet. Snow clung to his clothes, his hat, his pants.

Kyle clapped his hands for warmth. If Salmon would not turn back, at least darkness would stop them.

"There's a real bunch of crazies in that crowd behind us," Salmon said. "You'll see."

"Did you bandage where you were shot?"

"Taped it up. We need to find a place to camp before dark."

"I camped a mile or so ahead last night," Kyle said. "I left some firewood. Good spot. Trees cut the wind."

"Let's go for it."

They plodded on. It began to grow dark and Kyle glimpsed through the blowing snow a familiar circle of trees.

Salmon flopped on the ground. They discussed whose tent to use and chose Kyle's on the theory that it was larger. He set it up while Salmon poked around in the snow for leftover wood and started a fire. "I wouldn't object to a Scotch and water right now," he said.

"Jesus, yes. I thought about that last night."

"I heard the posse partying," Salmon said. "They definitely brought some flight fuel along."

"Who saw who first? What happened back there?"

"I heard them coming. A guy in a plaid coat pointed his gun at me so I shot him. Funny, I hadn't touched a gun in six months. Had the damn trigger tuned so tight I squeezed off two shots before I knew it. I think a helicopter came and carried him away."

"God damn it, Salmon." Kyle sat, shaking his head. He saw only trouble ahead,

"Judy wouldn't hike in this weather, would she? Did she and Ginny bring a tent?"

"They might have," Kyle said, "but police would have stopped them. I barely made it through myself."

"How did you?"

"Hiked up from Emerald Lake. They hadn't set up checkpoints yet."

They chewed almonds and dried apricots. Kyle stirred camper-store, freeze-dried chili into snow water and heated it on the fire. Salmon ate quickly. "Wind will cover our tracks," he said.

"Tomorrow?"

"We drop down into one of those canyons." Salmon jabbed with a stick at the fire and the wind trailed streaks of sparks. "We hike down to a logging road. There should be somebody waiting."

"The young guys?"

Salmon grunted. Kyle considered and decided he did not want to know. "Any idea who turned you in?" he asked.

"No. Could have been anybody."

"Fifty-thousand dollars – sixty now, I don't know if you heard..."

"Will buy a lot of beer, right."

"Remember," Kyle said, "Jeb Small doesn't want you dead. He wants to prosecute. He wants to star on TV."

"Therefore, I shouldn't surrender."

"You surrender, maybe Edgar Ware keeps the roads blocked until the state cuts you a deal. Maybe the Governor intervenes. Maybe you're a romantic hero."

"I don't want to surrender to these guys, Kyle."

"We wait for state police and you surrender to them."

Salmon stroked his chin. "I'm considering," he said.

Kyle clomped out into wind and snow to relieve himself. He looked back at their camp and it struck him how fragile, how tiny, their flickering flame appeared.

"I dreamed last night I could change one specific thing," Salmon said, sitting by the fire, "and if I choose the right one, I go home free. One thing. One thing only. What would it be? Not urge Edgar to barricade the roads? Not kill that first cow? You could say any of those acts led to all that followed. Take one of them away, tonight I'm home in bed with Judy."

"So what did you choose?"

"I would not have shot that guy this morning." They sat without speaking. Salmon rocked back and forth.

"What about where you got shot? Shouldn't we change the bandage or something?"

"Let's study it in the morning."

The night grew colder. Kyle dropped rocks on the fire to shield it from snow so burning coals might last to build up a blaze in the morning. That's the way they taught back in Boy Scouts. He and Salmon crawled into the tent and scrunched fully-clothed into their sleeping bags. Click. Click. Kyle listened to pellets of snow strike the tent. Click, click. The more he listened the more he disliked the sound.

Salmon muttered in the night and Kyle looked at his watch. Two a.m. "You know what day it is?" Salmon's muffled voice issued from deep in his sleeping bag.

"Saturday."

"Grizzlies and Bobcats today."

"By god, that's right!" Montana State versus the University of Montana. "Championship of the world," Kyle said. He and Salmon had played in three of these games, each time on the winning side.

He hoped for sun in the morning. Sun would bring helicopters, and they could surrender. But when next Kyle awoke he heard the clicking sound. He crawled outside. Snow fell gently, heavily.

He brushed away inches of the stuff, pulled away rocks and made a teepee of dead cedar twigs. He blew on surviving coals from last night until a flame licked up. He fed in larger twigs, huffing, puffing. A slender blaze wavered and rose.

Salmon wobbled away into the snow, took a long time at his morning toilet, and retraced his trail back. "There's blood in my stool," he said matter-of-factly.

# # #

CHAPTER 37

"Can we look at that bandage now?" There might be a good side to this, Kyle thought. Now maybe he will stop running and surrender.

Salmon stood at the fire and pulled up his sweater to expose his long underwear top. Kyle saw a circular, dark stain on the cloth, and in the midst of this something fresh and moist and bright. Salmon rolled the underwear upward, exposing a frayed bandage on his side a few inches above his waist. He peeled this bandage away and Kyle saw a ragged, purple mess.

"Jesus. You said he only nicked you."

"It looks worse than it is."

"You took a crap, blood came out?"

"Maybe it's bleeding into the intestine," Salmon said. "That can happen. We want to keep it disinfected, right? See what you can find in here." He tossed over his first aid kit.

Kyle read from a list of various bandages and medicines. "Antibacterial ointment. Maybe we should try that."

"Yes," Salmon said. "I think it's in a green and white packet."

Kyle picked through the contents of the plastic kit. "Got it." He held a spoon in the fire to sterilize it, let it cool, and used it to smear ointment around Salmon's wound. "What say we dab some iodine on too?"

"Do it."

Salmon jerked at the sting. A bubble of blood welled from a hole in back, maybe three or four inches behind the one in front.

"Look at this! There's a hole back here too. You need to go to a hospital."

"Of course there's a hole back there; bullet goes in, it wants to come out. It's through a fatty spot. Bandage it again, will you."

Kyle placed two-by-two inch sterilized gauze pads front and back and taped them down with adhesive. He poked through the plastic kit and found iodine antiseptic and alcohol prep pads. "Glory to god. There's a medicine cabinet in here."

"I've carried that first aid kit in my backpack for years and this is the first time I ever used it," Salmon said.

"Here's pills for 'pain, soreness and sprains.'"

"Give me some of those." Salmon put the packet of pills in his pocket.

"We could just stay here and wait for somebody to find us," Kyle said.

Salmon unfolded a forest service map and leaned to shield it from falling snow. "Here's us. Here..." – he indicated a spot further on – "...see how this ridge descends on the Hightown side. We slide down into Cottonwood Canyon and hike out to between where you left your car and the next ranch road." Salmon walked his fingers along a wavy line that curved outward to the plains.

"We use my car?"

"Not necessary. There's old logging roads all through here. Someone may be waiting."

"Not Judy," Kyle said.

"No. She doesn't know about this."

"This is dumb, Salmon. Blood's running out of you front and behind."

"Got to try."

"They'll follow our tracks."

"Look." Salmon pointed. Already wind and snow obliterated his footsteps of a few minutes ago.

Kyle shook his head. He had miscalculated in coming up here, just as he had miscalculated 17 years ago in taking his brother rafting down the Blackfoot River.

"Go back. Wait. Do what you want," Salmon said.

"Oh shit. I'll come." Kyle folded his tent and rolled his sleeping bag. He peeled and halved an orange. Salmon still had candy bars. The landscape around them dissolved into gray on white, white on gray. Ghost trees wavered in mist.

Knee-deep, lunging, they floundered downward through drifts. They reached bigger trees and fought through pine branches that spilled snow down their backs. Salmon carried his rifle slung on his pack and leaned on a walking stick he had cut to size. Kyle considered alternatives. Maybe he could knock Salmon down and hold him prisoner until someone official arrived to capture him. In Salmon's weakened state, maybe he could do it.

But if a court sentenced Salmon to death? To life in prison? Stay out of it, Kyle thought. Let the man choose. Besides, he doubted he could knock Salmon down anyway.

They dropped into a stretch of blowdown, a minefield of snapped trunks and tangled limbs. Kyle walked ahead, breaking trail. He planted one foot, probed with his hiking stick, planted the other foot. He sweated. Snow melted on his clothes. He felt trickles in his armpits and his pants and long underwear sagged wet and heavy. He brushed snow from a log so they could sit down. Salmon simply dropped his arms and let his pack slide to the snow. "I think it would help if I ate something sugary," he said.

Kyle found in his pack a Frosted Susan Apple Pie. He eased the pie from its aluminum plate, broke it into two, gave Salmon half. Brown shards of crust flaked on their fingers.

They lunged downward, reached a stand of pines. Branches grabbed their shoulders and whacked them in the face. Their chests rose and fell, their breath plumed. Salmon stopped, a curious uncertainty in his expression. "I'll just stand here a minute," he said. The gray sky above seemed to touch the tops of the trees.

"Why don't you throw away that goddamned gun."

"You could carry it," Salmon said.

"It's heavy. It's not only heavy, it's evidence."

"You got a point there." Salmon flung the black rifle into white snow as rippled as sand on a beach. The gun sank below the surface, a dark shark, a menace.

Down they plodded. A slope appeared on their left and a cleft developed between it and the next ridge, a canyon in the making.

Thick timber clumped at the bottom of this rift, so the two men stayed on the ridge's open crest.

They hit another stretch of blowdown more tangled, more cross-thatched than the one above. Salmon bared his teeth in apparent pain. They sat on the trunk of a downed tree and Salmon stared at his feet. "Maybe if I try eating again."

They shared a pop-top can of tuna. Kyle looked at Salmon and the loss of focus in his friend's eyes scared him. "Let's rest," he said, but already Salmon started on.

They worked their way lower, sliding, grabbing at tree trunks. Snow fell heavily, softly, and they scooped it up and swallowed as it melted in their mouths. It required continual handfuls to slack their thirsts.

Kyle stopped and looked back. A dark shape stumbled and sprawled in the snow. "I can't do it anymore," Salmon said.

Kyle tried to climb back but in deep snow made little progress. No way they could get back up to the high ridge, even if they wanted to. Salmon sat up, looked around as if confused, and slid on his back slowly downward.

"We ought to put the tent up," Kyle said. "That knoll down there looks level enough." At last, a solution, he thought: they stop, wait and let searchers find them. The knoll below extended to a porch-like eminence, a perfect place from which to see and be seen.

Salmon slid a few steps, rested, came slowly on. He sat in the snow while Kyle cleared a flat space and set up the tent.

"Something's wet," Salmon said. He dropped his pants. A sheen of blood reddened his thighs and he tried to wipe it away with a dirty t-shirt from his pack. "I'm bleeding again," he said matter-of-factly.

"Press hard," Kyle said. "Press hard."

Salmon wadded the t-shirt and sat on it seeking with the pressure of his weight to stop the bleeding. "Put your hat back on," Kyle said. "You ought to zip up your coat."

Salmon pulled on his hat. The weather did seem colder. He rose and felt behind his thighs. "It's working," he said.

"Bleeding stopped?"

"I think."

"Well, we've got no choice now," Kyle said. "We camp here." He looked around. Dead pines tumbled by forgotten cataclysms protruded from the snow like the ribs of old ships. Methodically he broke away branches to build a pile of firewood.

"Weather's clearing," Salmon said.

It did look brighter, and nearby trees cast what Kyle suddenly realized were shadows. Here, the snow had stopped falling. Above, like fog sliding uphill, grayness retreated toward the summit ridge of the Spirit Mountains.

Rents of blue sky opened above them. They glimpsed in the distance white prairie and crimson, puffball clouds. White mountain ranges appeared across the Judith Basin, peaks aflame in the dying sun.

"Rescue helicopter soon," Kyle said. "If not tonight, then the morning. They can't miss us. This is one bright orange tent."

He started a fire. He felt a sudden, vast relief. Salmon had not objected to the idea that someone might find them. He seemed to have accepted he could not run anymore.

"What do you think Judy's doing now?" Salmon asked.

"Probably looking for you."

"We tried, didn't we?"

"We sure as hell did. Salmon – Wovoka, I should say – there's something I want to know. Why did you tease me with that sign at the Chief Joseph Battlefield? '…Follow the Holy Road.' Jesus. If you knew the places I looked, the miles I traveled…"

"I didn't know the sign was there," Salmon said. "Honest. If you do find the Holy Road, I wish you'd tell me."

They devoured Kyle's last Frosted Susan Apple Pie and watched the lights of ranches wink on across the plains. Salmon took two of the pain pills and Kyle helped him change the bandage on his side. They left the fire burning and crawled into their sleeping bags. Kyle looked forward to the roar of a helicopter at first light in the morning.

Click, click. He awoke to the sound.

As boys, he and Terry never tired of snow. They ran outside to watch it swirl down in the arc of the streetlights. They measured every hour or so to see how much more had fallen.

One January morning, walking to school, Kyle came upon a cat dead in the snow. It lay with its eyes open and its teeth bared and next to it he saw two dead kittens, one only halfway out. It was thirty degrees below zero and the mother cat froze to death in the act of giving birth. Something chased her into this unsheltered field, and in her pregnant condition she stood no chance.

Kyle lay in his tent and listened to the click of falling snow. We're all on our own, he thought. Nature doesn't give a damn.

# # #

CHAPTER 38

The fugitive stirred in his sleeping bag. "Put it over there," Kyle heard Salmon Thirdkill say. Then, "Judy, it's cold."

Click, click; snow pinged against the tent. Salmon rolled over. "I'm not feeling good, Kyle."

"Let's eat something." But there wasn't much left. Kyle mixed a dusting of powdered milk and water in paper cups. Sitting up in their sleeping bags, he and Salmon spooned the last of their cereal.

Salmon peered outside. "Not good. I was looking forward to hitching a ride on a helicopter."

"Might happen," Kyle said.

"I hope so. I don't know if I'm strong enough to walk out of here."

"How far are we from that logging road you talked about?"

"Eight, nine miles. I'm hurting, Kyle. I think you should go down. Some football players I coached on the Fort Belknap Reservation may be waiting with a four-wheel drive. If you see them, tell them to go home. Then find some state patrolmen or deputy sheriffs. Tell them I'm ready to surrender. Tell them where I am. Find Judy too. Tell her I'm okay. I'll stay here in the tent."

Kyle studied his friend. Questions hung in the air. "Hell, I don't know one canyon from the next," he said.

"You'll drop into a canyon that's easier walking. Go around a few bends, and toward the end you'll climb over a ridge. You might even meet my friends on the way."

"Maybe they could hike up and carry you down."

"Let police do it. Or men in a helicopter. I don't want to get my guys in trouble. Tell them to go home."

"Say we wait an hour or two, see if it clears. See if the helicopter comes. Otherwise, I go down."

Kyle assembled remnants; a packet of freeze-dried chili, a few almonds, some cheese, a candy bar. "Look at this, a candy bar. I'll make you a pile of firewood, in case."

"Good thinking. Thanks, Lieutenant Loyalty."

Kyle broke dead tree limbs into burnable lengths while Salmon sat watching the falling snow. "Remember that Utah State game when Ardo McCullough threw the pass and hit the bird," he said. "They intercept, we lose. Why does that bullet hit me yesterday? Some things don't make any sense at all."

Kyle laughed, thankful for the opportunity. "That was one startled bird," he said.

He heard a sound, a sort of a gasp, and he glanced at Salmon. The look in his eyes held him. "You're strong and free to go," his gaze said. "I wish I could go with you, but I can't. I treasured life. I wish I had treasured it more." The intensity in his friend's eyes frightened him. The bottom seemed to have dropped from his soul.

The wind gusted. Salmon lifted his head. The blood appeared drained from his face. "Where's the sun? I want to feel the sun," he said. A vision flashed for Kyle, the old Indian he saw praying on Bear Butte.

Kyle grabbed him by his shoulders. He saw blood now, globs of it, on a log behind. Salmon's eyes closed. Kyle tried to lift him but he slid slowly downward, a ship sinking. He moved his lips as if he wanted to speak.

"Do you want water? Salmon? Do you hear me?"

Salmon's pants crackled like cellophane. Maybe the blood began to freeze. He had hemorrhaged, Kyle guessed. "Captain Courage. Talk to me."

How do you tell if a person's dead? Feel for a pulse? Hold a mirror up to see if they're breathing? Kyle did not need to do any of these things. He knew. He pulled Salmon inside the tent and covered him with his sleeping bag. He cuffed his friend on the shoulder.

Salmon looked, even now, as if he were planning something. In his alertness to people and their motives, he had often reminded Kyle of his own brother, Terry.

He sat for a while. The weather showed no sign of clearing. He rose and started down the mountain. He stopped to look back and glimpsed the orange of the tent. The next time he looked he did not see the tent anymore.

He tripped on something and somersaulted. What if he broke a leg? Fell over a cliff? Who would find him? Kyle considered all the things that could go wrong.

His mind groped, seeking solace. He had not dived into the Blackfoot River to try to save his brother, but, he told himself, at least he had climbed these mountains to try to help his friend. But the friend had died too, like his brother. Muttering, Kyle stumbled on.

Springtime floods swept a path of sorts along the floor of the canyon below and as he dropped toward it Kyle walked out of the falling snow. It took him a minute or two to realize this, and he looked up, startled. Above the mountain vanished into mist; down here the storm had stopped.

He chewed dried chili and studied his map. Four or five canyons twisted toward the prairie. Which canyon was his? Recent snow, heavier and softer down here, rose still above his hiking boots.

He slogged on. Trees grew higher and more tangled. Boulders bulked in the way. Gravity did not propel him as it had before, now that he walked more level terrain. Clouds smothered landmarks above, while in his canyon he saw only to the next bend. But at least he had descended from the steeps.

Kyle ate snow to ease his thirst. He took off his coat and tied it around his waist. He turned a bend and saw another bend. He reached this and saw another bend. He reached it and sighted on the next. He was moving. He was moving.

Concentrate, Kyle told himself. Sight on something close. He chose a tree and when he reached it chose a rock further on. Reaching the rock, he aimed at a tilted pine. Setting small goals, achieving them, he tried to fight back his fears.

He walked in stillness. Above him canyon walls vanished into mist. What's that, did the clouds rise? No, idiot, they don't rise, it's you who gradually descend.

He stared back at his tracks. They would melt in time or disappear beneath new snow. As with those men of mystery who followed the Old North Trail, nothing would remain to mark his passage.

"Hello," he yelled. 'Hello." No voice answered.

Kyle plodded on. He rounded bends. He slipped and fell. It's easy to get into trouble, he thought, not so easy to get out.

If he died, might he blame the last half inch of snow? The last hundredth? If he froze, what if he had reached warmth ten minutes earlier? If Salmon had received medical help yesterday? This morning? You drive yourself crazy with questions like this.

Kyle stumbled; his leg muscles burned. He rounded another bend and stopped. Something wrong: this canyon turned sharply ahead, but, according to his map, that direction led back into the mountains.

He studied his map, exhausted. This canyon should angle to the right, toward the prairie, but instead it turned exactly the wrong way. Kyle stared up at the canyon walls and tried to think. Should he make a snow cave, gather wood? He had no food left. It began to grow dark.

He saw movement. On a ridge above he saw a man. How long this man had watched him Kyle did not know. The man realized that Kyle saw him and slowly extended his arm. He pointed across to the opposite canyon wall, the wrong way, the side Kyle thought led back to the steeps.

"Go there," the man's gesture said. "Go there." Kyle looked more closely and saw that the man was his brother.

He studied the slope at which Terry pointed. It did not look so high, really, not so high at all.

Kyle looked back; he wanted to speak to Terry. But his brother was gone.

Kicking his boots into the snow, he slowly climbed the way Terry had pointed. He stopped several times to rest, and it was almost dark when he reached the top and looked down the other side. He saw lights moving across flats below, and he watched them for a minute or two.

He shouted. He waved his arms. The lights kept moving. Kyle shouted again, and the last man in line looked up and saw him.

# # #

CHAPTER 39

Five men followed Kyle Hansen's tracks into the mountains. One was a deputy sheriff, two had played football on teams that Salmon coached, and two were volunteers of the sort that editorial writers praise as "selfless," men with free time who assist at accidents for excitement and to get out of the house.

A state trooper gave Kyle a can of orange juice and drove him to his car at Emerald Lake. He used his lap top to contact his newspaper and to write a story and then he lay down in the back seat and slept until someone rapped on his car window to tell him the five men had brought Salmon's body down.

Kyle drove to Hightown, took a motel room, and went in search of Ginny Foster and Judy Thirdkill. He found them at Central Montana Hospital, where the local coroner had already performed an autopsy.

Salmon had died, the coroner's report said, of loss of blood and exposure. "How far did he walk after he was shot?" a doctor asked Kyle.

"Fifteen miles," Kyle guessed. The doctor shook his head.

Ghost Dance

Ginny Foster sipped coffee in the hospital cafeteria. "Judy's with Salmon. I don't think she'd mind if we went in."

Judy Thirdkill sat in a bright room beside her husband's body. She nodded toward Kyle. Salmon looked gray, defenseless. He looked like what he was, a Sioux Indian from up on Montana's High Line.

A clomping noise sounded and several men entered. "We were up there looking for him," one said. Apparently they had served as members of the posse.

Judy jumped up. "Who told you you could come in here?"

"Sheriff said it was okay."

"Get out!" She pushed them toward the door. She slammed it and turned, biting her lip. She walked to Salmon and looked at him. "Idiot," she said. "What were you thinking?" Then she seemed to relent. Judy leaned toward her husband. She touched his face. "Don't go, Salmon," she said softly. "Don't go."

Kyle's eyes moisted, and Ginny motioned him to leave. He bumped into the Fergus County Sheriff outside in the hall.

"My friend's wife is in there, and she's pregnant. Why the hell did you let those vigilantes bust in on her?" Kyle saw a uniform, and he unleashed frustrations.

"I didn't. I just told them where he was. The young man that Thirdkill killed had a wife and two kids. Did you know that?" The sheriff adjusted his hat with its little gold star. "Mister, if you don't mind, I'll need a statement from you."

They talked; the sheriff jotted notes. "I'm not going to charge you with a crime," he said, "because they tell me you are a member of the media. I want you to know, though, that as far as I'm concerned you acted as an accomplice in an murderer's attempt to escape."

Kyle walked away. As a former police reporter he had often observed the law in action, and he did not care to press his luck today. The two young Indians who waited with their pickup truck for Salmon to come down from the mountains were not charged with any crime either. They could have driven away immediately, but they wanted to help bring Salmon's body down. Now that he was dead, public sympathy appeared to swing in his direction.

250

Ginny emerged and she and Kyle stood at a window staring at a gray tedium of sky. The hospital sat on a hill above Hightown, with views all around. "Can't see the mountains," Kyle said. He imagined their orange tent still up there, sagging with snow.

"Judy and I camped below Half Moon Canyon," Ginny said. "We heard on police radio last night that Salmon died. Judy didn't believe it. She waited until they brought his body down. The funeral's tomorrow in Browning. We're driving over there in the morning."

"I'll follow you," Kyle said.

"Let's the three of us meet for dinner," Ginny said. She and Judy and Kyle stayed at different motels. "Judy wants to hear everything that happened between you and Salmon up in the mountains."

"I'll be ready," Kyle said.

"Edgar Ware and the Blackfeet pulled down their road barricades," Ginny said. "Governor Cloninger says he will offer full amnesty to the other cattle killers."

"I heard. I hope this time he means it. I heard the Bobcats beat the Grizzlies Saturday. Harley got his undefeated season."

"I'm happy for him," Ginny said.

"I'm not. The bastard broke my brother's arm."

Kyle wrote yesterday in his story for his newspaper, "...In the end, the second Wovoka's medicine failed, just as the first one's had...'" Today he made the usual rounds. Eldon Lauder sounded detached, Clinton Mosby drunk, Lars Bjornson and Edgar Ware tired and sleepy.

Kyle Hansen walked the sidewalks of his old home town. He drove up Main Street, turned and drove down again. Old cowboys crossed against the light from the Mint to the Stockman Bars.

He drove by his former home on Eighth Avenue South. He passed the Judith Theater, where Lance waited outside for him and Terry and he and Glenda Lodermeier necked in the balcony. He drove down Fifth Avenue to the Civic Center. "Okay if I shoot a few?"

"That's what it's here for," the janitor said.

Kyle shed his coat in the basement locker room. Someone had taped a note on the wall: "Whoever Goddamn bastard took my boat shoes please bring them back." Under this a different hand had printed: "What are boat shoes? Please explain."

What were boat shoes? Salmon would have enjoyed speculating on this. Kyle climbed the stairs to the big, high-ceiling gym. A basketball lay in the middle of the polished floor. He picked it up. He lofted a jump shot and chased down the ball. He felt the presence of his brother, Terry.

Terry eyed him, one hand on his hip, that old crooked grin on his face. Kyle, in his mind, tossed him the basketball. Terry nodded as if to say, "Watch me." He drove the lane, shed a defender with a shoulder-shrug, soared, banked it in. Ah. Kyle wanted to see that again.

Terry lobbed the ball back. "Your turn," his expression seemed to say. "Your turn. We're even."

Judy Thirdkill asked Kyle many questions at dinner, and Kyle tried to remember, not to exaggerate. Judy listened, soft and teary, nodding occasionally. She and Kyle touched fingers and she and Ginny departed to their motel.

They drove in tandem across northern Montana the next day, Kyle in one car, Judy and Ginny in another. The sky cleared and he looked back at the dark line of the Spirit Mountains. Bleak Browning lay ahead in the vastness of the Blackfoot Indian Reservation.

The funeral in Browning began at three in the afternoon. It was almost December and the mountains of Glacier Park rose luminous in the background. Beams of sunlight played on the high school field where Salmon ran for so many touchdowns. Judy sat in the first row of chairs, flanked by Ginny Foster and Judy's old sodbuster father.

Kyle sat with some of his and Salmon's old University of Montana football teammates. Indians, some in native dress, also attended. Some of Salmon's current and former students came.

Edgar Ware spoke, as chairman of the Blackfoot Council. He talked about Salmon as a teacher, a coach and a man. "Mother Earth weeps for Salmon Thirdkill," he said.

Several of Salmon's friends, including Kyle, also spoke. "I remember how he ran with a football," Kyle said. "That high stride. How he pumped his knees. Ah, he was something to see..."

Judy did not try to talk. She trembled when she stepped forward to look down at her husband's coffin.

# # #

CHAPTER 40

Kyle Hansen and Ginny Foster faced each other across a restaurant table in Great Falls, Montana. They had spent the night together and in two hours Kyle would board a plane to fly back East, where his dispatches from Montana had for several months appeared almost daily in the Washington Herald. Ginny asked about his series on Lewis and Clark, which, as yet, she had not seen.

"Well, in the final of the four, I tell about the later lives of Lewis and Clark."

"Lewis shot himself."

"That's right. In an inn on the Natchez Trace in Tennessee. He shot himself and sliced himself with a razor. President Jefferson appointed him Governor of the Mountains, so to speak, but he became a land speculator and lapsed into drinking and melancholy. He told people that Clark knew he was in trouble and was 'coming on' to help him. He died alone."

"Clark did better."

"That's right. He worked with Indians for many years, and it appears they liked him."

"Sacajawea?"

"She died in 1812, probably of smallpox, at an army post in North Dakota where her husband worked as an interpreter. She was about twenty-five years old. Clark paid for her son's education."

They asked for second cups of coffee. "I've no primary opposition yet in my campaign for the Legislature and I've a year yet to solicit campaign contributions," Ginny said. She wore a tight black dress and leaned forward at their table, her forehead almost touching his.

"That doesn't mean another Democrat won't appear, and there will be a Republican candidate too, one would think."

"One would think," Ginny said. "Yes. It wouldn't be any fun if it was too easy."

"You'll be tested in the white hot crucible of politics."

"And not found wanting, I hope."

Kyle chuckled. "And Harley, the big D, that's on the tracks?" He felt that today he lacked his usual brashness. Salmon hovered on his mind, and Terry, and places he had seen these last months. Last night, arriving in separate cars at a motel near the airport, he and Ginny had kissed almost chastely. After that they did not get a lot of sleep.

"Harley's not contesting the divorce. Montana State wants to extend his coaching contract for four more years, but I hear he's got an offer from Missouri or some place in the Midwest. Meanwhile he keeps the house, I buy the condo. It's got a terrace and it's near the college library and a wine store."

"Might be a good thing if Harley goes to Missouri."

"That thought occurred to me."

"The Mod Shop: can you still handle it if you get elected to the Legislature?"

"The Legislature's only in a session a few months a year. Marta could mind the store."

"My editor says a beat on Capitol Hill comes up for grabs. That doesn't mean I'd get it."

"It's what you wanted."

"I try to imagine my future in Washington. I get better assignments on the national desk, but I still spend years working my way higher. I look for political trends to ride and controversies to exploit as a way of getting my stories on the front page. Eventually, if I'm promoted to covering Congress or the State Department, I appear on those Sunday morning TV news analysis programs and stay up late on weeknights to do thirty-second interviews with cable news anchors. I might speak at an occasional small college graduation."

"People might recognize you on the street," Ginny said.

"On the other hand, I have received – or obliquely solicited– several job offers from newspapers in Montana, me hailing from Hightown and all. I'd want equity, a piece of ownership. Chances are, they won't give it to me."

"So?"

"Or they might. It doesn't matter. Either way I come back to Montana." Kyle felt confident about his professional life. It was his personal life that needed work.

Ginny tossed her hair, the now familiar gesture. "You want my opinion?"

"Yes."

"The skiing is better out here."

Kyle slid back his chair. "Good point."

"I called Judy yesterday," Ginny said. "She was sitting in the kitchen hoping to hear Salmon's car, to see him come busting through the door. I might drive up this weekend."

"Good. She'll like that. I'll call her before I go."

"Well. I feel we're making progress, you and I."

"If this were a movie, we'd flip a coin," Kyle said. "Heads, you move east. Tails I move west. If it lands sideways, we both go to El Salvador." He eyed her across their table.

Ginny grinned. "I'll toss the coin," she said.

"Here's a quarter."

"Is this one of those moments we'll look back on for the rest of our lonely, unsatisfying lives and think that if only back in November, 2003, in Great Falls, Montana, the coin had landed differently?"

"Let's do it and see."

"You call it," Ginny said.

"Tails, me Montana. Heads, you move to Washington. You flip."

She did. It fell on the floor and they leaned to see. "Tails," Ginny said.

They laughed. "If it landed heads?" Kyle asked.

"I would have asked for a do-over."

Kyle had returned his rental car last night, so Ginny drove him to the Great Falls Airport.

He got his ticket. She saw somebody she knew from Save the Land and plunged into conversation. He called Jack Leventhal in Washington. "Jack, I'm on my way."

It rained in the nation's capital, the older man said. He sounded pensive. "Did you ever find that Holy Road?" Kyle visualized him scratching his balding head.

"I'm still looking. What about you, Jack? What do national editors do when they've seen it all?"

"To tell the truth, I'd like a little newspaper of my own."

"A weekly? A small daily? What section of the country?"

"A weekly. Twice a week maybe. New England."

Kyle returned to Ginny. "How about that? My editor wants to buy a weekly newspaper. That's the first time we ever talked about anything other than softball or the next story."

A skim of snow coated the ground, a pale sun struggled low in the sky. Kyle had not told Ginny how up in the mountains his brother had pointed his way to safety, and he considered telling her now. Perhaps he had hallucinated. But it was Terry. He knew his own brother.

I'll tell her another time, he thought. Over drinks, maybe late at night. Now he wanted to talk to Edgar Ware. He punched the Blackfoot Tribal Chairman's home number into his cell phone and listened as it rang five or six times. "What else is new? Never could reach Edgar when I wanted to."

"You can talk to him when you come back," Ginny said.

"He probably won't answer the phone then either."

Kyle telephoned Judy Thirdkill in Havre. "Yep, at the airport. Wanted to hear your voice. Ginny's here. She tells me you might get involved in politics."

"We'll see. First, though, I think I'd like to have Salmon's baby."

"You had it checked? Boy? Girl?"

"I'd rather be surprised. If it's a boy, I suppose he'll want to play football."

"He probably will," Kyle said. "He probably will."

"Listen," Judy said. "Don't you let Ginny get away. You hear me? Hold on to this one. Don't let her get away."

"I won't," Kyle said. "I'm coming back."

"Did you tell her that?"

"Yes. She knows."

He and Ginny kissed. Kyle walked outside, mountains in the distance, the great spaces. His plane lifted off over wheat fields and the Missouri River, turned east. In a few minutes Kyle saw the Spirit Mountains high and white ahead. That ridge, that canyon... He searched the snowy landscape, hoping to glimpse an orange tent.

The mountains slid behind and little towns and isolated schools began to appear. Kyle tried to spot the football fields and basketball gymnasiums. He and his brother had played on those fields and in those gymnasiums and he recalled golden autumns and the winters of his youth.

Kyle Hansen gazed south across wandering rivers, looking for a white monument. Too far; he could not see it today, but he knew it still stood, up there in the wind. He knew he would return to the Little Bighorn Battlefield and walk that bare ridge again, just to see where the Indians had won.

The End

Made in the USA
Charleston, SC
25 January 2013